ALSO BY CHANDA HAHN

THE UNFORTUNATE FAIRY TALES

UnEnchanted

Fairest

Fable

Reign

Forever

THE IRON BUTTERFLY

The Iron Butterfly

The Steele Wolf

The Silver Siren

THE NEVERWOOD CHRONICLES

Lost Girl

Lost Boy

Lost Shadow

THE DAUGHTERS OF EVILLE

Of Beast and Beauty

Of Glass and Glamour

Of Sea and Song

Of Thorn and Thread

Of Mist and Murder

Of Gold and Greed

Of Secrets and Slippers

THE GRIMM TIDES

CHANDA HAHN

The Grimm Tides

Copyright © 2024 by Chanda Hahn

Neverwood Press

Editor: Hot Tree Editing

Cover Design: Covers by Aura

www.chandahahn.com

Paperback ISBN: 978-1-950440450

Hardcover ISBN: 978-1-950440467

Ingram ISBN: 978-1-950440474

For my kids,
One day, you will get around to reading this book
and see the dedication.
I love you.

PROLOGUE

As a slow fog drifted in, it covered the harbor like a white blanket. Ship bells rang out, warning sailors to be alert and cautious in the growing mist. The ships gently swayed against the wooden dock as waves splashed against their hulls. On the edge of the next pier, a group of seals slept, cuddling together like a pack of puppies.

A light beam from the lighthouse pierced the darkness at the other end of the harbor. From the ocean's depths, a haunting melody drifted up—a song of desire, need, and hunger.

On a fishing vessel, two men were late coming in from a long and productive day of fishing.

"Do you hear that, Jerome?" Nicky asked his shipmate as he secured a line to the dock cleat. He paused to listen intently into the near darkness.

"Hear what, Nicky?" Jerome replied gruffly.

"That sound." Nicky pointed toward the foggy bay.

Jerome tilted his head to listen. "I hear the waves. Watch the rope, Nicky. You're getting sloppy."

"No, I swear I hear something. You're just half-deaf," Nicky snapped back. He secured the rope and continued down the dock, heading toward the moored boats, his silhouette disappearing into the fog.

"I may be half-deaf, but I'm not half-dumb. You never go investigate strange sounds, especially in the middle of the night," Jerome called out after him, but Nicky didn't respond. "That stupid kid thinks he knows everything," Jerome muttered as he watched the dock, waiting for Nicky to return. "Nicky?" he called out again.

Echo Bay was famous for its strange sounds and haunting songs too. Many caves were only visible during low tide, and the wind whistling through those caverns created an eerie melody. Most of the time, it could be ignored. Other times, it was a call that dared one to investigate. But Jerome knew better. He knew never to approach the water's edge when he heard the call.

A heavy thud reverberated off the end of the pier.

"Nicky!" Jerome yelled out in worry. He dropped the rope, grabbed a lantern, and stepped off his fishing boat. He pulled his fish knife from his hip and walked along, scouring the shapes of each vessel, noting their empty decks. *Jolly Dodger*, an old-fashioned pirate ship, was permanently docked and gave tourists a pirate dinner adventure filled with rum tasting or nonalcoholic brews, bawdy songs, and even a fully choreographed fight. The ship's sides had been extended with seating along the docks lifted on platforms, giving the impression of a giant bowl around the boat.

Jerome lifted the lantern high, and nothing moved. He limped along the pier, his old age slowing him down as he searched the fog and took note of an empty berth, where the *Tosallas* fishing crew had either already headed out for the morning or had never returned from the night before.

"It's not funny, Nicky," Jerome called, sweeping the lantern from side to side. He was nearing the end of this dock, and only a few crates were left between him and the edge.

Jerome turned as a figure flew out of the sky.

"Gotcha!" Nicky yelled as he swung onto the dock from the stunt rope off the *Jolly Dodger*.

"Oh, you rascal." Jerome grabbed his chest in startlement.

Nicky let go of the rope and laughed, bending over to rest his hands on his knees. "You should have seen the look on your face, old man. You looked like you saw a ghost."

"With my cataracts, you idiot, everything looks like a ghost."

Nicky chuckled, wiped his nose, and surveyed the depths again. His head cocked like he heard a noise. "Do you really believe the rumors of treasure hidden in Echo Bay?"

"No, if there were treasure, my grandfather would have found it already." Jerome scoffed and waved a swollen hand at Nicky to follow him back to the boat.

"But what if the treasure's real?" Nicky reached into his pocket, his fingers playing with his lucky coin. "If the treasure's real, does that mean the curse is too?"

"Where's your head at, boy? It's a ploy by the travel committee to bring tourists to Echo Bay. That's all," Jerome said as he studied Nicky, taking in his transfixed expression as he continued his scrutiny of the water. "Come, we have fish to unload. Since I ain't got a fleet, I have to bring in twice their load to pay the bills." Jerome shuffled back, his pace picking up because he was irritated that he let the young pup get one over on him. When he didn't hear Nicky's footsteps following, he turned.

Nicky was kneeling at the end of the dock, staring into the water.

"What are you doing, kid?" Jerome called out.

But Nicky didn't seem to hear. He slowly stood, his head turned to Jerome, his eyes glazed over as if he was sleepwalking.

There was a zipping noise, and Jerome caught sight of a line of rope that had laid coiled on the edge of the dock and was now being yanked into the water with great force.

"Hey!" Jerome yelled to warn Nicky, but it was too late. One second, Nicky stood on the edge of the dock; the next, his foot was snagged in the outgoing line without a sound. Then he was gone, swallowed by the waves.

"Nicky!" Jerome ran as fast as he could, the morning light causing the waves to turn from inky black to a dark green. Through the misty fog, he could see a trail of darkness where Nicky's body was being dragged underwater out into the bay like a fish on a rope line—pulled by an unseen force. There was no ship in sight.

"Sweet Mary and Joseph." Jerome grabbed his knit hat in shock and tried to calm his heart. A terrible squeezing pressure filled his chest. He dropped to his knees, feeling lightheaded, and fell to his side. His eyes struggled to focus on the shadowy image that climbed out of the water at the end of the dock. It was covered in seaweed and slowly crawled toward him like a predatory creature. Dark eyes reflected nothing, and a mouth gaped open with razor-like teeth inside.

"Noo!" Jerome gasped out as his head hit the dock, and then he heard it—a whispering echo of a song that chilled his bones. One he had once heard long ago. A melody that always preludes death.

CHAPTER 1

"WHAT IS THAT AWFUL SOUND?" EVERLY SAID, COVERING her ears. She stood at the bottom of the stairs leading to the attic room. Everly carefully stepped over the stray socks and the folded towels waiting to be carried up. Ignoring the piles, Everly ran up the stairs and looked around the vaulted attic bedroom. It was quaint. A dusty, overstuffed chair was covered with piles of clothes—hopefully clean, but Everly doubted it. A full-size mirror and a few mannequins with old dresses stood in the corner near steamer trunks. On one side of the attic was the opened dormer window and her aunt's single wrought iron bed directly underneath. Another propped open skylight did bring in a single breeze, but the room was quite stifling, as it didn't have air-conditioning.

The commotion of noise came from an old Victrola. The record spinning and the wailing coming from it was not pleasant.

Everly rushed across the room and pulled the needle off the mini record with an accidental scratch. The wailing stopped.

She breathed a sigh of relief.

"I was listening to that." A muffled voice came from beneath a pile of clothes on the chair. "It's soothing."

Everly turned, and the blob of clothes moved. A slender arm rose in the air and pulled a compress off her face, revealing the red eyes of her aunt Summer.

Summer was her father's—Everick Hart's—sister. Her brown curly hair was pulled back in one of her many tie-dyed headbands, and despite the warmth of the attic, she was bundled in a teal bathrobe, her feet curled up beneath her. She moved in after Everly's father passed away from cancer. Summer's boyfriend had broken up with her, and she was wallowing in self-pity and enough heartache to be the inspiration for numerous Taylor Swift songs.

"Yeah, well, it sounds like a cat in heat." Ever lifted the record and looked at the faded markings. The title was barely legible—something followed by the words "Tantric Echoes." The music label icon had a swirl in the corner. "Play it much longer, and we'll have all the tomcats in the neighborhood prowling our yard."

Summer moaned, turning sideways in the chair, draping her legs over the armrest and an arm over her puffy eyes. "Well, at least someone could have a chance at love."

"You only knew him for three days. That's barely enough time to know if he's an ax murderer."

Summer gave her an ugly look. "He was a Sagittarius with a dairy allergy. I'm an Aries, and I hate blue cheese. It was like a match made in the stars." Summer sighed dramatically.

"Yeah, that's not a stretch because *nobody* likes blue cheese." Everly pinched her lips together and tried to hold back her frustration at her aunt. Summer had always been carefree and a bit off. But then, every one of her family members had been different.

Everly came from a line of grievers—people who can see grimms, supernatural creatures from beyond. But the gift of sight only came when they were young and if they witnessed someone close to them die. Hence their name, griever. Her whole family were grievers going back generations. Her grandfather was the county coroner, her grandmother was his medical assistant, and her dad was the Misty Creek homicide detective.

She now attended a private school called Gravemark that trains grievers in hunting rogue grimms. She has an omen—a talking raven that helps her and acts like a familiar. Weird was definitely a character trait for the Hart family.

Everly looked around the Victrola for the open trunk and found an empty sleeve for the old record, noting the unique circular pattern. She slipped it back onto the stack of other old recordings that seemed like they hadn't seen the light of day in years.

"You wouldn't understand what it's like to love someone so hard and it be one-sided." Summer sighed.

Everly felt a tug in her chest. *She knew.* For years, she'd had a crush on Hunter Abernathy, her best friend's older brother. She'd been trying to ignore his handsome smile and charm. He'd always been off-limits, dating other girls or one in particular—Aimee Stillwell. That was until a week ago. But then, after an altercation near Hollow Lake where Sergeant Mitchell tried to burn her alive in a cabin to cover up his and Ranger Danville's murderous crimes, Hunter had kissed her.

Almost? she thought. *Maybe?*

The more she tried to replay the moment in her head, the more she began to believe it was just a figment of her imagination. She thought there was a mere brush of contact on her lips. Maybe it was a brush of his hand?

She sighed.

Everly had spent countless nights obsessing over the moment that had happened in the blink of an eye, and before she could even talk to Hunter, he was gone—shipped off on a secret griever assignment to who knows where.

If Holland found out that Everly had almost—maybe—kissed her brother, she might lose her best friend. It was a sore spot between them. Holland stated that people were only ever friends with her to date her brother. She would never do that to Holland. She couldn't betray her best friend, but simultaneously, she was betraying her heart.

She looked over at her aunt, who had crumpled back into the chair and pulled the cloth over her eyes. Burying herself into the cushions, she faded into the mound and seemed to disappear into the piles of clothes around her.

A muffled sob came from the pile, and Everly stood awkwardly, watching her aunt cry. She wanted to comfort her.

"Do you want me to bring you a cup of tea?" Everly asked.

"No, thank you," Summer said softly.

Everly turned to head back downstairs, and the mound of clothes moved again. "But I'll take an iced vanilla coffee with a dab of whipped cream."

"But I would have to drive to Deja Brew, which is across town—"

"And a muffin. Whatever flavor they have," Summer interrupted Everly.

"Fine," Everly muttered, storming down the stairs to the second-floor landing. She paused and glanced at the blue floral wallpaper, which was slightly more welcoming than the red fleur-de-lis wallpaper on the first floor. Holland had called her red-painted Victorian house, with its dark shutters and old medical examiner's office slash morgue in the backyard, creepy. To her, it was home.

She continued downstairs to the charming kitchen with faded cabinets and an eat-in kitchen table. A door by the stairs led to the basement and backdoor outside. Off the kitchen was a solarium. Grandma Birdie was watering her plants, which ranged from medicinal to deadly and were kept in various colorful pots, speaking to Birdie's colorful personality.

Everly grabbed her keys from the dish on the counter and headed for the back door.

"What does she want now?" Birdie asked without turning around. She was still beautiful in her seventies. She once had the same strawberry blonde hair as Everly's, but hers had faded to a soft golden white with hints of red. Her eyes were lighter, and her skin was still flawless and pale. Like her daughter, Summer, Birdie always chose bright colors to accent her look. Today, it was a bright yellow shirt and pink capri pants with a polka-dot work apron. She had a rainbow silk scarf around her neck.

"Iced coffee from Deja Brew and a muffin."

Birdie shook her head and motioned Everly to follow her to the fancy dining room that no one ever used. In it, there was a white lace tablecloth covering a beautiful Queen Anne dining room set, glass lamps, and a china cabinet. Birdie went to the bottom cupboard in the china cabinet and pulled out a sleeve of plastic cups with the purple bean logo of Deja Brew. She took a dome lid, wrapped straw, and paper bag from the stack.

"What are you doing?" Everly asked in awe.

"Some things never change." Birdie took a cup, went into the kitchen, added ice cubes, pulled out a bottle of iced coffee she had tucked away in the back behind the orange juice, poured it into the plastic cup, and added a tablespoon of Monin's vanilla syrup, whipped topping, and put the dome lid on it. She pushed it across the counter at Everly.

"What about the muffin?" Everly asked, somewhat in awe.

Birdie pulled an individually vacuum sealed muffin from another cupboard and slipped it into a paper bag. "Now let it sit for ten minutes so the ice starts to melt and the cup gets condensation, then bring it up to her."

"How?" Everly shook her head in surprise.

"Hey, I may not claim her, but I raised her. She has always craved the same thing after a breakup. I learned this trick years ago. I'm just thankful that Deja Brew hasn't changed their logo or menu all that time, or I'd be broke from all her coffee runs."

"She doesn't know the difference?"

"She hasn't bought herself coffee from there in fifteen years. Has to do with her boycotting them because of some offense committed years ago."

"What offense?" Everly asked.

"Your aunt played her ukulele for open mic night, and

the manager banned her. Summer still craves their coffee but refuses to patronize the place in person."

Everly frowned. In some ways, she understood that her aunt tended to be a bit much and hard to handle, but that made her unique. She definitely didn't have a musical gene in her body. Neither did Everly. But that didn't stop Summer from trying. Despite having zero talent, she was determined to be the next Janis Joplin.

Birdie pulled a chair from the table and sat, avoiding the chair that Everick, her father, always sat in. "So tell me, how have you been?"

Everly leaned against the counter, pulling her strawberry blonde braid over her shoulder and trying to avoid this conversation. She started to roll the ends of her green plaid shirt between her fingers. "Fine," she answered.

Birdie's blue eyes narrowed. "Fine. My daughter falls head over heels for a guy within three days, and when he doesn't return her calls, she mourns for days. You've lost your father, had your life turned upside down within a few weeks, and were almost burned alive in a cabin in the woods. I think I need more than just 'fine.'"

"I lost my dad, but you lost your son," Everly corrected. "How are you handling it?"

Birdie's painted lips thinned, and she knowingly wagged her finger at Everly. "Don't change the subject. I'm old. I've known my fair share of death and have grieved for years. I've learned to deal with the pain. You're a recent griever, and the PTSD comes back sometimes at the most inopportune time. Like flashbacks. So are you still going to stick with 'fine'?" Her eyes narrowed to slits.

Everly sucked in her breath and watched as her grandma

noticed her tell. She thought she had been hiding it, but who was she fooling? It was why she had started returning home each evening after class and driving to school in the morning. She hoped to be able to sleep at home in bed, hoped the bad dreams would disappear. Instead, they just intensified.

"I can tell when a griever is hiding things," Birdie said.

"Just nightmares." Everly shrugged, playing it off.

"Oh, bug." Birdie placed her hand, covered with rings, on Everly's shoulder. "How about I make you one of my special teas? I've got just the one for nightmares. I call it 'Nox.'"

"Sure." Everly sat at the table as her grandma went into her solarium and started to pull a few leaves and petals from various plants; then she went to her dried-leaf tea tins. All her tea blends were homemade.

When she was done, she poured her tea into a home-made tea bag and attached a label. She pushed it across the table toward Everly.

Everly took the tea bag and sniffed the contents—hints of lavender, lemon, and something she didn't recognize but smelled relaxing.

"Now," Birdie said softly. "Never stir this one. Let it steep only."

"Why?"

Birde placed her hands on her hips and harrumphed at her. "Tradition, that's why."

"Superstitious is what you are." Everly put the tea bag on the counter and leaned back to close her eyes. She was rubbing her temples. She couldn't help but still hear that record's echoing vibrant, trashy noise. It seemed to reverberate through her head.

No. Wait. That vibration was the phone in her pocket.

Everly slipped her phone out and saw the text from Holland.

> You coming?

> Yes, I have a free period this morning. I'm coming in late.

> Is everything okay? I feel like you're avoiding me.

Everly's heart stopped in her chest. *Did Holland suspect the almost kiss with her brother?*

> My family needs me right now.

It was always easier to lie in a text since she didn't have to look someone in the eye.

> K, just text me when you get here.

> I will.

And as if thinking about boy problems wasn't enough, another text alert popped up. This time, it was from Ian.

> Stop sulking. Get to school.

She could almost hear him barking through the phone at her. She stared at the text. *Sulk.* She didn't sulk.

Everly groaned.

"You can't avoid him forever," Birdie said slyly.

"Avoid who?" Everly's head snapped up so fast her phone dropped onto the table with a clatter.

"The other person on the line. From how your face just changed to the color of a crab apple and immediately paled, I'd have to say... a boy."

"He's not a boy."

"Oh, excuse me, man." Birdie's lips pursed into a knowing smile, which made Everly groan.

Birdie's eyes drew to the newspaper sitting in her father's spot, and that smile turned down. This time, it was Birdie's face that went white.

"What is it?" Everly asked.

Birdie took the paper and tucked it under her arm. "Nothing that concerns you. I just missed the sale on roast beef at the Kwik Mart." Birdie's eyes flickered away, and she got up from the table. Everly watched her out of the side of her eye, and Birdie casually slid the paper into the garbage can. One thing her detective father taught her was how to spot a lie, and her grandma had about three different tells.

When the to-go glass had enough condensation on the counter, Everly decided it was time. She went and slammed the back kitchen door and carried the drink up to her aunt, placing it on the coffee table next to the chair.

A hand reached out and picked up the drink. After fumbling with the straw, Summer placed it in the lid and took a long sip.

"So good. Deja Brew's iced coffee is the best."

Everly didn't stay but headed back downstairs. Birdie had left the kitchen. Everly quietly lifted the lid and unfolded the newspaper to see what her grandma was trying to hide from her.

On the front page was another article about Sergeant Mitchell, the police officer who had tried to kill Everly because she figured out he was behind the Hollow Lake killings. But Everly and her friends knew better. She knew that Sergeant Mitchell was working with Ranger Danville, a werewolf who was once a griever and happened to be Ian Holmes's—her school mentor's—father. The two had some twisted deal involving blackmail that ended in Ranger Danville's death, shot by Mitchell. Mitchell was then killed by Officer Stevens, who caught him in the act of trying to burn her alive in a cabin.

Except now, there was a new detail released to the press. There was a small picture of her from last year's Misty Creek High School yearbook photo. It wasn't a horrible photo. At least she was smiling and wearing her favorite denim jacket that accented her blue eyes, making them seem significant, doe-like. The image printed made her pale skin look almost sickly. Her high cheekbones had a hint of blush —one of the few times a year she wore makeup. Her strawberry blonde hair fell past her shoulders. Everything about the picture felt average.

In the article, she read, "Everly Hart is the daughter of recently passed Misty Creek Homicide Detective Everick Hart."

Officer Stevens said he would try to keep her name out of the press. Well, that didn't happen.

"Uh-oh." Everly crumpled the paper into the garbage can. Just as a flash of light blinded her, she looked into a camera lens and saw a photographer standing on her back porch.

She blinked, and a beautiful brunette beside the photographer tapped the window frantically. "Everly, do you want to tell us about your close encounter with death?" The reporter smiled. It was beautiful, pearly white, and had all the allure of a crocodile waiting to eat her alive.

The flashbulb went off again, and she noticed a video camera on a third person's shoulder.

Everly dove into the back hall and pressed against the wall to hide. The wall of picture frames of the generations of Harts dug into her back.

"There's even more out front," Birdie snapped, storming from the front entryway.

Everly made her way to the front door and looked out the sidelight.

"News vans from all the three local channels, and even that gossipy online podcast. What's his name?" Birdie tapped the window to point to the elderly gentleman with pepper-gray hair and mustache. He looked like he came out of a Poirot mystery novel with his tan jacket and hat.

Birdie wasn't fooling Everly. She knew the name of the podcaster. Gerald Petrovich. He was her online nemesis, and she was secretly obsessed with everything he produced, which mainly consisted of supernatural events and gossip relating too close to her family's line of work. But every once in a while, he landed on a nugget of truth. Everly even helped Birdie make an online account so she could log in and leave him scathing comments about his detective abilities. She lived to prove him wrong.

"How do I get to school?" Everly asked. "Once I leave, they will be all over me."

Birdie gave her a wry smile. "Oh, you just leave it to me and Corvis. Give us five minutes." Birdie disappeared into the house, and a few minutes later, she heard an upper-floor window open.

Everly grinned when she figured out what Birdie was doing. As one of the few grievers who could talk to birds, she never outgrew that gift even though it was destined for grievers to lose their ability to see grimms and any other gift they might have gotten once they reached a certain age. Everly saw a dark shape fly past the window. It was Corvis. It pained her to think that she might lose her ability to hear him one day.

Everly grabbed her bag and keys, headed to the back hall, and waited for the signal. A dark shadow, a flock of ravens called an unkindness, grew overhead. They began to land in trees on the neighbor's roof, and other birds, large and small, began to assemble.

"You ready?" Birdie called from upstairs.

"Yep!" Everly stayed hidden, waiting, listening.

Then there was a screech. And a thud, followed by more screaming.

Everly peeked around the corner to see the reporter and camera operators running down the back porch steps as the birds began to dive-bomb them, sweeping past, flapping their wings into their faces. The expensive camera fell to the ground, and the reporter tripped. The cameraman helped her to her feet, and they took off running toward the street.

"Now!" Corvis yelled.

Everly dashed outside and into the front seat of her white Mini Cooper convertible. She locked the door, turned the car on, and backed out of the drive, almost hitting another reporter. She turned her wheel as more cameras flashed and bolted, driving away as fast as possible, heading toward the mountains.

Her heart thudded heavily in her chest as she drove toward Gravemark. She checked her rearview mirror for over twenty minutes to see if she was followed. It wasn't until she came to the stone gargoyles that guarded the entrance to the school and spoke the secret password to pass through the misty gates that she felt she was safe.

CHAPTER 2

"You need to learn to take a better photo." Holland came into Everly's dorm and jumped on her bed. She held up her phone to show the giant image of Everly splashed across the news article.

Everly couldn't help but feel like a pale ghost compared to Holland. Her best friend had luscious brown hair with just a hint of highlights; her tan accented her beautiful skin, and she always seemed to glow. Holland had an enthusiastic personality that attracted people—especially boys.

Everly was the odd one—the bookworm who preferred reading, drawing, and making costumes over a Sunday brunch and TrendTok. But like opposite sides of a coin, they somehow completed each other. Everly had never had a best friend before, and she valued that friendship above all else, even if it meant ignoring her longtime crush, Hunter.

Everly dumped her backpack onto the side of the bed and changed into her school uniform. She donned her green blazer jacket with their school crest on the pocket—a criss-crossed sword and ax behind a gray half-oval shield with the letter G. The whole emblem resembled a headstone, which was fitting considering how dangerous their school assignments were. It had earned the academy the nickname "Graveyard."

"We're supposed to keep a low profile, but now everyone will know my face from here to Timbuktu," Everly grumbled.

"Yeah, I don't think this will benefit your griever career." Holland pocketed her phone. "You're going to be grounded," Holland said, using the griever term for not being allowed out to reap grimms. "You can't go out to neighboring towns without drawing unnecessary attention."

"I know," Everly said as she sat on her bed and draped her arms over her knees. "What am I going to do?"

Holland awkwardly patted Everly's back. "It will pass. It just takes some time. I know from experience. Sometimes, the vultures need to find another juicy story."

Everly flopped backward on the bed to stare up at the ceiling. Holland understood. Her family was surrounded by the controversy of her mother's sudden death. The day she met Holland and Hunter Abernathy was when her father investigated the death of Pamela Abernathy. A tragic fall down the stairs ruled accidental, but Everly learned the truth. A grimm killed their mother.

Everly looked through TrendTok and saw Hunter's story photos had been updated—pictures of him drinking coffee at a nondescript cafe.

It was vague on purpose because all the photos were carefully planned and photographed weeks ahead of time by the GCS team. GCS stood for Griever Cover Stories. That particular cafe table came out of the prop room in the photography studio, and Katherine Dorn, or Kat, made the coffee he was drinking.

The next photo gave Everly pause. It was Hunter with his arms wrapped around Aimee Stillwell's waist. His face was buried in her shoulder as if snuggling her. With her shoulder-length brown hair, Aimee was making a peace sign at the camera. They looked happy, in love.

Everly frowned as she tried to study Hunter's hair. *Was it shorter than when she last saw him? Longer?*

There was no way to tell *when* this photo was taken because it could have been from months ago and only recently posted. Each of the grievers created background stories scheduled to be posted while the grievers were on cases. No one would believe a teen would disappear from social media for weeks. Each of their profiles was carefully curated to create a living, breathing alibi. Everly had spent hours taking similar shots with Ian Holmes as her "cover boyfriend." She felt that every photo of Ian and her looked like it came from a romance novel cover. But that was because he had the bad-boy vibe, and Everly was the innocent book nerd.

"Have you heard from your brother?" Everly asked, trying not to sound hopeful.

Holland made a face. "Nope, he was sent out on an assignment with Aimee, believe it or not. Which means he is incommunicado. What are the chances that those two would get paired after their breakup?" She adjusted her sock. "I bet you they're already dating again. He's always been a sucker for damsels in distress, and Aimee can be the worst."

Everly's heart sank.

Holland glanced at her watch. "Time to go." She

checked her makeup in Everly's mirror and then headed into the hall.

Everly groaned and pushed herself up, grabbing her crossbody. Underneath, she saw a white envelope with a red wax seal on top of a black gift box. It was the same as the one she got from the society inviting her to come to Gravemark. She ran her finger under the wax and opened the envelope.

Inside were two lines.

Courtyard.
Midnight.

Everly tucked the envelope into her bag, hiding her smile, and lifted the box. Inside was a robe, and she knew there would be a secret ceremony. She wondered why it was being held in the courtyard, not the secret hall. How was she ever going to focus on classes? She wanted to ask Holland about it but knew keeping things like this a secret was better. Not all sibs, or siblings of grievers, were allowed to come to the Grimm Society's meetings.

———

Everly kept pulling on her neckline as she adjusted the green robe. She assumed she needed to wear the robe since it was in the box that accompanied the extremely vague instructions.

Her nerves had gotten the best of her, and she had paced most of the night until her clock read 11:45 p.m. She left her room silently, making sure the door didn't make a noise as she closed it and headed down the back stairwell. She had already learned the layout of the whole campus because that was what her father had drilled into her. *"Learn the details and commit them to memory. It may save your life one day."*

She held one hand on the brick wall as she navigated the stairs by the glow of the emergency lights to the first floor. Her breathing was normal, and her heart was calm, as she had a vague idea of what would happen. She had heard the whispers from the other students. It was a night for omens. It was an event that only happened once a year, where grievers could present themselves and get chosen by an omen.

Everly had asked about her father's owl the day she met Corvis, and her grandma had joyfully explained the omen ceremony.

"What kind of omens are there?"

"Oh, it depends on the student and what they attract—bats, cats, spiders. One year, a student even had a butterfly." Birdie laughed. *"It was hard to keep your father's omen, Orly, from eating it."*

Everly came to the last step, pushed the heavy metal exit door, and left the school. The first thing she noticed was the chill in the air brushing against her hair and the bright moon's light on the white rock path that seemed to glow. She followed the path, twisting through the hedgerows until she came to the courtyard's center. It was a round dais with ten pillars of varying height around the semicircle. At the head was someone in a dark robe, their face and head covered by the hood. Behind them were rows upon rows of other students in green hoods. Everly moved to stand among them.

The leader in the hood spoke, their voice low and gravelly, genderless. "Welcome. Tonight is a special night where omens choose grievers to bestow their gifts upon. In doing so, they will share a bond with you, a life with you, and will be your companion, your guide, and your protector. However, not everyone is ready for the responsibility. The omen and the omen alone do the choosing."

As if on cue, an omen from each genus flew, hopped, crawled, or slithered onto one of the pedestals and specially designed perches. She recognized a horned owl, a bat, and Corvis, her raven. She spotted a fox, hound, and black cat on the lower pedestals. On the pedestals that touched the ground were frogs, ferrets, and even a beetle.

Everly felt the wind change, and she looked up and saw bats fluttering in the belfry. She could see eyes staring at her from the bushes. A reflective glance told her a fox or two might have been waiting in the bushes.

The sky became alight with even more fluttering. The sound was so loud that Everly covered her ears, looked up at the sky, and saw it was covered with wings. Birds of all sizes began to flock to the roofs and perch along the decorative balconies.

"Never before has it been this attended." The master of ceremonies looked up in awe as a cauldron of bats swarmed in a circular motion. "A strong griever is here, which attracts omens of equally strong fortitude." They motioned with their arm to the students lined up along the sides. "Any of our students who would like to present themselves forward for selection may do so now."

A crunch of gravel made Everly turn, and Holland removed her hood and nervously stepped from among the others in green cloaks. Her dark hair was in a braided crown. She took off her robe and discarded it on the ground. She was dressed in white and stepped up on the platform closest to Everly.

Holland turned and caught Everly's gaze and gave her a small smile. Everly gave her a thumbs-up of encouragement. "You got this," Everly whispered.

Then Thomas, a young sib with a mole on his cheek, joined Holland on the dais.

Two more students came forward. The rest stayed where they were; either they already had an omen or were too nervous to get rejected by the omens. Or, like Hunter, off on an assignment.

Everly could see Holland's hand trembling, so she reached out and grasped it, giving it a reassuring squeeze.

"You," the voice commanded, pointing to Thomas. "Stand on the dais and say—"

"I choose you, Pikachu!" a dry voice cut in.

"Corvis, what did I tell you about speaking out of turn? You're ruining it." The leader's voice rose to a familiar pitch.

Birdie! Everly chuckled when she recognized the fearsome Grimm Society master of ceremonies as her grandmother.

"What's going on?" Holland asked, her face contorted in confusion.

"Oh, it's the raven delegate. He's talking back to the speaker."

Even as she whispered to Holland, Birdie and the raven were having a full-on conversation about respecting elders and bringing cartoons into a ceremony.

Holland looked around the dais and saw the raven sitting on one of the columns. "I don't hear anything."

"Oh, um...." Unsure what to say, Everly clammed up when she forgot not everyone could hear omens as she could. Usually, you could only hear the omen you were bonded to unless you had a gift like Everly and Birdie. It made perfect sense to have Birdie, who never lost her gift of speaking to omens, oversee this particular ceremony. She was the only one who could.

Thomas, who was called upon, stepped forward into the center of the dais. He turned slowly to look each omen in the eye and waited an excruciatingly long time.

From what was explained to her, if an omen chose a griever, the delegate would announce their choosing, and then one of the omens waiting in the wings would volunteer. Omens were amplifiers of the griever's natural gifting, so they were attracted to certain traits of a griever. If none felt a match, they wouldn't present themselves.

"Step back, young initiate. This is not your year," the hooded voice of her grandmother commanded.

Everly could feel her leg start to bounce in nervousness for Holland. Would a sib get a griever?

"You can do it," Everly encouraged Holland.

Holland lifted her chin and whispered back, "Of course I can. This is my year. I know it." Holland released Everly's hand and stepped toward the center. She put on the brightest smile and looked around at the omens expectantly.

A small voice came from a bat hanging upside down on his pedestal's perch. "This griever can't hear, and her sight is weak. The bats will help this human. Who will pair with her, my brethren?" After the announcement, there was a long pause.

Holland, who had heard none of the exchange, was starting to doubt herself and back away from the dais. She was looking at each of the podiums in hope. The sky was empty except for one shadow flapping toward her from the belfry.

"Oh no. Not you. Anyone but you!" But the bat didn't hear her. Holland opened her mouth to scream as a furry black form dove right for her head. "I change my mind. I don't want an omen." Holland tried to scramble back into the crowd, but it was too late; a small fruit bat haphazardly crashed into her and clung to the back of her dress.

She looked at the beast clinging to her shoulder straps. Her mouth kept dropping, and she whimpered in fear and moved to stand next to Everly. "It's a flying rat."

"Bats are cool." Everly tried to comfort her.

"Why, thank you. I do think we are as well," the small bat spoke. "Got any food?"

"Did it just speak?" Holland asked, a look of amazement in her eyes as she realized she could hear the bat speak.

"Yeah, it did," Everly said encouragingly.

"Got any food?" the bat asked again.

"No, um. Not right now, but I do in my room." Holland's face softened, her expression turning to one of wonder as she gently cupped the bat. She broke into a bright smile.

Two more students went forward and didn't receive an omen, and Everly began to realize how rare it was. She did see someone from Drake Hall get paired with a salamander. Gemma Kane was rejected as well.

Someone tried to move through the crowd, and she got shoved from behind and fell forward onto the dais. Everly's hands pinwheeled, and she tried not to fall over, but her hood fell back. As soon as she stepped onto the dais, there was an eruption of fluttering wings and barking as every single omen seemed to launch into the air right toward her before anyone spoke.

"Mine" came a high screech from a podium.

"No, mine!"

"We claim her!"

Yipping and snapping followed as a black fox dashed forward, and a cat lunged for him, cutting him off from approaching. A hawk flew at Everly's head, and she tried to duck but then tripped over the cat. She landed hard on her hip and looked up as a wolf was knocking over students and racing toward her, and then a hawk attacked him midair. One by one, each of the omens seemed to go crazy and attack one another, and Everly was right in the middle of the foray of screaming animals and claws. She felt a clip of wings hit her face, and part of a claw nicked her cheek.

Her heart was racing. This wasn't what she wanted.

"Something's wrong!" Birdie cried out, waving her arms. "It's never been like this before. Everly, get back!"

She could see the students stepping back in fear through the chaos of attacking omens. Her eyes met Ian's as he dropped his hood and tried to escape the mob. He stepped forward, and the omens thought he was there to hurt her, so they turned on him.

"Stay back!" a hawk screeched and, claws extended, swooped for Ian's head.

"No. Stop!" Everly commanded, and the hawk swerved upward at the last minute. She heard a scream as a wolf bit a girl's robe, trying to drag her away from Everly.

"Corvis, help me!" Everly cried out in terror as something brushed against her face, and she felt a sting of pain.

As if reacting to Everly's fear, Corvis dove from his

pedestal and, in a flash, grew ten times his size and let out a blast of light, which scattered the other ravens into the sky.

As the bright white light lit up the sky, Everly could feel a sudden jolt of fear coursing through her veins. She could barely see through the bright lights until she noticed the faint outline of a portal in front of her. Then, all was quiet. The omens haunting her were gone, and the night was silent. All the students stared at her in awe, as if she had just performed some dark magic.

Still holding her bat tightly, Holland asked, "Where are all the omens?"

Without answering, Birdie grabbed Everly's arm and pulled her through the garden. The aftereffects of the light still blinded her, and she couldn't see where her grandma led her. She heard the slamming of a garden gate and felt warmth as they headed inside a building, and then a door slid open, and they were alone. It was a relief to avoid the chaos and confusion, but Everly couldn't help but wonder what had just happened and what was yet to come.

A clink of a chain and a bare bulb flicked overhead, and Everly realized they were inside what looked like a small broom cupboard.

Birdie gently pulled back her own hood and reached to touch Everly's face, examining the scratch on her cheek. Despite a few scratches and cuts on her arms from trying to protect Everly, Birdie was more concerned about her well-being. "Bug, are you all right?" she asked, using the child-hood nickname that always brought a smile to Everly's face.

"I'm fine. But I didn't know that you would be overseeing the ceremony?"

"Just because I'm old doesn't mean I'm not useful. As a

guardian of the omen ceremony, I am crucial in communicating with all the omens and preserving their secrets. It's an honor and a responsibility that I take very seriously."

"Secrets?" Everly asked, her curiosity piqued.

"Never mind." Birdie's eyes widened when she realized her slip.

Everly crossed her arms. "Fine, but explain to me what happened. It was like all the omens went crazy."

"You stepped on the platform, and the omens responded and tried to claim you."

"But I already have an omen. I have Corvis. Can a griever have more than one?"

"It's not been done because the bond between an omen and griever is so close. It's not usually safe to have more than one, but maybe it's because your bond is so new." She pressed her fingers to her forehead. "There's a lot of firsts that are happening with you that I just don't have answers to."

"You mean when I chose Corvis as my omen when it is usually the other way around."

"Yes, that was highly unusual, but that is kind of the way Harts do things. But changing the status quo has made people question how things are done. Your choosing Corvis marks you as special, and now every omen from here to the sea wants to be paired with you. You're just lucky that you got Corvis, and he is strong enough to protect you."

"Where is Corvis?" Everly asked worriedly. "I saw a bright light, and then he and the other omens disappeared."

"He sent them all away." Birdie fidgeted with a ring on her finger, her eyes downcast. Her voice dropped, and she whispered, "He did something he wasn't allowed to do, and because of that, it will take some time for him to recover from the magic used and, um... get back from wherever he took them."

"Get back from where? Is he okay?"

"He's fine, I think... I've only seen one other omen attempt to do what yours did. Normally, it's done when you summon an omen, but Corvis... did the opposite, which is forbidden. He will probably be in trouble with the Grimm Society for what he did."

"That's not fair," Everly said. "He was only trying to protect me."

Birdie pressed her lips together. "I know, Everly, but omens have their own system of rules they must follow, and he knowingly broke them."

"So what, is the ceremony over since the omens are gone?" Everly had a sinking feeling that what had happened might have made it so no one else would get an omen until the next ceremony.

"Yes, my dear. It's over. I have to report to Ms. March and the society. It would be best to go to your room and not speak with anyone. Let me deal with the repercussions."

"But, Grandma."

Birdie pushed on the wall, and Everly realized they had gone into a secret compartment. When they went into the hall, the panel disappeared, and Everly couldn't even see a crack in the seam of the wood. What other secrets did the school hide?

"Go!" Birdie shooed Everly away and headed off at a quick pace toward Ms. March's living quarters.

CHAPTER 3

Everly woke up with a pounding headache. It was as if she could hear Corvis, but he was far away, trying to speak to her through mud. She rubbed her temples, sat cross-legged in her dorm room, and tried to focus on him.

She could hear him faintly, but it was more feelings. She pressed her hand to her chest.

"I'm okay," she breathed out. Immediately, a feeling of relief came over her. They were both okay. Then, their connection broke, like a phone call that lost signal and disconnected. She could still feel Corvis but didn't know where he was.

She got dressed, ran a brush through her hair, and noticed that, like Birdie, she didn't exactly get away unscathed. There was a scratch on her cheek that had already scabbed over. In all the commotion, she didn't even feel it. She brushed her blonde hair down, doing her best to hide the mark on her forehead. She added mini gold hoop earrings and her dad's watch, completing her "I don't care if I'm poor" ensemble.

She turned and looked at her mother's journal on the nightstand and flipped open one of the random pages.

October 10, 2005
I've been trying to do some extra research on the Holmes family and the differences between types of curses.

Since Eugene was bitten, he is the carrier of the werewolf curse. Ian is under the generational curse—passed down from father to son or mother to daughter. As long as Ian doesn't succumb to his wolf, his children will be less likely to be wolf-cursed. It may take generations, but there is a chance for his child to grow up normal. Ways to keep the werewolf under control?

Wolfsbane?

Poison or cure?

Maybe the answer lies in studying curse breaking.

Everly flipped the pages but didn't find anything else of note. It was the end of that journal. She would have to go and pick up her mother's second journal, but she wasn't sure if she wanted to learn more about the woman that everyone else looked up to but was a stranger to Everly.

Her phone buzzed with a notification about a change in her morning class.

> Please meet in the school foyer at
> 8:15 a.m.

Everly looked at her father's watch and realized she would have to get going. She shoved the journal in her brown crossbody bag, headed out of her dorm, and passed the living room.

From the outside, Gravemark Academy looked like a creepy castle used to film horror shows, but inside, it was warm and welcoming. There were four resident halls for the older griever students: Liberty, Serenity, Lupine, and Drake Hall. Holland lived in Liberty while Everly was in Serenity. Each hall had twelve dorms—six boys were down one hallway, and six girls had rooms down the other. They shared a kitchen and commons area. Just outside the entrance to each hall was the resident advisor's apartment. She passed Ms. Bellcamp's apartment on her way to the main foyer.

Unfortunately, not all halls were filled; being a griever was dangerous. There were currently around thirty students old enough to be grievers, while those too young were across the campus in Colgate Cottage—a smaller home for foundlings, kids orphaned at a young age with the gift of sight. They wouldn't survive in foster homes, as many would mistake their gift of sight for schizophrenia or mental illness. Gravemark and the other griever schools would house and educate them until they were ready to begin full griever training.

Everly was preoccupied with her thoughts as she jogged down the grand steps and into the school's main foyer, with its polished white tiles and high stained-glass window. It was still late morning, and the light flickering through created a rainbow of colors on the floor. Everly was surprised to see about fifteen students had gathered. When she entered, there were quite a few stares her way and whispers. She knew they were whispering and talking about last night's unusual omen ceremony. She stood in the middle of the room, her hands in her blazer pockets as she pretended not to hear the jabs.

"It was crazy. Every omen tried to attack her."

"Her? Why would they attack her?"

"There must be something wrong or evil about her."

"But didn't she already get an omen? Why was she even on the platform? Is she just that greedy?"

Everly tried to keep her head up and not acknowledge all the whispers and conjectures that were getting it wrong.

Everly almost returned to her room, but then Holland appeared with a big grin, and she kept subtly petting her blazer pocket.

"Don't tell me." Everly chuckled. "Your omen is in your pocket."

"He said his wings are tired, and he wants me to carry him." Holland gave the cheesiest grin.

Everly was proud when she didn't roll her eyes at how easily Holland was being manipulated. "I think he's being lazy and found someone who will spoil him rotten."

"Shh, did you see how itty-bitty he is?" Holland admonished.

"You called him a flying rat yesterday."

"I'm a woman. I'm allowed to change my mind."

Everly spotted a long black clawed hand reach up out of the green pocket and feel around. Immediately, Holland pulled a date out of a baggie and handed it to the omen. No matter what she initially thought of having a bat as her familiar, she was officially smitten.

"Does he have a name?" she asked Holland.

"I am Batman," the little bat muttered through a mouthful of chewy date.

"No," Holland said, not having heard him. It seemed even with an omen, she still struggled to hear.

"I am vengeance. Fear me.... Mmm, food." Her pocket wiggled again as the bat kept eating.

"Maybe you should call him Bruce," Everly suggested.

"I don't like Bruce" came from the pocket.

"As in Bruce Wayne, alter ego of Batman," Everly added, speaking to the bat.

"Yes, I am Bruce the Batman," the bat in the pocket responded.

Holland frowned at her omen. "Did he just say something? I swore he said something."

"Yes, he likes the name Bruce."

"Like Springsteen?" Holland asked, her eyebrows raised in excitement.

"Exactly." Everly chuckled, giving up.

Holland's phone buzzed, and she looked at the screen, her brows knitted together in worry. She looked around the foyer, a look of panic on her face.

"What's wrong?" Everly asked.

"N-nothing," Holland stammered, her hands trembling as she quickly stuffed her phone into her pocket. Her complexion had turned several shades paler, indicating her distress.

"Are you sure you're okay?" Everly insisted, sensing something was wrong.

"I'm fine," Holland snapped. "Drop it, okay?"

Something was definitely wrong with Holland, and she acted funny, hiding something. Maybe it had to do with her new bond with her omen or boy problems. Everly was about to ask her when she felt the energy in the room shift as Ian

Holmes—the boy her mother wrote about in her journal—entered the foyer.

There was an unmistakable aura of power about Ian. He was the strongest griever in the school—part talent, part because he was born werewolf cursed. Something that he tried to hide from most here. He kept his werewolf under control by drinking wolfsbane, and whenever a full moon was near, Ms. Bellcamp would take him and lock him away in a cage of silver to control him. The more he shifted, the stronger his werewolf side became, and the deadly hunger for blood grew.

When Everly's life was in danger, Ian overpowered his fear of the consequences. Without the moon to aid him, he purposefully shifted and broke the chains on the cellar door to save her. Although it was only a partial shift, it brought him dangerously close to making his curse permanent.

As Everly gazed at Ian's disheveled appearance, she couldn't help but blame herself for the incident that had driven a wedge between them. That night, Ian let his werewolf curse take over to save her from the burning cabin. He had barely spoken to her since then, except for biting remarks through text messages. It seemed like he silently held her responsible for making him rescue her.

Ian's usually wavy blond hair seemed even more out of control today, and his piercing blue eyes were bloodshot and tired. As Everly tried to wave at him, she noticed his back stiffen, and he turned away, avoiding her immediate presence. The tension between them was palpable, and she couldn't help but wonder if they could ever mend their relationship.

Everly felt a range of mixed emotions. While she was

grateful for his heroic act, she now carried a heavy burden of guilt. A burden Ian must feel as well because he kept avoiding her. The whole situation had strained their relationship, and Everly was unsure how to move forward.

"What's with you two?" Holland noticed the dismissal by Ian. "Isn't he supposed to be your mentor?"

"He was. But he's not acting like my mentor anymore," she said, frowning. "He's barely talking to me. Just texts."

"What did you do, kill his dog or something?"

"Uh," Everly said, reminding Holland. "His dad died."

Holland's eyes widened in surprise. "That's right! I forgot that the grimm hunting in the mountains and murdering people was his father," she said without tact and a little too loudly. Ian's wolf hearing picked up the comment, and then those icy eyes met hers, and she could feel his fury.

Everly took a deep breath. Most of the students believed Ian's dad died years ago. They weren't in the hall when she revealed his family lineage. Only the members of the Grimm Society, Holland, Hunter, and Cass—the changeling—knew.

As Everly thought about changelings, she suddenly felt a gentle pressure against her arm. Turning, she saw Cass, who had transformed into her fae form, standing beside her. Despite her petite stature, Cass exuded an otherworldly aura that made her seem both fragile and dangerous at the same time. Her porcelain skin, dark eyes, and white hair added to her mystique.

As Cass nervously fidgeted with her hands, Everly couldn't help but notice her striking appearance, especially when she was wearing the Gravemark green blazer and plaid skirt. However, Everly also knew that Cass wasn't her real name and that she was hiding something beneath her timid demeanor. Although Cass was a master at mimicking others and taking on their personas, she seemed uncomfortable in her skin. Despite her small size, Everly knew better than to underestimate Cass's strength and cunning.

Everly reached into her crossbody bag and pulled a sucker out, and before it even cleared the opening, she felt Cass's tiny fingers snake it away.

Seconds later, the wrapper was discarded on the floor, and the girl was almost giddy with joy at the red lollipop in her mouth. Changelings had a soft spot for sugar.

"Cass," Ian called, and like a lost puppy, Cass obeyed and went to stand next to Ian, looking up at him with wide, adoring eyes. His mouth turned down, and he started to point toward the doors, explaining things to her.

"Well, I guess he's *her* mentor now," Holland observed. "You've graduated. Congratulations... I think?"

"What a tangled web," Everly muttered under her breath and looked down at her black boots, noticing one of the laces had come untied.

"Web? Spider? Where?" She could hear Bruce and his excitement at possibly eating a spider.

"*No,*" Everly thought back at him.

As she sensed his disappointment, she glanced around the room, searching for Corvis. But he was nowhere to be found. She usually found him perched on the top buttress or outside on a nearby tree. Although he was supposed to be with the other omens in the vivarium, he felt it was beneath him to hang out there. Plus, there was no TV in the vivarium, and Corvis was addicted to watching cartoons. She hoped that he would return soon.

"Okay, students," Mr. Jensen called out as he bounded

down the stairs. He was the youngest of the staff members and a former griever, like most teachers here. He had short brown hair, a bright smile, and too much energy. He clapped his hands. "I've got a special treat for you today! Field trip."

The students groaned despite Mr. Jensen's exuberance. Field trips usually meant time to slack off, but with the number of groans, she knew it was probably hard work.

"But I didn't change my shoes!" Lacie exclaimed.

"What's so bad about a field trip?" Everly turned to Holland, who had scrunched up her face in disgust.

"It's a field test," Holland said, shoving another date into her pocket. Her dark hair was pulled into a high ponytail, her cute dimple showing. "It's like a pop quiz for grievers."

Everly felt a moment of panic. She was still new to being a griever, even though she had been cleared to hunt grimms. It didn't mean she was ready for a test. Most of her knowledge came from reading her family's past griever journals.

Holland leaned over and whispered, "It's okay, you've got this. It's just like the 'guess how he died' game your dad played, but, um... worse and not fun." She tried to smile, but the smile didn't reach her eyes.

Mr. Jensen motioned out the doors to where two minibuses lined up along the curb. Everly saw that Mr. Wilcox, the biology teacher, was in the driver's seat of the first bus, and the second was empty.

Everly stuck close to Holland.

"Okay, I need all the sibs on Mr. Wilcox's bus. The rest of you come with me."

Holland turned and waved sadly at Everly. "Good luck," she mouthed and marched up the steps to sit on the half-empty bus with Thomas Golding and Anna Winthrop. Sibs were usually the siblings of grievers whose gifts hadn't surfaced yet. There was usually only one super strong gifted griever per family; it was unusual to have more than two. But for the Abernathy family, there were three, and Holland's gifts weren't that developed yet. Some believed it was because of buried trauma. She didn't remember being in a car accident with Kerrigan, her older sister, that led to the death of Kerrigan's boyfriend—Dean. Because of that, her gifts didn't fully develop. Sibs were treated like grievers in training, with all the knowledge but without the gifts.

Everly sighed and was the first student onto the second bus. There were only four rows of two seats on each side. She headed toward the back of the bus, more to hide than anything. Slipping into a seat on the left, she put her crossbody bag on her lap.

She watched as Gemma Kane got on the bus. She froze when she saw where Everly sat, and a quick look of disgust flashed across her face before she sat in the front. The other seats filled in around her. Maddox took the back across from Everly and gave her a nod in greeting. Ian boarded next, and Everly looked right at him, but he turned and took the second seat from the front, Cass sliding in next to him like it was the most natural thing in the world.

Mr. Jensen turned on the engine, and the bus pulled out of the parking lot.

Everly looked down and fiddled with her crossbody bag; a shadow passed, and Lacie took the seat next to her. She started talking about clothes, makeup, and boys.

Maddox's eyes widened in horror, and he pulled out his headphones and covered his ears to play a game on his phone.

It wasn't the easiest of conversations for Everly to jump into, but she tried because she was used to listening to Holland.

Every once in a while, she could feel someone watching her, and she glanced up to meet Ian's icy gaze. She saw him take a swig of wolfsbane from his flask before leaning against the window and closing his eyes. A white head popped up, and Cass looked back and grinned at Everly before plopping back down into the seat next to Ian.

A sour feeling filled her stomach. *Was it jealousy?*

Then it hit her—the reason Ian was assigned to mentor Cass. They shared a bond. They were both grimms—or were-cursed grimm in Ian's case.

When she first learned of the grimms, Everly never expected to be tutored by one. Most believed them to be vicious killers. But some grimms were good, like Professor Stubbs, her history teacher and a dryad, and Mr. Halsey, the librarian. So it would make sense to give the changeling a mentor who could relate to her.

She should be excited for Cass. Instead, she was morose.

They drove further into the woods, the tree line growing closer together. The high mountains cut off light, and the air felt chillier. Out of nowhere, the bus stopped in front of an old, abandoned two-story house. Its once vibrant paint had faded, and the roof was littered with holes. Ivy crept up the sides of the old house, obscuring the windows. The front screen door swung and creaked ominously as it swayed back and forth in the gentle breeze. The stones leading up to the porch were buried beneath dead grass and pine needles. Along the outside of the house was an old-fashioned cellar and coal shoot.

The bus doors opened, and the students piled off and gathered in groups. Everly tucked her hands into the pockets of her navy blue peacoat and hung by the back.

Something wasn't right. She couldn't put her finger on it but did not want to go anywhere near that house.

Everly found herself seeking out Ian, moving to stand by him. "How are you?" she asked.

"Fine," Ian said, refusing to make eye contact. Instead, he focused on their surroundings, his eyes narrowing. "If you haven't noticed, I'm not your mentor anymore. I've been reassigned," he stated. His eyes flickered briefly to Cass, who was sniffing the air.

"I smell candy," Cass said, licking her lips.

Ian lifted his face and gave a cursory sniff. He shook his head as if disagreeing.

"Do you smell something?" Everly asked. "Because I smelled—"

"This is a test," Ian cut her off. He finally turned to look down on her, raising an eyebrow. "Trying to cheat?"

"I didn't expect you to," Everly remarked. "I was just trying to make conversation. We haven't talked since—"

"You got yourself captured," Ian interjected, "and almost killed."

"That was an accident. I trusted Sergeant Mitchell. I didn't expect him to turn on me."

"That is the hardest lesson to learn. That sometimes, it's not the grimms that are the most deceitful. It's humans." When Ian said humans, his mouth curled like the word was distasteful.

Confused at the change in Ian's demeanor, she stepped back, deciding to avoid him altogether.

"Okay, here is your field test. Behind me is a house that is grimm occupied. What kind of grimm? That is for you to find out. You will go inside in groups of three and do your best to identify the grimm. Don't catch or attack. Just make observations." Mr. Jensen rocked on the balls of his feet and looked over the unenthusiastic students. "Volunteers? No." He looked at his clipboard. "Okay, let's do Lacie, Grayson, and Simon."

Everly watched as Lacie made eye contact briefly before moving to the front of the steps, waiting for Grayson and Simon. Lacie immediately took the lead, her cute demeanor gone as she began to bark orders. She was pointing up at the house, directing her teammates, and making a plan of action. Everly could see why she was a griever team lead. Lacie Duvall came from a long line of grievers. She was a legacy, a great-great-granddaughter of one of the founding members of their school. So when it came to hunting grimms, Lacie had a killer instinct and sharp intuition, cleverly concealed behind her perfectly polished smile and shimmering lip gloss.

"Griever bags?" Lacie asked Mr. Jensen, referring to the bags with their reaping tools—iron and silver weapons—they would use to fight and capture grimms. But telling them they wouldn't need a gun almost guaranteed it was a level one—trickster, pixie, or gnome. Harmless for the most part when left alone.

The level of grimms ranged from one to five. Level twos—haunters—were ghost types. Threes—lures—were mermaids, sirens, etc. Level fours—titans—were giants, minotaurs, and any other grimms whose largest asset was strength. Level five, known as the hunters, were the cold-blooded killer type. These included werewolves, vampires, and carnivorous grimms.

"You won't need them," the teacher assured them, pulling out a stopwatch.

Lacie nodded, and the three of them headed toward the house. She took the front step. Simon flanked right; Grayson went left.

Ten minutes passed, and Mr. Jensen looked at his stopwatch and said, "Okay, next group."

"But they haven't come out yet?" Maddox gestured toward the house.

Mr. Jensen folded his arms across his chest. "How long would you wait before sending in backup?"

"Well, I—ten minutes, but you said we wouldn't need our griever bags." Maddox seemed uncomfortable.

"I did."

"But if they haven't come out, then—"

"They failed." Mr. Jensen pointed to Maddox, Deena, and Dom.

The three grievers headed into the house, this time all of them taking the front steps.

Everly listened for sounds of fighting and watched the windows for any shadows that passed, but it was silent. Nothing came from the other teams.

This time, it was Ian who approached her. They were the last group left. It was up to them to work together. "I don't like this. We sent six grievers in; we should have heard or seen something."

"Oh, now you want to work together? I thought this was a test. Isn't this cheating?"

The corner of Ian's mouth twitched. "Cheating or winning? You want to get a good grade, right?"

"What kind of grimm could it be?" Everly asked.

"I don't know." Ian crossed his arms and sniffed the air again. "I know it sounds stupid, but to answer your earlier question, I smelled pizza."

"Pizza? Really?" Everly said in surprise. Her brain was working a million miles a minute. She reached into her crossbody bag, pulled out her journal, and began to scan her notes compiled from her family's griever journals, searching for any clue as to what grimm would inhabit a house.

She turned the pages. There was something there. Something she remembered reading about a certain grimm with different lure abilities. *Will-o'-the-wisps...?* She immediately discarded that thought.

After another ten minutes, Mr. Jensen motioned for Everly, Cass, and Ian to go in last.

Ian bolted toward the house.

"Ian," Everly called, reading the last page but still feeling helpless.

Ian didn't wait. He ran straight for the front door, kicking it open with immeasurable strength. Cass was right on his heels. As soon as they crossed the threshold, he turned, his fists up to fight, but she saw his shocked face as the door slammed behind him with a thud.

Cass squealed, and then all was quiet.

Everly stood there on the front sidewalk alone, looking up at the house with trepidation. What happened to the other grievers? Why didn't anyone come out?

She walked up to the front stoop, raising her foot to step

on the first of the wooden porch steps, and froze, slowly dropping it back down to the gravel path.

Holland would call it her spidey sense, but her dad would say it was her gut and intuition. There was something wrong with this picture. With the test. With the house.

Corvis? She called out to her omen, but he was silent. Either not allowed to interfere in this test, or still too far away.

Everly kept her distance and slowly walked the perimeter. Her skin crawled with goose bumps, and she listened for sounds of life within, but again, there was nothing. It was as if the animals in the woods had also gone silent. Was there anything she had read that could give her a read on the situation?

She closed her eyes and tried to follow the other grievers' routes. They all entered the house. Group two had gone similar routes, but someone had used a window and the back door. Ian had all but barged in the front.

The closed shutters could indicate a grimm that hated the light, but it could also be haunted. Bogarts, ghosts, and even hobbs liked to live in abandoned houses.

But she didn't think it was a low-level grimm.

It was as if the *house* ate the grievers.

But this was different. It reminded her of the children's story.

"It's a trap," Everly said, turning toward Mr. Jensen.

Mr. Jenson looked up from his clipboard, a look of surprise in his eyes. "What do you mean?"

"The whole house is a trap. A lure set by a level-three grimm. Like the story of Hansel and Gretel and the gingerbread house used to lure children."

"But you haven't identified the type of grimm," Mr. Jensen said smugly.

"Witch," Everly said.

Mr. Jensen's grin grew wider. "Again, I asked what kind."

"What kind?" Everly tucked a stray strand of blonde hair behind her ear and quickly began to run through the various kinds of grimm witches. There were ones whose talent lay in casting curses and granting wishes, but then there were others whose giftings were reminiscent of the seven deadly sins. Gluttony was the witch in the Hansel and Gretel story.

"A deadly sin witch," Everly answered. "Gluttony."

Mr. Jenson's eyebrows rose high on his head, and he gave a clap. "Bravo!" He brought his fingers up to his lips and gave a piercing whistle. The house opened up, and with a loud bellow, the grievers came tumbling out of the house as if expelled by a giant burp.

Lacie came rolling down the steps, covered in cobwebs and dirt and wrapped in fur coats. She was followed by Simon, who was tangled in old curtains. A giant steamer trunk fell down the steps; the lid crashed against the ground, and Ian tumbled out.

Cass walked down the steps, wrapped up in Christmas tree tinsel. "I'm so sparkly!" she giggled.

Everly went over to help Lacie up. "It was horrible." Lacie shivered and wiped at invisible cobwebs. "It was like a bad episode of *Hoarders.* As soon as I entered the house, the closet opened and pulled me inside it."

"The furnace swallowed me up," Dom said. "Luckily, it was off."

"At least you weren't eaten by the sofa. Look, I found

two dollars in change." Maddox held up the coins and coughed up a piece of sofa foam.

Ian got up and stormed away. He was not even willing to admit that he fell for the trap.

"How did you know?" Lacie asked in disbelief. "I refuse to believe that you weren't tipped off. No one caught that the house was enchanted."

"I didn't. Except that something felt off."

"It was because we didn't come out," Grayson said. "If you had gone first, you would have fallen into the trap just like us."

"I don't know about that," Mr. Jensen said. "Everly was hesitant since she got off the bus, weren't you? Tell us what you were feeling."

"It wasn't so much of feeling as smelling." Everly looked around at the surrounding woods. "It didn't smell like the woods near my house. I couldn't smell pine or dirt. Cass said she smelled candy. Ian smelled pizza. I smelled—uh, never mind." She felt her cheeks grow warm from embarrassment; she wasn't about to admit she smelled Hunter's brand of aftershave. "It smelled differently to each of us. It reminded me of the tale of Hansel and Gretel, who were starving and came upon the gingerbread house. That house would have turned into whatever the desire of the traveler was. You all smelled what you most longed for."

"But what kind of grimm is a house?" Maddox shot back, hands on his hips, determined to prove Everly wrong.

Everly looked at Mr. Jensen, and he gave his nod of approval. "It's not a grimm at all, but what I believe are the remnants of an old lure charm. Mr. Jenson just asked us to identify what type of grimm inhabited the house. Past tense.

If there were a level-three witch, he would have equipped us with griever bags."

"That's correct, Ms. Hart," Mr. Jenson said excitedly. "This was one of the first grimms I encountered over twenty years ago. The witch was a hoarder with a gift of gluttony but has since passed on. The essence of her spell is still powerful to this day, so we keep it boarded up and hide it away. This can happen with spells and curses. Their strength doesn't always diminish over time, even with the passing of the caster."

"That house could have killed us," Deena snapped.

"Nonsense, it is only strong enough to hold you in an enchantment for about an hour, tops. Then you are, um..." He moved his hand to cover his mouth and his laughter. "Released from the spell."

"Don't you mean ex-spelled," Maddox said, unable to contain his humor in the situation.

Lacie rolled her eyes, and Ian held back a smile. He gave Everly a nod, and she felt a warm feeling run down her body.

The sound of wheels on the gravel made everyone turn to gaze down the road as a news van slowly made its way up the path to the house.

"Oh no!" Everly groaned. "How did they find me way out here?"

"Oh, um." Lacie held up her phone and grinned sheepishly. "I may have tagged you in my picture."

"On the bus!" Mr. Jenson ordered. "Quickly, we don't want them to see the house."

In a mad rush, the grievers ran back onto the bus as Mr. Jenson jumped into the driver's seat and gunned it. The bus's wheels turned over on the gravel as they sped away, kicking up dust. Hopefully, the news reporters would pass on by the enchanted house.

"Well, this is exciting," Lacie said. "I've never been chased by reporters before."

Ian grumbled, expressing his discontent with the situation. "It's not exciting. It almost put us all at risk of exposing one of the Grimm Society's secrets. Everly's newfound fame is a liability."

Hearing this, Everly felt her anger rising. She couldn't believe what she was hearing from Ian. "That's not true," she said, trying to control her frustration. This was not the Ian she knew. He changed overnight.

Ian's blue eyes darkened, and he pointed at the dust cloud of the news van following them. "Okay, then what do you call that?"

"A complication," Everly sighed.

"Neither is good."

Everly held onto the back of the seat and watched as the van got farther behind them. They didn't stop at the enchanted house but followed them right to the front gates of Gravemark.

CHAPTER 4

"THIS IS GOING TO BE A PROBLEM," MS. MARCH SAID, looking at her computer screen. She turned the monitor so Everly could see the live security feed.

Only a few hours after Everly returned from the field test, Ms. March called her into her office. Ms. March, the headmistress, wore a pale yellow dress with a jacket, the raven brooch still pinned on her chest. Her hair was carefully pulled back into a coif. She was shorter than Everly, probably only reaching four foot ten, but her heels gave her the illusion of being taller. But not much.

Ms. March's office had close to two dozen doilies. On the armrests, under a potted plant, under a picture frame showing a young Ms. March with a tennis trophy in front of Gravemark Academy.

"It will pass," Everly said, hopefully thinking about what Holland had promised.

"Yes, but the real question is when? I don't think it is going to die down anytime soon. As you know, our students must keep a low profile. We can't have our faces broadcasted across the state. It ruins our grievers' anonymity. And it makes it increasingly difficult for them to go on reaping assignments with news cameras watching every move they make."

"Then what do you suggest I do?" Everly's fingernails dug into the wooden chair. She leaned forward, her knees bouncing in worry.

Ms. March's hands steepled together, and she pressed her fingers against her chin. "The Grimm Society has decided it would be best for you to leave Gravemark for now."

Everly's stomach dropped, the world began to tilt, and she couldn't regain her footing. "Leave? But I only just got here. You can't—"

"I can," she corrected sternly. "Plus, it is for the best. Pack only what you need. You will be escorted off campus within the hour." Ms. March folded her hands; her nails were a soft baby pink color, one that Everly had heard Queen Elizabeth used to wear.

"But why?"

"For the safety of our school and our students. That's why," Ms. March said.

"Is this because of what Ian Holmes said?" Everly asked, her voice coming out bitter.

"No, this decision is based on Mr. Jensen's recommendations, and I have to agree with him." Ms. March pulled out a white vellum envelope with a wax seal on the cover. It was similar to the one she was given when she was first accepted into Gravemark but not identical.

This wax seal was gold. Not red. Was there any significance to the color of the wax? Different sender?

Her fingers trembled as she held the letter in her lap, unable to open it and read the words inside. What would happen next?

Everly felt a single tear slide down her cheek. She tried to wipe it away, but another one followed. "Is there anything I can do? Anyone I can talk to?" she pleaded.

"No, it has been strictly forbidden for you to speak with anyone. Do you understand?"

Everly nodded numbly. She felt that she was being unfairly punished.

"Good, that will be all." Ms. March nodded and dismissed Everly with a wave.

Her feet felt glued to the floor, and when she pushed the chair back, it scraped loudly against the floor. When she stood, she did so automatically, her feet walking back to her dorm while her mind was a million miles elsewhere.

She had failed. She was dismissed from the school. She was probably the first in her family to do so. She walked up the stairs, her hands running along the fence, feeling sentimental.

How could she get so attached to this school so fast?

When she went into Serenity's common room, it was empty. Everly looked at her watch. It made sense. Most of the students were in classes for a few more hours. There wouldn't be anyone to see her leave in disgrace. It was probably better this way, she thought.

She unlocked her room, went to the wardrobe to pull out her duffel, and began to pack all her clothes, leaving behind the school uniforms. The school provided those, so she felt bad taking them with her. Besides, they would only serve as a reminder that she had failed at being a griever.

"It's not fair," Everly muttered again as she vehemently shoved a pair of socks deep into her bag. She cleared out her nightstand drawer, grabbing the can of pink pepper spray, hairbrush, and—

Her hand wavered over her mother's griever journal. It was one thing to feel exhilarated at reading her heroic father's journal entries. But they had a different connotation when she found out it was her mother's exploits she was reading.

Her mother had left when she was eight years old. Walked out the door and never came back. Under the journal was another envelope from the Grimm Society. It only held two words—*well done*—and she recognized the handwriting.

It was the same as the journals.

It was a letter from her mother.

Everly slammed the nightstand closed, leaving the journal and letter, and moved to the computer desk. She took her laptop and tucked it into her bag. Then she grabbed her father's picture on the desk—a framed photo of Everly and her dad sitting on their front porch.

"Sorry, Dad, I guess I wasn't that good at being a griever." She ran her fingers down the glass, wrapped it in a flannel shirt, and carefully packed it in her duffel. It didn't take her an hour to pack. Maybe twenty minutes at most, and the rest of the time, Everly just sat on the edge of her bed and worried, chewing on her bottom lip. She'd have to return to regular high school, walk through those doors, and pretend to be normal.

She tried to text Holland, but her messages when unread.

When the hour was up, Everly grabbed her duffel bag and backpack. She opened the dorm room to see Ms. Bellcamp standing there with her hand raised to knock. Her blue eyes opened in surprise.

"Oh, right on time," Ms. Bellcamp said. She glanced down at the duffel and bag in Everly's hand and nodded. "Good, you're packed. Let's go." She turned and beckoned Everly to follow. Her resident advisor was normally all about fashion, preferring pencil skirts and fancy blouses. Usually, she was decked in pearls and bright nail polish. Today, she wore dark jeans and sneakers. Her hair was pulled into a ponytail and hidden underneath a black hat.

Like an assassin. Or someone that buried the bodies for an assassin. Why did her brain always go to the morbid?

Everly followed her advisor down the back stairwell, the one closest to her room. She had teased Ms. Bellcamp about living in murder central her first day at Gravemark. Today, that joke seemed less funny.

The stairwell was dark, lit only by the emergency exit lights, which created a reddish glow. Everly was surprised that they were taking the back exit. Was this part of the plan to make her disappear from class? No one can see or speak to her if they sneak her out the back way.

As Everly walked down the stairs, her heart sank with each step. Instead of heading toward the parking lot, Ms. Bellcamp turned to the basement level. The corridor led them through an underground passage. Ms. Bellcamp didn't stop there and proceeded to push through another door and climb another set of stairs. Eventually, they reached a keypad and security box, and Ms. Bellcamp swiped her badge. The door unlocked, and they found themselves in an underground garage.

"Whoa," Everly said as they approached various delivery trucks and vans.

There were three vehicles parked in the garage: an electrical service van, a plain white box van, and a flower delivery truck. A ramp led up to a heavily secured metal door with security cameras and digital codes.

Ms. Bellcamp came up to the back of the white box van, slid the door up, rolled up the belt, and came to an abrupt stop. Inside were three silver food cases on wheels, used for delivering food.

"Ready?" Ms. Bellcamp smiled.

Everly didn't feel like answering; her mouth was as dry as the Sahara. "No."

"I thought you would be excited," Ms. Bellcamp said, and she opened the second case's door; it turned out to be a mere facade that led to the inner truck, which was decked out with a computer with multiple screens, a bunk bed above it on one side, and a padded bench seat that doubled as a couch on the other. Below the bench seat were drawers, and a tall locker with weapons stood at the back. Furthermore, she discovered a small compartment that slid open to the front cab; above it, there was a bunk bed. They must have used this for a few stakeouts.

Cass was sitting at the computer desk in the swivel chair.

"Hey," Everly greeted, and Cass waved, then pushed off and spun the chair. She wore gray sweatpants, an oversized sweatshirt that made her seem even more childlike, and white sneakers. Her white hair was pulled back out of her face.

Cass bobbed her head, turned to the desk, and carefully moved the mouse. Being a grimm, she was still learning and had little technology experience. She was a quick study, but some oddities in how she acted did not seem quite human.

The front cab compartment slid open, and Ian's stern face appeared from the passenger seat. "Ready?" Ian was also in dark, nondescript clothes, a gray jacket, and a black hat.

Ms. Bellcamp ducked under the door into the front cab and gestured for him to move as she slid into the driver's seat and turned the truck on. "Get in the back."

Ms. Bellcamp put on a pair of sunglasses and hit the remote on the garage door. It slid open, and the truck began to drive out of the underground parking.

Cass leaned back in her chair, gave Everly a cheeky grin, and reached for a box of donuts. She looked through the different flavors and settled on powder.

"Never thought we would be doing a reverse grimm sweep," Ian said. He folded his arms and took the second chair next to Cass. He was not quite making eye contact with her, but at least he was making conversation.

"What do you mean 'reverse sweep'?" Everly sat on the bench seat and looked for a seat belt.

"We use different delivery trucks and systems to sneak the captured grimms into the school grounds. Then we transfer them to the oubliette. Today, we are using our cover trucks to sneak *you* out," Ian explained.

"I never imagined that's how you do it," she answered.

"Yeah, I'd get weird looks if I strapped an ogre to the top of my Bronco," he said.

"But normal people can't see grimms," Everly stated.

"Yes, but you forget that quite a few still can see something. They definitely wouldn't see an ogre on a Bronco, but they certainly wouldn't see a large buck. But then, sometimes, those with latent gifts will still see a grimm," Ian answered.

Ian sat at the desk and began to type. He was slower than Kat, but he knew what he was doing. Different security cameras from the school popped up, aimed at the front gate. "There are still two news vans outside the school. We may have to take Memorial Way."

"Let's just wait a bit longer for our plan," Ms. Bellcamp said. She pulled over on a back road and turned over her shoulder to watch the security screen.

"Come on," Ian muttered under his breath and leaned forward, his hand gripping the edge of the desk.

Everly, now caught up in the intrigue, was also staring at the screen when a familiar car pulled up to the school's front gate. "Hey, wait a minute, that's Sheldon. I mean, my car. Who's driving it?"

"Holland," Ian said over his shoulder.

Ian hit a button, and the camera swung to the side for another view. They could see Holland in a blonde wig, driving Everly's Mini Cooper. When the gates opened, she slowly drove out, and the reporters moved in to shoot. Holland could be seen holding her hand to hide her face as she pulled out of the school and headed down the mountain road.

"I should be doing that." Cass pointed at the screen. "I make a much better Everly." Like melting butter, she shifted, growing taller, her face filled out, and her eyes lightened to a shade of blue, her hair turning the same shade of strawberry blonde. Cass still wore the same clothes but was now the perfect replica of Everly.

"Just one problem with that." Ian smirked.

"What? What's the problem?" Cass spoke with Everly's voice but had a different inflection.

"You don't know how to drive."

Cass rolled her eyes and flumped back into the chair dramatically.

At least she had the perfect teenage reaction nailed down, or teenage theatrics were not race-specific. Everly could almost imagine a teenage giant throwing a similar fit and accidentally destroying a whole town.

The car in the security screen slowed and stopped as Holland was still getting used to driving an older vehicle.

"I know the way she drives," Everly said. "I just got the hood replaced. She better not put a dent in my car."

"Would anyone notice a new dent?" Ian teased. "It was pretty dinged up before."

"Ha ha," Everly answered back.

"Look, it worked." Cass pointed at the screen as the news vans pulled out after the Mini Cooper.

"Not all of them," Ian sighed. There was still a lone station wagon driven by Gerald Petrovich, the spook investigator.

"He didn't fall for it. I wonder why?" Ms. Bellcamp said.

"Because I don't think he is necessarily interested in me, but the school," Everly added. "His last few articles about the paranormal have hinted at Gravemark Academy."

Ms. Bellcamp pinched her lips. "Okay, we are taking Memorial Way. Please turn off your phones now so we can't be tracked." She pressed on the gas, and the van lurched forward; then she stopped when a black wolf slinked in front of their path.

Shadow, Ms. Bellcamp's omen. She rolled the window and spoke with him softly. "Not today."

"Yes, because of the day. You're sad," Shadow said.

Ms. Bellcamp looked through the rearview mirror to see if Everly was listening to her and her omen's private conversation. Everly pretended to look the opposite way, focused on the headstones and not eavesdropping.

"I'm always sad, Shadow. My burden is great."

"I come, share."

"No, you stay." She rolled up the window and ignored him when he began to chase after the van. Everly could understand how hard it would be to leave an omen, but she didn't know why he was being left behind. Everly wondered if there were secrets her teacher was worried she would overhear.

A few minutes later, they were on a hidden gravel road. It was almost nonexistent except for the random headstone every few hundred feet.

"Why are the headstones so far apart?" Everly asked when they passed a large stack of stones and a few monuments that were covered with moss.

"A hundred years ago, there was a full-scale attack on Gravemark. Many died protecting the school and the foundlings. Gravemark decided to bury the grievers where they died in battle, as a reminder of how dangerous grimms are and how close they came to decimating the school and our society."

Everly sat stunned as she passed another grave marker. There must have been forty headstones scattered. This many people had died, but why? Why the sudden attack on Gravemark?

"Has it happened before?" she asked.

Ms. Bellcamp's gaze met Everly's through the rearview mirror. Her voice trembled as she spoke. "Seven years ago, another such event occurred at a school called Crypthaven. The school no longer exists, and all the students and staff who were there that day perished." Her words hung heavy in the air, and Everly couldn't help but feel a chill run down her spine.

Crypthaven. She remembered the leader of the Grimm Society mentioning the other griever school and giving a verbal warning that she didn't want what happened to Crypthaven to occur at Gravemark.

Soon, they came to another secured gate, which ended up by a crematorium. The van passed through with a flash of a security badge, and they were on their way.

"Where are we going?" Everly finally gathered the courage to ask.

"The Grimm Society decided you were bringing too much attention to the school. So we're sending you away," Ms. Bellcamp answered.

"Oh." Everly felt her heart sink. "Is this like witness protection... or something?"

"Or something," Ms. Bellcamp said, her face severe before slowly breaking into a sly smile. "It's your first reaping assignment." She tilted her head. "Mr. Jenson said that you passed your field test with flying colors and recommended you for this assignment. It just happened that with the extra security and eyes on the school, the Grimm Society decided to send you away for a while. Far away."

Ian turned in his chair and pointed at the Google map on the computer screen. "We're going here."

Everly squinted, trying to make out the area on the map. It was a whole lot of blue, which meant the ocean. "Where's here?"

"Echo Bay," Ian answered.

"Echo Bay," Everly repeated numbly. *Was this some weird coincidence?* She had *just* found the file folder in her dad's desk with all the newspaper clippings and articles about Echo Bay and the following odd events. Every seven years, the town would be hit with a string of mysterious deaths, and they were always connected to the rumored appearance of a dark ocean tide.

Maybe the file was on the top because this was year seven, and Everick Hart was preparing to solve the case once and for all before he passed away from cancer.

Ms. Bellcamp spoke up from the driver's seat. "Echo Bay was part of Crypthaven's territory, but it has become ours since the school was destroyed. It's farther than our usual cases, so Mr. Jensen suggested bringing you. Maybe you won't be recognized way out there."

Ms. Bellcamp began to hum a song that was so off-key it was unbearable, like a weird hummingbird mixed with chainsaws. Everly flinched at the unexpected sound.

"So I'm not expelled from school?" Everly asked, looking toward Ms. Bellcamp in surprise at how out of tune she hummed.

Cass seemed immune to the noise, while Ian seemed prepared.

"Not yet." Ian leaned back in his chair and lifted the headphones to cover his ears, looking directly at their teacher. "Give it a few hours. Being expelled may start to sound like a vacation." He pushed play on his phone and closed his eyes to relax.

Everly narrowed her eyes and plugged her ears. "Speak for yourself." But no one heard her over the cackling.

Ms. Bellcamp continued her humming, this song almost sounding like one of her aunt Summer's love ballads. *This is going to be a long ride.*

CHAPTER 5

"We're here," Ms. Bellcamp called out as the van slowed and they started to turn downtown.

During the car ride up, Everly eventually fell asleep despite the unpleasant sound. She sat up and stretched her arms over her head. Cass had crawled up to the top bunk, and one foot was hanging over the bed as she slept. When it was deemed safe from cameras, Ian had moved up to the passenger seat.

As they arrived, the refreshing scent of the ocean filled the air.

Everly leaned through the compartment door and saw Ms. Bellcamp pull into a public parking lot and park the van.

The view was stunning. Across the lot was a charming row of businesses. Each storefront had a unique pirate or mermaid theme painted, giving the street a whimsical and adventurous feel. The shops included salons, cafes, gift shops, and the Treasured Antique Bookstore.

Everly's gaze went to the marina and the vast ocean beyond it. The water shimmered in the sunlight, and she saw over a hundred ships lining the docks. The private vessels, including sleek sailing ships and luxurious cruisers, were on one side. On the other side were the fishing vessels, mainly consisting of large fleets with a few tugboats and smaller fishing boats.

But the main focal point was the magnificent pirate ship. It was a stunning sight, with its black-and-white sails and intricate details painted on the ship's hull. It was like it had just sailed in from a swashbuckling adventure on the high seas.

Ms. Bellcamp hopped out of the truck and stared at the cove, unable to hide her gaze. She swallowed and grabbed her iPad. "Coming?" She gestured to a side road to the marina's left. Unsure of what to do, Everly grabbed her bags and followed Ms. Bellcamp down the private drive, which opened up to a spread of beach houses with private beach access. Most of the houses looked closed up for winter since owners probably only visited during the warmer months. There weren't any cars in the drive, but again, most probably used the much larger lot above instead of the small driveways that could only fit one car.

Ms. Bellcamp walked up to one of the houses, approached the back door, punched in a code, and took a key out of a compartment.

"Okay, this house will be your headquarters for the next week. That's how long we have until the tide disappears for another seven years. So pick an empty bed. Change and get ready for debriefing."

Ms. Bellcamp opened the door, which swung into the back hall. They passed the kitchen and were greeted by a familiar face.

Katherine Dorn was standing at the counter frosting pink cupcakes and wearing Dr. Martens boots, striped socks, and baggy jeans with holes large enough to fit a dog. Her long fuchsia-colored hair was in two braids. She gave Everly a bright smile. "Yo!"

"Kat, you're here?" Everly asked in surprise.

"Of course." Kat grinned, carefully putting down one of the cupcakes. She picked up a second and began piping yellow frosting on the new cupcake. "Been here for what seems like forever, but it was only a few days. As soon as I got the message that you'd be joining us, I began assembling your portfolio." She nodded with her chin toward a manila envelope on the counter.

"Where do I put my stuff?" Everly asked.

Kat flung an arm over her head, pointing to the hall. "Bunk with me. First room on the right."

Everly did a quick tour of the home. The downstairs had a kitchen, dining room, living room, and two bedrooms, each with twin beds. Upstairs was the master bedroom and another guest room.

Everly went into the first bedroom and dropped her duffel and backpack on the twin bed nearest the door. She noticed Kat had already claimed the other bed, which was covered with clothes and comic books.

A painting of a lighthouse hung on the wall above each bed. The whole room was white with touches of a beach theme, including an en suite bathroom with seagulls, starfish, and netting for decor. Their bedroom and the living room each had a slider door that opened to the deck, and within ten feet, she could walk on the beach. She had a full view of the marina to the right from the patio and a great view of the private beach. To the south was a lighthouse, and Everly gazed at the photo above her bed and wondered if it was the same.

When she headed out past the kitchen, she saw that Cass had tried to grab a cupcake, but Kat became defensive. "Cass, drop it. If you take one bite of those, I will annihilate you and everything you hold dear. Do you understand?" Kat said it with a scary smile, and it terrified Cass enough that she put the cupcake down.

"Good girl." Kat opened a cupboard, pulled a sleeve of Oreos from a bulk pack, and tossed them to the girl. "Here, these are safe for you to eat."

Cass caught them, and her smile was restored as she headed to the couch.

"Catch us up," Ian said with a cold soda already in his hand. He reached for a swipe of the frosting, and Kat swatted his hand away before he got any. He gave up and moved to sit on the edge of the couch, popped open the can, and took a swig.

Everly was eager to know the plan as well. She didn't precisely understand how grieving assignments worked.

Ms. Bellcamp held out her iPad and flipped through various articles—the same ones her dad had compiled from seven and fourteen years ago. "It's a phenomenon we've nicknamed the grimm tide. It happens every seven years during October when the moon wanes, and it brings about a string of mysterious deaths in Echo Bay. Locals chalk it up to unfortunate accidents, as living by the sea and deep-sea fishing can be very dangerous."

"Is it always the fishermen?" Everly asked.

Ms. Bellcamp seemed uneasy and unfocused. She

looked down at her iPad and had to remember what she was doing. "The deaths always seem to be random, affecting people of different ages, but always locals." As she picked up a brochure about treasure hunting, she continued, "There are many small caves along the coastline. People die yearly from getting trapped in some caves during high tide. It's possible that there could be a natural explanation for these deaths."

Kat raised her hand. "But highly unlikely because there's rumor of the tide. Many have claimed to see the ocean suddenly turn dark before each death, like a bad omen."

"What did the Crypthaven griever team uncover in their earlier investigations?" Everly asked.

Ms. Bellcamp grew even more uncomfortable, fidgeting with the iPad pencil. "Their records were lost when the school was destroyed. We know what to expect, and you all know my history here. I have every hope that you will be the one to stop these senseless deaths. So we first need to establish your backgrounds and get you acclimated into Echo Bay's life quickly." Ms. Bellcamp looked toward Kat. "What were you able to get?"

Kat cracked her knuckles. "It wasn't easy, but with the start of the school year, most of the summer help has gone back to school or cut jobs for the season. There are only a few part-time gigs, and I managed to get both of you interviews on the *Jolly Dodger*." Kat pointed at Everly. "Your interview is tomorrow at three. Ian, you go after her. Don't screw it up."

"Nice," Ian said. "I approve."

"Yeah, well, wait until you see what I said your skills were."

"Skills?" Ian seemed a little worried, and Kat was having an absolute blast.

"Trampoline, aerial acrobatics, and stunt work."

"But I can't do any of those?" Ian said.

"Yeah, well, I may have lied on your résumé." She grinned. "Plus, maybe I wanted to see you without your shirt off. Oh, but you're *not* Ian Holmes—" She pulled out a manila envelope, sliding the fake paperwork, a burner phone, a stack of bills, and a driver's license toward him. "—your name is Duke Harrington. You're nineteen and from Southern California."

"What?" Ian said in disbelief. "Do I look like a Duke?"

"Well, I remember you complaining about your name on your last assignment."

"You named me Buzz."

"Stop whining. I created your persona after one of the greatest astronauts ever," Kat chastised.

"And a Pixar cartoon," Everly added, biting her lip.

Kat waved at Everly to shush. "Not everyone is going to make that connection."

"To infinity and beyond!" Cass clapped her hands excitedly.

Ian's hand shot straight out to point at Cass in frustration. "See, even Cass has seen it."

Kat raised her chin, deciding to ignore Ian's mini tantrum. Everly felt that Kat lived for teasing Ian with his alias.

Kat grabbed a second envelope, getting a smear of buttercream on the outside, and handed it to Everly.

Everly wasn't sure she even wanted to open the file. She dumped out the contents and saw a picture of her, taken a few weeks ago with the GCS— Griever Cover Stories —team.

"You're Eve Blakeman. Started you with something easy. It's close enough to Everly that I don't think you will screw up too badly. We usually age our grievers up and mark those we can't as homeschooled. You also have an interview. There's one show a day, so you should have plenty of time to investigate the weird things happening here. And with four grievers and a changeling, we got this in the bag."

"Four?" Ian's brows knit together.

"I said you would need to report to your team lead." Ms. Bellcamp sat in the chair facing the window, and she seemed to be lost in thought.

"I just assumed that I would be the team lead?" Ian didn't sound pleased at the prospect of working with another griever.

"I selected them specifically because they're already well-known with locals here. Aimee Stillwell's family owns this house and has a boat, so it will make getting around easier."

Aimee? Everly could already feel the trepidation as she realized what this meant. *This team is well-known together.* Grieving assignment. It could only mean...

Hunter.

Voices came from outside, the front door opened, and in came Hunter, carrying a grocery bag. Hunter was tall, tan, and muscled. His light brown tousled hair was cover model worthy, and his eyes were a deep green with hints of gold. He seemed comfortable wearing a denim jacket, dark jeans, and white sneakers.

He paused in surprise at seeing a room full of people.

Then his eyes lit on Everly, and she saw he couldn't contain his smile.

Aimee Stillwell came in on his heels and pushed past him, only to stop in disgust when she saw Everly and Ian sitting there. "What gives? We could have handled this case by ourselves."

Ms. Bellcamp didn't even look up from her iPad. "Trouble back at the school. Decided to bring out another team here till it cools down."

"What kind of trouble?" Hunter's eyes darted toward Everly, his expression filled with concern.

"Nothing that a little time away won't cure," Ms. Bell-camp answered.

Aimee took the second grocery bag and entered the kitchen to put the items in the cupboards. She kept flashing jealous gazes at Everly, and Everly took the chance to escape. She headed toward Ms. Bellcamp, who was grabbing her purse and slinging it over her shoulder.

"You're not staying?" Everly asked Ms. Bellcamp, who had not brought in any suitcases.

"I can't do what you can do, Everly. I'm not a griever anymore. I will keep in touch via Facetime and return in a few days. If you need anything, call me, but I find it highly unlikely you'll need help."

Something in Ms. Bellcamp's posture and tone of voice betrayed her true feelings.

"You don't think we'll find anything, do you?" Everly said in sudden realization.

Ms. Bellcamp blinked quickly and looked away. Her lips trembled, and she let out a long sigh. "No, I don't think you can stop what plagues this town."

"Why is that?"

"This isn't my first time here in Echo Bay. I once led a team of the best and brightest grievers from Crypthaven in an attempt to stop the grimm tide. But we never could. Then seven years ago, the finfolk—nasty, murderous grimms—attacked the school. Only those of us here in Echo Bay survived. I keep thinking, if only I could have stopped the attack." Ms. Bellcamp's voice trembled with emotion as she recalled the tragedy that befell her.

Her hands clenched into fists, and she sniffed, looking away. She wiped at her eyes with a tissue. "Ms. March contacted me and brought me on staff at Gravemark. But this is like torture. I can't be here, Everly. I wouldn't be helpful to you."

"It's guilt," Everly said.

Ms. Bellcamp nodded. "I can't stand being here for very long. It brings back too many memories, and none are good." Her hands clenched into balls. "I will leave you the truck and take my leave." She placed the two keys on the coffee table and headed out the front door.

When her advisor departed, Everly moved to the front window. She watched Ms. Bellcamp get into a taxi, which she must have ordered from her tablet a while ago.

"That was weird," Everly said out loud.

"Oh, you get used to it," Kat said, coming out of the bedroom with another laptop bag. She set it up next to her first one and plugged it in.

Hunter opened the fridge to reveal that it had already been fully stocked with milk, orange juice, bottled water, soda, lunch meat, steaks, chicken, vegetables, and fruit.

Everly went into the kitchen and looked through the

cupboards to see potato chips, bread, cereal, Pop-Tarts, and everything a teen could want, including ramen. She opened the freezer to reveal frozen pizza and pints of Ben & Jerry's ice cream.

"You hungry?" Hunter asked, pulling out fresh ground beef. "I grill a mean cheeseburger."

"I'll take a burger," Kat announced loudly. "Well done."

Hunter shot her a look. "Hockey puck coming up."

"Yes," she cheered.

"Medium rare," Ian called out, turning the TV on.

"What about you? Do you have any special requests?" he asked. His eyes met hers briefly before he kneeled to pull a cutting board from under the counter and portion the beef into patties. Without looking, he pulled out a hidden spice rack and took down the onion powder, garlic powder, and other seasonings.

"I'll eat whatever you make. As long as it's not mooing," Everly said.

"Good answer," he said, chopping away.

It was like watching a master chef at work, how Hunter knew his way around the house with familiarity. He handed her the meat plate and told her to follow him to the deck, where he started the gas grill.

She put the meat on the patio table next to the grill while he made sure the grill was clean. She took the chair farthest from Hunter and sat awkwardly. She was still trying to figure out what to talk about. They hadn't conversed since that night of the fire.

"You sure know your way around this house," Everly said, immediately wanting to put her foot in her mouth. That sounded precisely like something a jealous girlfriend would say.

Hunter's gaze fell on her, and he knew what she was asking. "I've stayed here before. This house belongs to the Stillwell family. I used to come out here during the summer."

"You mean with Aimee when you were dating," Everly said. *Why did that sentence seem to stick in the back of my throat like a rogue popcorn kernel trying to choke me?*

"Yes, when we used to date." Hunter took the plate of meat and set it on the hot grill. A satisfying sizzle followed.

He was giving her the bare minimum of answers. Not enough to satisfy her curiosity.

The sliding door opened, and Aimee came out to join them. She wore white shorts and an oversized pink sweater top with sandals. Her brown hair was shoulder-length and flat ironed straight. It shined with enough oil to reflect the setting sun. The girl practically screamed Posh Spice. She moved to stand next to Hunter and placed her hand around his waist.

"Good evening, Mrs. Bulechek!" Aimee waved to a woman in running gear walking her golden retriever along the beach.

"Evening, Aimee! How's your family been?" Mrs. Bulechek's hair was pulled into a ponytail. Even though she was in running gear, there was enough jewelry to know it was more for looks than actual running.

"They've been doing great. We all needed a break from the city and had to come out here to relax." Aimee put her head on Hunter's shoulder, and he didn't move away.

"That's nice. How have you been, Hunter?" The fact

that Mrs. Bulechek knew Hunter by name explained how often he had been out here.

Hunter closed the grill lid and reluctantly slid his hand around Aimee's waist. In response, Aimee's face lit up.

"Doing good, ma'am," Hunter replied.

"You don't let that one get away now. Her dad and I go way back." Mrs. Bulechek tossed a ball, and the dog ran down the beach. "Will we see you at the pirate festival next summer?"

"Wouldn't dream of missing it." Hunter smiled tightly.

The retriever returned with the tennis ball, and Mrs. Bulechek ran up the porch of the house next door and cast one more adoring look at the young couple as if she could bask in their young love.

When the slider closed, Hunter pulled himself from Aimee's grasp, his smile falling. His gaze flickered to Everly, who stood there with her heart in her throat—frozen in time and caught in the most awkward situation.

Was it an act? Probably, but the way Hunter leaned into her and how Aimee clung to him with such familiarity told her it was too soon to know.

Aimee grinned gleefully as if she had won her boyfriend back. She bit her lip seductively and ran her hand along his shoulders. "See you inside, babe."

Hunter's shoulders twitched, and he winced at the word "babe."

When they were alone, he looked over at Everly. "I can explain."

"Explain what?" Everly stood up. She thought he and Aimee had broken up, but maybe that was an act, and this was real.

"Aimee isn't my girlfriend. I mean, she was, but then she wasn't. Only while we're here is she my girlfriend."

"You don't need to explain anything to me," Everly cut him off, moved to the door, and looked back toward the grill. "Except you may have to explain to Ian why you burned all the burgers."

Smoke was coming from under the hood, and Hunter yelped and flipped the lid open to see eight pieces of black charcoal. Everly left him to deal with the mess he made.

CHAPTER 6

"It says 'ere that you don't have any experience as a server?" Roy Marksman, captain of the *Jolly Dodger*, said, pointing at her application.

"I don't," Everly said nervously, recalling her uncoordinated accidents. The most recent was when she knocked a drink out of Ian's hands at school.

The *Jolly Dodger* dinner show encompassed more real estate than the pirate ship. It also included a white warehouse situated near the pirate ship. The exterior of the building was adorned with different-sized harpoon guns, darts, oars, and anchors. And there even a replica cannon attached to the cement sidewalk for photos.

As Everly stepped inside, she noticed a training arena for the stunt-show workers and double doors where she glimpsed a fully equipped kitchen. Seeing how they managed to feed so many people for the show was fascinating.

The interview room was nothing like she had imagined—just a simple plastic table near a back wall of photos and memorabilia from famous guests. Captain Roy, the interviewer, was half-dressed in his pirate costume, looking like a cross between Santa Claus and Long John Silver's mascot. He had a red stocking hat, a gold tooth, and a decorative pirate coat draped across his chair. Even his eye patch caught her attention, but Everly couldn't tell if it was decorative or functional. She found out when he lifted the patch to look at her application, which had been wholly falsified thanks to Kat Dorn.

"I don't like to hire anyone without serving experience, but this is our offseason, and most of my regular cast takes off this month. We used to do three shows daily during the summer, but shows have been reduced to one in the evening."

"I'm homeschooled, so my schedule is flexible, and I could use the experience for my college applications. Plus, I'm also available for odd jobs like cleaning and errands."

Captain Roy sucked on the inside of his cheek and studied her. She could tell it wasn't going to work.

A phone rang, and Captain Roy excused himself to pick up the phone next to the appointment book. "'Ello? What do you mean you can't come in?" He turned his back, and his voice became muffled as he spoke to his employee. A few minutes later, he returned and sat down, the chair squeaking under his weight.

Her gaze landed on the photo wall behind him and the various fishing vessels and snapshots. One frame was a little more worn than the others and lacked dust, so the glass had been polished as if it held more meaning. She studied the photo. It looked to be Captain Roy when he was younger, holding up a fish, and next to him was an older gentleman who could pass as a family member. *Father? No. Too old. Grandfather?* On the dock, near his feet, was a Jack Russell terrier with a bandana around his neck. Everly took a chance.

"I love boats. That's part of the reason why I wanted this job, working on a ship and so close to the water. They bring back so many memories of when I would go on fishing trips with my grandpa and his dog; it was a little scruffy terrier named Bruno," Everly lied through her teeth, hoping he wouldn't see right through her charade.

"Really?" he asked. "Me too; I had a terrier named Russ."

"What are the odds?" Everly pretended awe. "I even remember my first time catching a rockfish. It was so ugly I begged my grandpa to throw it back."

Captain Roy slapped his knee and leaned forward as he laughed. "I loved fishing with my gramps. He was the one who taught me the importance of respecting the sea."

He leaned back in the metal chair that groaned under his weight. He didn't ask any other server-type or food-handling questions. Instead, he began to relay his childhood story of growing up on his grandpa's boat and how he used to explore all the caves in the cove in search of the famed pirate Lennox's treasure.

Everly sat enraptured or pretending to be invested. She nodded at all the right places and asked open-ended questions about his life, like how he went from a fisherman to the captain of the *Jolly Dodger*.

"Once, long ago, the *Jolly Dodger* used to be known as something far more notorious. She was the beauty known as the *Siren's Revenge*, and my great-great-grandfather served as a boatswain on her during the reign of the notorious pirate Lennox. However, there's not much left of the real *Revenge*. When she was no longer seaworthy, she was refurbished, reconstructed, and transformed into the new *Jolly Dodger*, leaving only a few traces of its original glory."

By the end of the interview, it was as if Everly had switched the conversation, and she was the interviewer.

When her time was up, Roy stood up, held out his beefy hand, and gave hers a shake. "Welcome, Eve, to the *Jolly Dodger* dinner show. You're our new serving wench. Report to Marnie for your uniform and training. I have to interview my next future pirate."

As Everly stood up, she was in a daze. She got the job because of her observation skills. When she pushed out of her chair, she saw more photos of Captain Roy's Russell in different Halloween costumes posted on the wall.

A shadow appeared in the open doorway, and Ian stood there waiting with his application in hand. He had changed and was in khakis, a white shirt, and his jacket. He had showered since that morning, his hair a bit damp, and when she walked up to him, she could smell his aftershave. He didn't move out of the doorway but stood there, blocking her. They were playing a game of chicken.

"Everly," Ian whispered.

"You must be Duke!" Roy yelled jovially. "Come in, come in."

Everly slowed and bumped him in the arm to get his attention. "You have a retriever, Russ, and you love to dress him up in holiday costumes."

"What?" Ian said in surprise.

"Trust me." Everly stepped past Ian and let him into the

room, hoping that he nailed his interview. Despite Kat's expertise at forgery, it only went so far when it came to selling a character.

Everly went around the warehouse to a side room that Roy had directed her to. She came around to a staff entrance door. Everly entered the door and headed down the hall until she got to the wardrobe department.

Everly knocked.

"Come in. It's open," a feminine voice said.

Everly stepped into the room. It was packed with clothing racks, hats, nets, and various outfits ranging from wench corsets to boots. A woman with wild straw-colored hair was present in the room. There were beads braided throughout her hair, and she wore a white flowing top with several gold bangles. Her fingernails were painted green, an unusual color that complemented the beads in her hair. She had green wing-tipped glasses on and had sewing pins in her mouth while running a pair of pants through a serger. She looked up through the bottle-like glasses and smiled from the corner of her mouth.

"Can I help you," she said legibly, despite the stack of pins between her lips.

"Mr. Marksman said I should come talk to you about getting my uniform for the show tonight?"

"Captain Roy," she corrected gently. "Okay, let's see what I have that will fit you." She put the pins down and moved over to the racks of clothes. "It's a bit colder going into our offseason, so something with long sleeves."

A window in the workroom was open to the ocean, and a slight breeze blew through, making the sea glass and shell wind chime hanging from the frame clink.

Marnie stopped her sorting and looked out the window toward the sea.

"It's beautiful," Everly said, referring to the wind chime, her attempt at making conversation.

"The natural items always make the best tones," Marnie agreed. She took her yellow measuring tape and quickly took Everly's measurements, nodding as she mentally figured out her sizes.

"How long have you worked here?" Everly asked as Marnie moved to measure her waist.

"Since the run of the very first show thirty-five years ago. I was Captain Roy's first hire," she bragged. "I started as a serving wench, like you, and worked my way up through the ranks, and now I'm co-owner. This place would fall apart without me." She smiled and played with a gold key on a chain around her neck.

"My grandma almost didn't want me to get a job here in Echo Bay; she was a bit superstitious about all the accidents," Everly lied, trying to pry out information.

"Accidents?" Marnie pulled out a drawer and began to sort skirts by size.

"Well, that's what she called them. There seems to be an unlucky string of deaths every few years. Surely, you've heard the rumors, having been here thirty-five years?"

"I can assure you that it's nothing but rumors." Marnie didn't even turn around to look at her.

Everly moved to sit on an old trunk, and Marnie spun around before she even settled her weight down. "No, don't sit there!" She shooed Everly away, picked up the trunk, and moved it out of reach.

"I'm sorry." Everly felt terrible.

"It holds our most valuable heirlooms," she said, checking to ensure the trunk wasn't damaged. "It's been in the family for generations."

"Again, I'm very sorry."

Marnie noticed that Everly's apology was sincere, so she resumed sorting through her piles of clothes. However, it seemed she couldn't help but keep an eye on Everly, almost as if she expected her to do something mean again, like accidentally creasing her skirt.

Finally, she focused back on her piles and drawers, opening and shutting them, until she came away with a black, flowy long-sleeve top, green knee-length skirt, and long, striped socks.

"Shoe size?" Marnie asked.

"Seven and a half."

Marnie pulled out a pair of calf boots with custom soles so as not to slip on the deck. "Hair must be pulled out of your face, but it doesn't have to be up. Makeup, well, that's up to personal preference. Nail polish can be any color."

"What color is the one you're wearing?" Everly asked.

Marnie blinked and seemed surprised. "Oh, I've had this shade for so long the label on the bottle wore off." She moved on and gave Everly a black apron with pockets. "Okay, I think that's everything. You go ahead and get dressed in the dressing room down the hall and then go to the kitchen area, where you will work under Starla. She's the lead tonight and will run you through tonight's service."

"Got it," Everly said.

Marnie waved her off, her head already back down as she hummed a sweet song while focusing on sewing a hem. Her voice was full and confident.

Everly closed the door and headed farther down the hall until she found the separate guys' and girls' dressing areas. Even the dressing room was decorated like the inside of a pirate ship with portholes and wood paneling, wooden lockers, and fake electric candles.

Everly quickly dressed, pulled out her makeup kit, and decided to darken her eyeshadow and eyeliner, opting for a more theatrical look. She left her blonde hair down but did pull the front back and braid a few strands. Then, she took a purple bandana and wore it in her hair. The striped socks and even the boots were more for fun than period accuracy. The skirt was definitely a lot shorter than she would have liked, but the socks helped cover her legs.

She did a spin in the mirror and couldn't help but smile in excitement. She liked the idea of going undercover. It was almost like a dream. She might not be the most extroverted regarding personality, but she was an observant introvert, and she hoped those skills would come in handy.

After getting dressed, the sound of activity caught her attention, and she decided to follow it. She walked down the slightly sloped hallway until she reached the kitchen. Inside, three men were working furiously in a large industrial kitchen. A chef was busy putting trays of half chicken into rows of ovens while one was tasting and perfecting the gravy, and another was filling the pastries with their delicious contents. The aroma of the cooked food filled the air, making her stomach grumble in anticipation.

Everly moved past the kitchen and went into a back room. Starla looked a few years older than Everly and had red hair. Her makeup was on point for a wench, and she even had added extra bangles and an antique necklace. She was focused on the latest Samsung phone that had only come out a few days ago.

"Starla?" Everly called out her name.

"Who wants to know?" Starla's snarky response came back.

"I'm Eve, a new hire. I was told to come back here for training."

Starla looked up from her phone, and Everly's stomach dropped. All preconceived ideas that this would be a fun job went out the window when she was sized up, and the girl found Everly lacking.

"Don't they realize I have enough to do without training someone?" Starla sighed dramatically and stood up, dropping her phone into her apron pocket. "Follow me," she said.

Starla's training was almost nonexistent. She pointed to the kitchen, the warming carts, and the ramp leading up to the ship. "We get the food, put it in those wheelie things, and move it up the ramp and into the storage. We serve it. When we're done, we clean dishes, put them on trays and back into the carts, and wheel them back into the kitchen. Got it?"

"Got it. What about the menu?" Everly asked.

Starla turned and put her hands on her hips. "Look, kid, it's pretty simple. Everyone pre-orders their food when they buy the ticket online. It's a chicken, fish, vegan, or allergy-friendly option. It's pre-assigned seating, so we know who gets what. It's a colored-coded map." She pointed to the map of the ship. And that's when Everly saw the inner workings of the *Jolly Dodger*.

Everly noticed a grand ship with an arena only partially built onto the dock. The seating arrangements were divided into four groups. On the port side, there were long benches with yellow-and-red seating, while on the starboard side, it was green and blue.

The show began with a spectacle of aerial work, sword fighting, and stunt performances. The middle of the floor rolled back, revealing trampolines that took the excitement to a new level.

Four pirate performers were already warming up, stretching and jumping on the trampoline with their shirts off. Everly stared a little too long at the muscled back of one of the younger performers who was doing full twists and backflips on the trampoline. Then, he was called over to a pirate in green. They began to go through some sword work, and then one pirate pretended to stab the other, and he had to fake fall over.

"Oh, hey," Starla said. "Fresh meat." She paused and gave a longing look at the pirate with the red sash around his waist.

Everly stopped to cast a glance at who Starla was ogling. Her cheeks went red when she noticed it was Ian.

He must have passed his interview with flying colors and was already being incorporated into the show.

"Looks like Dylan has some competition for the hottest pirate."

"Who's Dylan?"

Starla pointed to the pirate in green. "We date, sometimes. So he's off-limits. Too bad the new guy is a red shirt. He won't get much stage time."

"Red shirt?"

Starla laughed. "Yeah, red shirts always die first. Cannon fodder for the senior pirates. They run on during the battle scenes, get beat up, and have to fake die or fall off the boat. It is tedious, but one doesn't stay fodder for long. He's way too hot to be falling off the boat." She fanned herself, and Everly could already see the girl had set her sights on Ian.

"Okay, our first set of guests arrive in an hour. Let's start filling the ice bins."

CHAPTER 7

"WATCH OUT," SOMEONE YELLED AS A CART ROLLED down the ramp straight toward her.

Everly was struggling to get her own cart down the ramp when she suddenly noticed the runaway food cart headed straight toward her. Without wasting a moment, she turned and shifted her weight to catch the cart with her shoulder and back, grunting in pain. Luckily, she had a heads-up, or else she could have been seriously hurt. However, the disappointed look on Starla's face gave her all the hint she needed. Clearly, Starla had intentionally lost control of the cart, which was both unfair and dangerous.

Dinner service was more manageable than Everly had first thought. What was difficult was figuring out the cues for the show on when to serve because she had zero training from Starla. She focused on the servers across the way from her and figured out the courses from there. Soup, salad, dinner, dessert. It was easy, and she had a section of twenty-five people, and she only spilled two drinks and dropped one plate of food.

Not bad for her first day of work. She had made a little improv joke about how she would have to swab the deck because of her serving skills. The patrons laughed and even gave her a nice tip. She probably wouldn't have dropped anything if she hadn't been glued onto the show and focused on Ian when he made his first appearance.

Starla was right. The generic pirates wore either a red hat, vest, or sash, were fought off dramatically, and they had to fall. Her heart was in her chest when Ian had to climb up a rope ladder and then was stabbed and had to fall into a safety net. A few moments later, he climbed up another rope ladder and was back into the fray of the fight. Dylan dispatched Ian again with almost the same three-combo move, and then Ian had to throw himself backward over a railing onto the mat below.

Everly's keen eyes watched the show in awe at first, amazed at how Ian could add himself to the show seamlessly, but then she realized there was a dance to it. A three-combo move that preceded every choreographed death. A distinct three combo that ended with a gut wound. The person would keel over, grasping his gut. A combo that started with a punch would end up with someone falling backward over something—a person, a railing, or a barrel. Most people wouldn't pick up the fight choreography and the tells. It would end with falling into the net, trampoline, or water.

When she first saw Ian fall, she dropped the cup she was trying to hand to a patron. The plate of food hit the dirt when Ian hit the water.

After that, she was able to pull herself together. Until she had the jarring run-in with the food cart.

Everly sucked a breath in between her teeth. Her shoulder, which had taken the brunt of the cart weight, was now sore, but the cart hadn't rolled off the ramp or fallen over. She rolled both carts to the side, lifted her arm, and checked the rotation.

"Are you okay?" a male voice asked, his hand touching her elbow.

"Yeah, I'm good," Everly answered and turned to see she was speaking with Dylan, the pirate in green. He was five foot ten, with dark golden eyes and brown hair. He had already changed out of his pirate garb and was in shorts, a white polo, and sneakers. Without all the stage makeup around his eyes and mascara, he wasn't bad to look at. She could understand Starla's infatuation with him.

"You need to take more care!" Dylan snapped out at Starla, who was looking very sheepish.

"Sorry, Dylan. I wasn't strong enough to hold it. You know I need help moving it down the ramp," she said, simpering and playing the weak female role.

Everly could feel Dylan's hand tense at Starla's actions, and he released.

"The new girl had no problem carrying her cart and catching yours."

"But I'm not built like a workhorse, like her." Starla pouted.

Everly's eyes widened at the insult, but she didn't let it faze her. Immediately, her mouth kicked into defense mode. "That's because my mom was a draft horse and my dad a stud."

Dylan let out a hearty laugh, unable to contain his amusement. He had to turn his head away to hide his grin, not wanting to offend anyone. Starla's expression made it clear that she was not pleased with the result, and she glared at Everly as she descended the ramp. Starla grabbed her cart and pushed it toward the kitchen as if it weighed a ton. The tension in the air was palpable, and she hoped the situation would diffuse soon.

"That was a good comeback," Dylan said, affirming. "You seem to know the art of a tactful insult."

"Yeah, well, I'm used to fighting a different way." She turned, grabbed her cart, and began pushing it across the dock to the kitchen.

"Here, let me help. Your shoulder's hurt."

"I got it—"

Dylan stepped in front of Everly and started to push the cart. Everly walked beside him awkwardly, trying to figure out what to do or say.

"I'm Dylan," he said, pausing to hold out his hand. "Most people call me Dylan."

Everly laughed at his joke. "I'm Eve," she said, easily converting to her fake name.

"So, you're new in town?"

"How do you know that?"

"I haven't seen you before, and I know most of the locals."

"Oh, yeah." Everly tucked a strand of hair behind her ear. "Just moved into Echo Bay."

"Yeah, so did that other guy." Dylan used his head to gesture to Ian, who was coming down the ramp behind them. "Never seen a first timer take so many hits on their first show."

"Really? What do you mean?"

"Usually, we teach them one combo, and they fall once

for their first show. It's a one-and-done kind of thing. But we had some last-minute call-ins and were short about three stuntmen, and he learned all their spots and nailed them on his first try." Dylan had tried to compliment Ian, but behind it, she could hear the tang of jealousy. Ian would have to be careful not to make enemies.

"So, what can you tell me about Echo Bay?" Everly asked, slowing her steps and watching as Dylan did the same.

"What do you want to know?"

"What's fun to do around here? Where's the local hang-outs or any scary haunts?"

"Haunts?"

"You know, rumors, ghost stories. In the show, Captain Roy talked about a cursed treasure. There has to be a bit of truth to it, right?"

Dylan picked up his pace. "I don't know if there's truth to cursed treasure, but some weird things have happened here." His eyes started to sparkle with mischief. "Especially in Howler's Cove."

"Where's that?" Everly asked eagerly. "I've never heard of it."

Dylan made it to the kitchen and pushed the cart near the sink and industrial dishwasher; he opened the cart's door to reveal the tray with dirty dishes.

The dishwasher was a glum man with a long gray mustache; his eyes were a dull blue, and he reached for one of the trays and began to dump the leftover food into the trash.

"It's our secret hangout. Maybe I'll take you there if you're interested?"

Everly headed out of the side kitchen door after Dylan and paused, looking up toward the ship. The other three servers had already left the kitchen and headed back to wipe up the tables and finish for the night. She wanted to go and ask him questions. Isn't this what they were supposed to do? Interview the locals? But at the same time, she just got this job, and she wasn't done.

With his hands in his pockets, Dylan saw her dilemma and eased her fears. "It seems you still have work. Tell you what, new girl. Tomorrow night, I'll take you to Howler's Cove."

Everly couldn't hide her smile of anticipation. "Can't wait to hear how it got that name."

Dylan grinned. "It is quite surprising." He turned, kicking a rock with his shoe, and headed off into the night, passing under a streetlight.

Everly watched him go, marveling at how easy it was to fit in. A little starstruck at her luck, she turned and ran into someone.

"Oh, sorry," she said breathlessly, stepping back to assess who she ran into. Ian still wore his pirate costume, and up close, she could see that he wore the outfit with disdain. "You did amazing out there tonight. All the *oofs, uhs,* and *ahhs.*" She added sound effects to getting punched, stabbed, and falling with an echoing cry. "It looked like fun."

Ian looked away uncomfortably. "This isn't fun. It's insulting. I'm going to kill Katherine Dorn."

"You had fun, admit it."

Ian grumbled, "It's all stage work—nothing that would help anyone. Plus the props couldn't hurt a fly. Their sword work was sloppy and slow, and I could see the blows coming a mile away. I would have knocked them all into the sea if this was a real fight." Ian reached into his pocket and took a sip of his flask. He made a face as he swallowed the bitter wolfsbane.

Everly bit her lip. "I think being a pirate suits you."

Ian ran his hands through his hair. "Because I'm dashing?" he said slowly, fishing for a compliment.

Everly bit her lip to hide the smile. "Because you're ruthless."

He frowned. "Well, we got our first assignment done. Now, we need to work on part two."

"Which is?"

"Fit in with the locals. There's something that we're missing. That all the other teams from Crypthaven have missed."

"What do you think it is?"

"I don't know. The sooner we find the answer, the sooner we can go home. By the way—" He let out a breath. "—good call on the dog. I didn't think I would get hired until you gave me that hint. It totally got Captain Roy on my side. Not to mention that during the interview three separate stunt pirates called in sick."

"You're kidding," Everly said. "Someone called out during my interview too."

"Glad it all worked out."

Everly saw Cleo waving for her to finish cleaning her section, so she excused herself.

As Everly continued to work, she felt more at ease with Ian. She grabbed a bucket of bleach water and a rag and cleaned the tables in her section. As she had been talking to Ian for a while, she was the last to finish, and she didn't know where everything was kept. While cleaning, she thought she saw someone swinging off the boat's portside with one of the stunt ropes, but she dismissed it as one of the employees and continued with her work.

After sweeping and mopping, Everly was putting away the mop bucket when she heard a faint call over the water. The sound chilled her bones, and she froze, staring out over the dark ocean, trying to listen to it again. But all she could hear was the sound of the waves lapping against the shoreline.

Could it have been her imagination?

Maybe. It never came again. Perhaps it was just a noise, a trick of the ocean. But what if it wasn't? If she encountered one, she didn't have any weapons to fight a grimm. She didn't hear that sound again as she finished putting everything away.

When she descended the ramp, she headed inside the warehouse to clock out. She was exhausted after a full day. She hadn't expected to jump into work and start after interviewing.

"What did ya think of the show?" Captain Roy came to stand by the time clock, where she punched in her number.

"It was amazing," Everly gushed. "I've never seen anything like it."

Captain Roy beamed with pleasure. "That's what I want to hear. And how did training go with Starla?"

Everly thought carefully about her words, knowing insulting your superiors would never bode well. "It was good. I learned a lot as the night went on."

Captain Roy frowned. "Which means she taught you nothing, and you had to fend for yourself." He let out a long sigh. "Nothing I can do about that. She's family. Can't fire her, or else—" He drew a thick finger across his throat. "—I'll never hear the end from my sister."

"No, really, she was fine." Everly tried to put her new boss at ease.

"I apologize for not being able to train you better. Unfortunately, we were short-staffed. Three of my stunt pirates and one of my servers are out sick due to food poisoning caused by cupcakes they received in a singing telegram from a girl with pink hair. Can you believe it?"

Everly held her breath and kept her face neutral. It was Kat. Kat had poisoned the staff of the *Jolly Dodger*, almost guaranteeing that she and Ian got the jobs.

"It's a good thing you could jump right in," Captain Roy said. "I thank you for that."

"No problem," Everly said. "I had a lot of fun. See you tomorrow." She waved at Captain Roy and headed through the hall to the main building and onto the dock.

It was dark except for a few lights that created halos on the ground. As Everly came to the edge of the dock, she felt the hairs on the back of her neck rise.

Someone was watching her. She headed up the marina to the street, and the feeling didn't go away, even as she turned the corner and headed down the block. A shadow moved as she passed a row of cars, and someone grabbed her arm.

Everly reacted. She grabbed the wrist, twisted, and flipped her attacker over her hip, and they hit the ground with a thud, but her attacker was prepared. She felt her body weight shift under her as they countered her attack with their own, and she came with them, falling. At the last second, they turned and took the brunt of the force with their body, and Everly landed on top of her attacker.

"Oh," Ian moaned, his eyes clenched as he held onto Everly's waist.

"Ian," she hissed. "What are you doing?"

"Escorting you home," he groaned. She tried to push off, but he whispered, "Don't move."

Everly stilled. She was afraid that, in her struggle to get away, she had hurt him. "Are you okay? I'm sorry. I didn't mean to hurt you. But you startled me."

Those blue eyes opened, and he looked up at her. "Maybe you should have been hired as the stunt pirate."

"Is that a compliment?" she asked weakly as she lay on Ian, his arms wrapped around her waist, her hands around his neck. He didn't seem in any hurry to move, and she was starting to panic. Maybe he was hurt more than he let on.

His eyes met hers, and she heard his intake of breath. His gaze lowered to her lips, and the corner of his mouth rose slightly, and he brought his face closer to hers.

She froze, unable to breathe.

"Nope. The compliment would go to your head, and it's big enough already," he whispered. "Okay, you can get off now."

"Oh, sorry." She started to move, but his hands tightened slightly around her waist as if he was reluctant to let her go. Then he released her.

She got up and moved to a safe distance, her heart rushing loudly in her ears as her embarrassment took over. "What are you doing, scaring me half to death?"

"I wanted to make sure you got back to the house. It's dark out."

"What?" She was struggling to think being so close to him.

"You never go out alone. Hunter ordered me to make sure you get back safe each night."

"Oh?" she said in surprise. "Of course."

Ian got up and rubbed his hip. "That hurt."

"That's because you didn't roll out of it," Everly answered. "You took the fall on your back to protect me. You shouldn't have done that."

Ian's eyes met hers in the dark, and he came up and brushed a loose strand of hair behind her ear. "Protect you?" he said in surprise. "That's our job to protect each other. You may not always approve of my methods, but I will do whatever it takes to ensure you are safe. Even if it means—"

Just then, a car alarm down the street went off. Everly turned to see a Tesla's lights flashing, and she frowned.

Ian tensed. His eyes scanned the darkness, sensing something she couldn't. "We need to go."

CHAPTER 8

"I can't believe you poisoned people to get us jobs," Everly chastised Kat when she headed into the house.

Kat was playing another game on her laptop at the dining room table. An open jar of peanut butter sat next to her. "Hey, I'm thorough. It's why I'm the best." She stuck a spoonful of peanut butter in her mouth.

"But you poisoned people," Everly argued.

Kat took the spoon out of her mouth and waved it at Everly. "Poisoned is a strong word. I just gave them ipecac to induce vomiting. They'll recover soon enough. The real tragedy is that I had to sing and dance. I don't sing."

Ian shook his head in disgust and plopped on the couch.

"Oh, sure. Where's the 'thank you, Kat, for all your hard work'? I also hacked into the *Jolly Dodger* email through the website and saw two interviews for today. I emailed the other applicants and told them the job was filled, then reworked you in," she said in a high-pitched voice.

"Was there no other way?" Everly asked.

"Hey, not everyone can charm their way into a job." She

looked over at Ian, who was sitting on the chair, arms crossed, glaring at her. "Cass, what did I tell you about those cupcakes? Put that down!" Kat yelled when she saw Cass pick up a chocolate cupcake with blue icing off the counter and start to peel the wrapper off.

Cass glanced over at Kat and put it down. She hesitantly pointed to the pink cupcake next with a hopeful look.

"Oh, yeah, no. The pink will make you go number two." Kat made a face. "Yeah, better just stay away from *all of them* to be safe."

Everly studied Kat's demeanor, the slight tilt of her shoulder, the quick smirk she tried to hide.

"They're all safe," Everly said, picking up a cupcake and holding it toward Cass. "The ones she was making yesterday were vanilla with yellow frosting. These are a different batch."

"Spoilsport," Kat pouted. "It's no fun having a human lie detector test living with you."

"Hey, we all have our gifts." Everly chuckled.

Cass's hand reached for a cupcake, and Kat shook her head and drew a finger across her throat. "Do you really want to risk it?" Kat taunted.

Everly picked up the same cupcake, took a bite, and watched Kat's face fall in defeat. The cupcake was soft and chocolaty, and the frosting was not overly sweet.

"It's fine." Everly handed it to Cass, who greedily finished the cupcake.

Everly rubbed her shoulder, realizing it was sore. Her whole body ached from catching that runaway cart.

"I'm going to bed," Everly announced, stealing another cupcake.

Ian was digging into the fridge, and Kat had returned to playing her game.

Everly went into her room, placed the cupcake on the nightstand, changed into her pajamas, and then sat cross-legged on her bed. She finally pulled out the envelope from the Grimm Society, broke the gold wax seal, and out fell articles about Echo Bay. They were similar to those her dad had clipped, but these were older, going back to the first mention of a tide.

Everly recognized the familiar handwriting on the notes; it was her mother's.

Everly opened the file folder and read through the titles of the articles: local died while scuba diving in a presumed oxygen tank mishap, elderly fisherman fell off a fishing boat during a storm, boy caught in a riptide was swept out to sea, the woman disappeared while paddleboarding.

Her mom wrote in red ink on the clippings.

Natural phenomena or grimm?
Why seven years?

And that was as far as she got before tapping on the glass interrupted her. She looked up in surprise to see Corvis outside her window. Without hesitation, she slid open the window to let him in, then tucked all the articles back into the envelope and shoved it in her crossbody bag.

"You made it."

Corvis flew into the room and landed on the nightstand. He dropped Ms. March's raven brooch on the table. "Always. I had to do a few things for Ms. March and the society as my penance for making the omens go poof." He fluffed his feathers and seemed quite proud of his achievement, even if it did land him in hot water.

"You shouldn't keep stealing from her." Everly picked up the famous pin that Corvis seemed obsessed with.

"She shouldn't lock it up in her jewelry box then." He shook his head and eyed the cupcake.

"How did you find me?" Everly asked, picking up the cupcake and slowly peeling the outer paper off.

"I'm your omen. I can always find you like a bird knows which way is north. It's instinctive. But I did some scouting while you were working on the pirate ship. Made some friends with the local seagulls."

"And—"

"They don't speak the same dialect. It's a lot of short speech, but apparently, something big comes in with the tide. Then disappears."

"That's it?" Everly asked, feeling deflated. "I already knew that."

"I will keep working on it, but they only wanted to talk about seals. It seems they have a hatred for the local seals. Call them uptight sewer dogs."

"Thank you for saving me the other night." Everly broke the cupcake into bite-size pieces and placed it on her nightstand for Corvis.

"Oh!" He flapped his wings and made a few shows of gobbling it up in one bite. "I'll gladly get into trouble if you keep feeding me cake."

They talked until Corvis had to head on another errand for the society. He was deemed their new intersociety messenger pigeon as punishment for his actions.

She had just laid down when she was abruptly awakened by a loud commotion outside. The sound of bullhorns filled the air while flashing red-and-blue emergency lights danced across the ceiling. She quickly jumped out of bed, ran to the window, and peered at the pier. There, she saw the harbor police and search and rescue boats frantically moving up and down the bay, accompanied by an ambulance and police cars. The scene below was a flurry of activity, leaving her wondering what could have happened.

She left her bedroom, headed to the living room, opened the slider, and stepped out onto the balcony. She wasn't the only one who had woken. Hunter came and stood next to her as she shivered in the morning air.

"What happened?" Everly asked, scanning the docks. Then there were more flashing lights, and one of the harbor boats pulled up their net. Even from a distance, they could see that what was caught in the net was bigger than a tuna and not moving.

"It's started," Hunter said, his voice full of dread. "The grimm tide is here."

CHAPTER 9

DESPITE THE BEAUTIFUL ARRAY OF WAFFLES, EGGS, AND jam prepared by Kat, the breakfast tasted bitter. The food was challenging to swallow as if weighed down by an invisible feeling of guilt.

No one wanted to speak of the death of the young fisherman, Nicky Delucca, who tragically died sometime in the middle of the night. The harbor police ruled it an accident because of an eyewitness to the incident—Jerome Miller—who was being treated nearby.

Kat's beautiful heterochromia eyes, one green and one brown, were filled with sadness. She pulled her knees up to her chest and rested her chin on them. "We didn't get here in time."

"It's not anyone's fault," Hunter said. "It could be a fluke."

"Or it's not a fluke," Kat argued, her words muffled behind her knees.

No matter what Hunter said, Kat would probably argue

with him. "The marina around the *Jolly Dodger* is closed, but we can still take the boat out and search."

Hunter held out a map of Echo Bay, pointing to the coastline. "This whole area is dotted with hidden caves. I think our first thing to do is go out at low tide and explore them."

"But they've already been searched," Aimee said.

"Not by us. Ian, Cass, I want you to go with Aimee, take her boat, and explore these northern caves. Kat, Everly, and I will take the southern side using these walking trails."

"But don't you think people will be suspicious if you're not with me—" Aimee started to argue, but Hunter cut her off.

"Let them. We don't have time to play house. We can't fail." His hand clenched the map, and Everly felt his frustration mirrored in her body.

That was four hours ago. They had started on the southern side of the cove and took to the private walking paths that would take them down to the caves. Kat wasn't thrilled at being dragged out into the sunlight. She wore a big floppy hat and shades large enough to cover half her face, doused herself with almost a bottle of sunscreen to protect her pale skin, and walked around with an umbrella to shade her.

Everly felt disheveled and embarrassed after a series of mishaps during their cave explorations. She dropped her flashlight, and the batteries fell out. Her white shorts were soaked after falling into a tide pool in the first cave, and in the second cave, she had lost a shoe in the sand, forcing her to hop out on one foot and tie her laces together. With the tide coming in and most of the caves filling with water, they had to abandon their exploration and head back. Their last stop was a remote area called High Point, where they had to walk along a rocky ledge that was only accessible at low tide to reach the cavern. However, with the tide rising, the path was disappearing, and they were at the mercy of the riptides.

"Nothing," Everly grumbled, slapping her hands against her leg to dust off the sand. "There's nothing in there except dead stinky crabs and old washed-up Coke bottles." The last cave was dark and difficult to explore even with their flashlights, with little pockets of pools and a shallow ceiling.

Kat had already headed around the point and was going up the path.

Hunter came out of the cave, and he followed her gaze as well. "Well, if we don't find anything here, we must search the other side of the beach and maybe even... underwater."

Everly felt her mouth go dry as she looked at the murky depths. So unclear. Anything could be hiding beneath those vicious waves, like a sea monster.

"Ever been scuba diving?" Hunter asked.

"No." She shook her head. "But you can't seriously think of going out there alone. It's too dangerous —too many boats and propellers. You could get injured," Everly argued.

"Well, we must keep searching, and we're running out of time."

"But I think the other grievers have already checked these caves. We have to start looking in other places where they haven't."

"What other places?" he said in exasperation.

"Places that aren't on the map. Places that only locals would know."

"You're right. We need to move faster."

Everly walked back to where Kat found a seat on a rock. She was on her phone, her fingers flying as she typed.

"You think you could hide from me?" Kat grinned as she spoke to the screen. "But I found you. Ha ha."

"Found who?" Hunter asked.

Kat had done her work, listening to the emergency radios and following all the blogs and news channels.

"The only witness, Jerome Miller," Kat said, "is now in the Saint Vinnie's Hospital."

"What for?"

"Stroke." Kat looked solemn. "It's time I go and visit my great-uncle Jeremy twice removed."

"Jerome," Everly corrected.

"I know that," Kat said. She pointed to her watch. "You two need to get going. Or you'll be late." She started to march away and then turned back with a wicked grin. "Want to have a little wager?"

"What kind? Hunter asked.

"First one to figure out the kind of grimm gets out of reporting duties."

"Deal," Hunter said eagerly.

Kat did a little fist pump and made her way up the path to the main road.

Everly gazed at Hunter, standing before her in a plain white shirt, board shorts, and sunglasses. Despite his relaxed outfit, she could sense the weight of his task. The burden seemed to have taken a toll on him, and she could see the gravity of his responsibilities etched onto his face.

They stood on the water's edge, alone for the first time. Everly suddenly felt self-conscious, tugging on her shirt to hide the dirt spot from when she fell earlier. She shifted her weight from foot to foot, unsure how to carry on now that it was just the two of them. Should she address what happened at the house? Or his recent breakup? No, maybe it would be better to pretend it never happened. If Hunter wasn't going to bring it up, neither would she. They stayed side by side and watched the tide slowly enter, admiring its deep green color. The water was beautiful and serene, and in no way did it look dangerous or mysterious.

"Why is it called the grimm tide?" she asked after enough time had passed that she felt she could pick up the pieces of her broken heart.

"Because it seems that this phenomenon happens every seven years during the new moon phase of October."

"New moon, that's when the moon is at its darkest, correct?"

Hunter nodded in agreement and then used his hands to demonstrate the phenomenon of the moon phases. "During the dark phase of the moon, when it is positioned between the earth and the sun, there is very little light. During this phase, the tides are at their highest and lowest of the month, and this seemingly ordinary town becomes the target of something sinister. The tide that comes in with the phase of the moon takes lives and then returns seven years later to take more."

"The grimm tide," Everly repeated in understanding.

"But I want to know why? Why only kill every seven years?" Hunter shoved his hands into his pockets and sighed. "The tide has come in, and we're going to get trapped out here on this point if we don't get going."

Everly turned to follow Hunter up to the beach when she heard a haunting echo.

A trick of her ears?

"Do you hear that?"

"Hear what?" Hunter responded, and when she didn't answer, he kept walking.

Everly paused and looked back toward a cave that they had already explored. But she heard it again. It was a song this time, and when she turned away, it grew fainter. She took a step closer, and the song grew louder. Following a hunch, she picked up her pace and headed back to the nearest cave.

They had already explored a tunnel that went back about twenty-five feet. The tunnel had a ninety-degree turn that led to water coming in. Maybe the water had uncovered something buried in the sand, which was now floating in the waves.

Holding her shoes in one hand, Everly waded through the chest-deep water back toward the cave entrance.

"Everly? What are you doing?" Hunter called out after her. He had already made it up to the walking path.

"I'll just be a second. I thought I heard something," she yelled and waved up at him.

"No, don't." He took off running back toward the beach.

She wasn't deterred, so she returned to the cave and looked around. "Come on." She looked through the water to the murky sand below. Her instinct said there was something here—something she was missing.

Then, a flash of light reflecting off the water revealed a secret tunnel hidden behind an outcropping and almost underwater. *Should she explore it?*

The song grew louder as soon as she saw it, and Everly knew to follow it.

Everly waded through the murky water, determined to follow the song; her gut told her she would find something at its crescendo. As she dipped under the ledge and emerged into a small cave, she was disappointed to find nothing but darkness. Despite the lack of light, she continued her search, feeling the water turn colder with each passing moment.

Then she heard it—a loud aria when she looked down.

Through the water, she could almost feel the music leading her. She took a deep breath and dove under the surface, her fingers brushing across the sandy bottom, digging, following the melody until it blasted in her ears. Then her fingertips brushed across something, and she picked it up. She stood up, took a deep breath, and brushed her wet hair out of her face so she could gaze at the gold doubloon in her hand. Treasure. *Was it real?* She felt a prickling sensation on her neck. It was as though she was being watched, and the feeling sent shivers down her spine. Turning around, she saw black, beady eyes staring at her just inches above the water.

CHAPTER 10

"What the grimm?" Everly yelled as the creature lifted the rest of its speckled head out of the water.

A harbor seal had followed her into the cave and blocked her exit.

Heart racing uncontrollably, she kept still, trying not to threaten the creature.

"It's okay," she soothed, edging around, trying to return to her quickly disappearing escape route. She would have to dive under the rock ledge and swim out if she stayed much longer.

The seal swam toward her, its long whiskers brushing against her arm before disappearing under the water.

"Oh, boy," she whimpered and looked away. She hoped that cute face didn't suddenly change into deadly. *Wasn't that what happened in horror movies? The cute and cuddly thing would either eat the wrong food, get wet, or have some curse that changed it from cute to rip your face off deadly.*

Everly's heart raced as the seal reappeared above the water. "Um," she hummed, trying to remain calm. "I'd like to leave now. So maybe you should... shoo!" She waved her hands, hoping the seal would leave, but instead, it pressed toward her again. Everly felt a wave of panic wash over her as she realized she was trapped. The water had filled up her small cave, and her exit was now fully encased in water. She pressed herself against the back of the cave, desperately searching for a way out.

As she held her breath and dunked under the water, she felt a rush of adrenaline coursing through her veins. She was grateful to see a pool of light still showing her the exit, but she knew she had to be brave and swim past the seal. But she stayed calm and collected, carefully observing the creature before her. After a moment of silence, the creature darted away, leaving Everly alone again with her flashlight. Suddenly, something grabbed her leg, startling her. She let out a scream, but it died in her throat as Hunter emerged from the water, his face only inches away from hers. The water trickled down his tanned face onto hers, and his green eyes looked turbulent, adding to her confusion and fear.

"What are you doing?" he growled, his hands reaching for her shoulders.

"The seal!" she cried out.

"What seal?" He glanced around with his flashlight.

"There was a seal right here a second ago."

"We need to go," he ordered. "Listen, it's a good fifteen-yard swim now underwater. You can do it. The problem is when you reach the entrance of the cave. There's a heavy current coming in. You need to fight your way out. Got it?"

Everly nodded, too ashamed to admit she was in the wrong. She shoved the coin in her pocket.

He grabbed her arm. "Three deep breaths, then swim for

all you've got. Let's go," he said, grasping her forearms. "On three. Ready?"

She could feel the strength and calmness emanating from Hunter as they treaded water together. Looking into his eyes, she knew that she was safe and protected. Together, they took a deep breath and plunged into the water, with Hunter gently pushing her ahead of him.

She cut through the water with her hands, which propelled her forward with each stroke. The light around them changed as they entered another chamber and grew brighter. It was hard to believe how far she had come, especially considering how short the distance had seemed when walking. Swimming required different strength and focus, and time seemed to slow down as she worked hard to keep moving forward.

But Hunter was right beside her, giving her the confidence she needed to keep going. Even as she felt exhaustion creeping in, she knew she could rely on him to keep her safe and help her reach the end of their journey.

She felt the strength of the current pushing her further back into the cave. And she almost panicked. She wasn't strong enough. She tried to cut through it, but another wave slowed her.

Panic began to build. She couldn't do it. Her lungs were burning.

Then Hunter was beside her, grabbing her by the arm; he pulled her after him. His willpower and strength were no match for the violent ocean. Then she felt him pull up, and they broke through the surface, gasping for air.

"Watch out!" he called, grabbing her as a wave slammed into them. Hunter wrapped his body around hers as the ocean slammed them into the sharp rocks above the entrance to the now-submerged cave.

Hunter's head snapped back against the rocky surface. He went limp, his grip on her lessening.

She clung to the rocks and grabbed onto his arm, afraid he would get washed back out to sea.

"Hunter!" she cried, seeing the water turn red with blood.

He didn't answer. He was unconscious.

Everly felt tears slide down her cheek, as they were now at the mercy of the waves that were slamming them repeatedly against the rocks. She was doing everything she could to keep his head above water.

Her free hand grasped a rock, and she held fast, her right arm around Hunter's head as she struggled to keep him from slipping beneath the waves.

"Help!" Everly cried out. "Someone help. Anyone!" She closed her eyes and knew that she was running out of strength. She couldn't save them both. Her whole body was cold, and her fingers were going numb. She couldn't hold on for much longer.

"Hunter," Everly sobbed. "Hunter, wake up. I need you. I can't do this without you!"

Her grasp on the rocky outcropping started to slip. She closed her eyes. "I'm so sorry," she whispered to Hunter. Another angry wave slammed into her, and Everly felt her grasp slip. She slid into the water, her head hitting the side of the cave, and she could feel herself start to black out.

Help! I need help!

A giant bubble erupted from the water around them, followed by a second, and then a stream of bubbles popped and flowed around her skin. She felt the water grow warm as her vision went black.

———

"Wake up!" a voice yelled.

Everly's eyes burned, and her skin felt on fire. No, not on fire. Like she had been through a spin cycle on a washing machine. A sudden pressure hit her abruptly on her chest, and Everly gasped.

"Wake up!" the voice said again and then started screaming. "No, no. Back off. Mine. You no... eat. Scram, rats."

Through the noise of Corvis's thoughts, she turned to her side and pushed herself up. She was on an unfamiliar beach, surrounded by dozens of seagulls watching her. Just waiting and watching, probably hoping that she was something dead.

Corvis was flapping his wings and hopping around her, trying to keep the seagulls at bay.

"Corvis?"

"I'm here."

Everly turned and saw the still form in the sand ten feet away.

"Hunter!" Everly crawled through the sand, her eyes burning with unshed tears. His back was to her, his white T-shirt shredded and covered with blood. Beneath it, his skin was raw.

She grasped his shoulder and turned to check his pulse. He was breathing.

Tears of relief slid down her face.

"Hunter." Everly gently cupped his face. His eyes fluttered open, and she had never been more excited to see those beautiful green eyes.

"Everly? Are you—" His voice was hoarse. He reached out and put his hand on top of hers.

She smiled, her heart melting.

"It's okay. I'm fine. Just a bump on the head. But you're scraped up quite a bit." She turned to show him their surroundings. "We're not in Kansas anymore."

"Go, you bastard mix of rat and pigeon!" Corvis continued to fly around and attack the seagulls. When Hunter sat up, they finally gave up on their prey and flew away.

"Where are we?" Hunter asked, releasing a sigh of pain as he sat up. He squinted and took in the shoreline and lack of lighthouse.

"I don't know." Everly looked over at Corvis. "Do you know where we are?"

"About three miles north of Echo Bay," Corvis answered. Corvis flew to land on a branch half stuck in the sand.

"How did we get here?" Everly asked.

"I don't know," Corvis answered. "I just found you here."

Everly relayed the information to Hunter, who squinted and looked at the terrain. "I don't recognize this beach."

"I don't think we just washed up here," Everly said.

"What do you mean?"

"It's against the current." She carefully got to her knees and then stood and studied their surroundings again. Her observant eyes were missing something. She moved to the water's edge and saw long, straight tracks in the sand. "Whatever made those tracks is how we got here." She pointed to the beach. "This is the only area of disturbance."

Everly spoke aloud her reasoning. "There's broken branches and deep gouges in the sand. Something heavy. Could be a boat or maybe a WaveRunner, but I don't know what these tracks are." There were sections of patterns in the sand that were slowly fading.

"We should call for help."

Everly patted her pockets and realized the burner phone Kat had given her was gone. "My phone is gone."

"Mine too." Hunter pushed himself to his feet.

"You need to rest," Everly shot out.

"I'm fine." He started looking around the beach in case their phones washed up. "What's that?" He pointed toward a dark speck on the water in the distance. As it drew nearer, the sound of the motor grew louder, and the boat became more visible. The sleek twenty-five-foot Yamaha jet boat glided smoothly through the water, creating gentle waves that stretched against the shore. As it came closer, Cass smiled and greeted them from the bow's seating.

At the helm, Aimee steered the vessel toward them but had to stay far enough back to not ground the expensive jet boat.

Ian jumped off the bow into the water and rushed over to them. His face was stern when he saw Hunter's bloody clothes. "What happened? You were supposed to be down south." He turned to Everly for an explanation.

Her face was red in embarrassment, and explaining it to Ian made it all the worse. "I, uh—"

"It was my fault," Hunter cut her off. "I thought I could explore a cave, but the incoming tide caught me off guard. Then we ended up here."

Ian cast Everly a look of disbelief, and she knew he didn't buy the story.

Thankfully, the jet boat had an integrated swim platform that was water level, making it easy for them to wade out into the ocean and get on board.

"Hunter! You're hurt!" Aimee cried out, rushed to grab the first aid kit under the bench seat, and kneeled to pull off Hunter's shirt. He turned to let her start cleaning and disinfecting the cuts, which looked pretty deep. Ian took the steering wheel, backed them into the ocean, and sped home.

Everly sat on the bench seat, her eyes closed as they sped back, the wind whipping at her face and hiding her tears as she listened to Aimee fuss over Hunter. As much as she disliked Aimee, she came from a family of doctors and was their assigned medic. She was the one who made the tough calls. She was so distracted she even let Ian drive her family's boat after threatening to sue him if he scratched it.

After a frantic boat ride, they finally slowed and pulled into the dock near Aimee's beach house. Seeing that familiar white beach house relieved Everly's racing heart. Ian quickly tied up the boat, and they rushed Hunter up the private dock, away from the prying eyes of their neighbors. Once they were safely inside, Aimee took charge and began giving orders. She directed Ian to bring Hunter to the main bedroom, where she stayed, and not the guest bedroom he usually used, probably because it had its own bathroom and bigger medicine cabinet. Aimee pulled out a pen flashlight and began to check Hunter's pupils, her face a picture of concern.

"You said he blacked out?" Aimee looked to Everly, who nodded.

"We both did."

Aimee directed Ian to help Hunter clean up his back in the bathroom. When the door closed, she turned her attention to Everly.

She grabbed a blanket and put it around Everly's body, which was still wet.

"Any nausea, vomiting, blurry vision?" Aimee moved over and began to check out Everly's pupils with the penlight.

"No, I'm fine. I hit my head and lost consciousness, but I'm okay. I'm more worried about Hunter."

Aimee's body was tense, no-nonsense. "You should be. He took a beating on those rocks. What were you doing?" she hissed under her breath. "He's never been careless on a mission. I don't care what he says. I blame you."

"You're right," Everly admitted. "It's my fault."

Aimee clicked the penlight off and sighed. "Your pupillary reaction is good. Where did you hit your head?"

Everly pointed. Aimee leaned up and felt the back of her scalp for a small bump, and Everly winced.

"I think you should be okay. Let's get some ice on your head. I will call Dr. Madsen at Gravemark and have him prescribe some antibiotics for Hunter's back. You. Bed rest. Now!" She pointed to the bed.

Everly took the blanket and crawled further up onto the master bedroom bed. It was a king-size bed, and a seventy-inch TV screen was across the room. Aimee went to the hall, and Everly heard her call Dr. Madsen. She was methodical in her notes and relaying information.

In the master bathroom, she heard the shower running and knew that Hunter was getting cleaned up.

She reached into her pocket and pulled out the coin.

It was flat, with a weird etching on it. When she rubbed her finger across the surface, she saw it change. Words appeared but not in a language she could read.

After a few minutes, the water shut off, and Hunter came out wearing a bathrobe. The deep V of the front exposed his chest, and it was covered with wrapped bandages. She averted her eyes. Ian went downstairs to speak with Aimee, leaving them alone.

There was an awkward tension between them.

"Are you okay?" Hunter started.

"I'm sorry," she said simultaneously but then continued. "This is all my fault."

"No, I've seen that look on your face before. You went back into that cave with a purpose. You found something, didn't you? Spill, Everly Hart. I know when you are keeping a secret."

Hunter sat on the edge of the bed, and Everly reached into her pocket and handed over the coin. She waited eagerly to see if it shifted the same for Hunter as it did for her, and then she heard it—his inhale of surprise. "What just happened?"

"Have you ever seen anything like this before? Is this grimm treasure?"

Hunter flipped the coin over and examined it closer. "I mean, when you think of them as a society, they would have to have a monetary system of their own before they assimilated into our culture."

"What do we do with it?" Everly asked.

"I think we should show it to Ms. Bellcamp and see if we can have Kat translate this."

Everly nodded and then got up from the bed. She was half dry, half wet, and sand clung to her body. It was in every crevice, and she was supposed to work in a few hours. She wanted to call off, but she couldn't when so much depended on their mission. She headed for the door, leaving Hunter with the coin.

"Hey, Everly." Hunter got up from the bed and reached for her hand. His grasp was warm around her wrist. "It's not your fault." His thumb brushed the underside of her palm. She paused and looked up into his worried gaze. "We're a team."

She nodded, though a knot formed in her throat. It was hard to swallow with all the guilt building.

CHAPTER 11

AFTER A REFRESHING HOT SHOWER, EVERLY FELT rejuvenated and ready to take on the challenges of the night. She quickly changed into her work clothes and headed toward the dining room. As she entered, she noticed Ian and Hunter huddled over a town map, deep in conversation.

"And this is where she found the coin?" Ian asked, pointing to a cave on the northern side.

"Yeah, in this cave. She said it called to her."

Ian was pensive. He picked up the coin and frowned. "Kat, what did you find when interviewing the old man?" Ian was also dressed for work. He had a red bandana around his head, a bare torso, and a red vest with black pants and boots.

Kat had pulled out a magnifying glass and was looking over the markings. It took her a moment to realize that Ian was talking to her. She shook her head. "Not much. He was half-hysterical and still recovering. I didn't get much else because the nurses came in to sedate him."

"What are your thoughts on this coin?" Ian asked Kat.

"I think it's freaking awesome, but it's not like I can just Google grimm dead languages. There's not an online database for that. However, if there is any information available, it would probably be at Crypthaven's secret library."

The room fell silent at the mention of the destroyed school. "They have a secret library?" Aimee asked in surprise.

"Of course, so does Gravemark," Kat said nonchalantly.

"Wait? You mean besides the normal one in the old church." Everly started to get excited.

"Of course, why do you think Mr. Halsey never leaves the library? There's a second library deep in an underground cavern; he guards it. Now, I bet Crypthaven has a secret library as well." Kat leaned back and tapped her chin in thought. "I bet if we could find it and gain access, we might be able to learn more about the coin and the grimm tides."

"But isn't the school destroyed?" Aimee seemed hesitant.

"Well, the main structure was completely decimated after the fire, but the underground is a maze of tunnels."

"How far away is the school?" Everly asked eagerly.

"It's only about an hour. If we leave early tomorrow morning, that should give us plenty of time for me to dig up old blueprints." Kat spun the gold coin on the table. It rolled across the map and landed right on the cartoon etching of the *Jolly Dodger*. "Look at that. Pirate ship. Pirate coin? Do you think they're connected?" she added.

"I don't know, but I feel like a pirate coin and pirate lore needs to be explored," Everly said.

"See if you can check around at work tonight," Hunter said, handing her the coin.

Everly took it and placed it in her crossbody bag.

"Ian." Hunter turned and gave him a cold glare. "Watch out for her."

Ian's lip curled. "I can take care of her, unlike you."

"Stop," Everly snapped. "Let's go." She headed out the door.

————

The night fell into a similar routine as the show before. Everly felt more confident after the second night. Dinner service was more manageable, and she was assigned to the opposite section of Starla, but it placed her right in Dylan and Ian's section.

During intermission, Everly took a quick break from her duties as a server and made her way to the gift shop in the corner of the warehouse. The shop was packed with pirate-themed souvenirs, such as flags, toy rifles, necklaces, and miniature treasure chests. However, none of these trinkets caught her eye as much as the glass display case showcasing more expensive replicas. Then, she noticed a treasure that looked similar to the coin she had in her pocket.

She even went so far as to approach the scruffy-looking pirate who ran the gift shop. He had a thin build and wore a red-and-white-striped shirt with a knitted hat. His name badge boldly displayed "Skittles."

"Yep, you can buy them individually or three for twenty," Skittles answered.

"Can I see one?"

Skittles reached into the case and pulled out a gold coin. Everly tested the weight and handed the coin back to Skittles. "Thanks."

"Looking for anything in particular?" he asked.

"A coin like this." Everly held it up.

Skittles's eyebrows rose in surprise. "Where did you find this? May I?" He held out his hand, and Everly handed it to him. Skittles placed the coin on a black velvet mat. He took out a long magnet and touched the coin.

"Most coins are fake and electroplated to look like gold. Silver and gold aren't magnetic. It looks like it could be one real gold coin." Skittles pulled out a headlight magnifier and leaned over the coin.

"What are you doing?"

"I'm a member of the Professional Numismatists Guild. I specialize in bullion and, most importantly, dating and identifying treasure. Most of the treasure this far north is from privateers' stashes. Despite that, I have personally identified several pieces from Echo Bay's famous pirate hoard, checking them against ledgers." He proudly pointed to several polaroids above his head, taken of treasure. A gold cup made with a skull head, a pendant necklace, and another smaller coin with a wing. As Everly leaned in close, the coin with the wing fluttered, and she held her breath. It was all grimm treasure.

"Who found those?" Everly asked. "I'd like to meet them."

"The owners' names are strictly confidential," Skittles added. "I take pride in my hobby and business. You're the new employee. If you want to leave the coin with me, give me say... till tomorrow, noon. I bet I can identify which hoard this coin actually came from. I will conduct a few tests on the metals, etc. But I won't do anything that harms the coin's value."

He was so excited that she didn't want to say no, when she was sure it was grimm treasure. If Skittles could identify where it came from, it might give her a clue about the origin faster than Kat or the school. But the real question was... did this have anything to do with the tide? It was the only grimm hint she had so far.

Everly bit her lip, debating. "I don't know."

The stage music started, alerting the guests that the intermission was over and the show was about to begin again.

"Tell you what. If this is part of the Lennox treasure, I will help put you in touch with the other finders." Skittles leaned over the counter and held the coin out to her, making the choice entirely hers.

That sold her. "Okay. I'll come get it tomorrow afternoon."

"Deal!" Skittles filled out a form and had Everly sign it, agreeing to the dating and identifying of the coin. He tore off the receipt slip and handed it to her.

Everly felt a sense of relief. She excused herself and went back to her post. Other than a screaming child that cried when the fake mechanical sea monster came up from the ship's side and started to swat the pirates in the final epic battle, her night was uneventful. She could even focus on the show's story a bit more. The *Jolly Dodger* was searching for a cursed treasure that a dragon protected. The dinner show incorporated a lot of laughs as the crew searched for the treasure only to realize that one of the pirates had it the whole time. And the finale was the ship being attacked by a giant dragon.

Everly watched in awe as the animatronic arms were lowered back into the ocean.

"It is something, isn't it." Marnie came and stood by her, watching the end of the show. "This is my favorite part. It took five years to build the dragon, and adding her to the show really brought up our revenue."

"It is such an interesting storyline," Everly said.

"I came up with that too." Marnie was in a long purple dress, her locks covered with another bandana, and bangles fell on her thin wrists, creating a soft tinkle sound whenever she moved. "Before, it was just about overthrowing a ruthless pirate captain. Now, it is much more fitting to Echo Bay's history."

"How so?" Everly asked.

"The cursed treasure of Lennox is a fascinating tale passed down through generations. Captain Lennox was a notoriously ruthless pirate, and his crew was so loyal they gave up their soul to serve by his side. His boat, the *Siren's Revenge*, ran aground here in Echo Bay, but there was no captain, crew, or treasure. The ship was barely afloat, half destroyed as if it tangled with a royal fleet. Some say Lennox's cursed treasure brought down the *Siren's Revenge*. Others say he threw the treasure overboard in the ocean. Others say there was never any treasure. My personal theory is that the pirate Lennox buried his lost treasure and killed anyone who touched it."

"That is quite the story," Everly agreed, excitement coursing through her body. But she could tell Marnie felt it was more than a child's tale. "You believe it?" she asked, watching Marnie for tells.

The woman looked out into the bay, her head nodding. "With every fiber of my body." Marnie leaned close to

Everly, her voice dropping to a whisper. "It is said that the treasure will either grant you power over the sea or death."

A chill came over Everly's whole body. Goose bumps ran up her arms as she looked into the woman's eyes. She believed every single word that came out of her mouth.

"So, where do you think this treasure is now?" Everly asked.

Marnie waved her hand out at the bay. "Who knows? Probably washed out to sea, buried under a coral reef or mounds of industrial waste."

It was time to collect the checks and cash out for the night, so Everly excused herself to return to her row of guests. That was a gold mine of information, and Everly was excited to share it with Ian.

She bussed the tables, wiped them down, and was getting ready to push the warming cart down the ramp when she heard giggling from near the stage.

As Everly wheeled her cart, she noticed the sounds of kissing and a soft sigh coming from behind one of the stage curtains near the mast. She slowed when she recognized Starla's laugh. Trying not to make any noise and disturb them, she continued moving the cart past the lovers. However, as luck would have it, the wheel got caught on the curtain and pulled it back with the cart, revealing Ian and Starla locked in a passionate embrace.

Everly's body went rigid as she stared at the unexpected sight before her. It was as though she had stumbled upon the cover of a steamy romance novel. Starla's eyes were half-closed, her cheeks flushed, and her lips swollen from her intimate encounter with Ian. As Ian looked up, he didn't seem surprised to see Everly there, but his eyes narrowed as he quickly pulled the curtain shut, plunging them back into the darkness.

Her heart wasn't sure what to make of that encounter. In one moment, she felt betrayed because he was her fake griever boyfriend, but he also hadn't shown any reaction to her over the last few days.

She grunted as she pushed the cart down the ramp. Her actions were hasty, her brain working overtime in anger. Everly had pulled out the last tray of dishes and emptied them onto the dishwasher's tub when she heard someone clear their throat.

"You ready?"

Everly spun in surprise. She didn't even hear Dylan come in. "For what?" she asked, wiping her hands on her apron.

"For the party."

"Oh, yeah. I just need to change." After Everly clocked out, she changed into shorts and a tank top with a sweatshirt and white sneakers. She folded her uniform into her bag. When she left the dressing room, Dylan swooped in and grabbed Everly's hand, pulling her after him. He led her down the dock to another four docks away.

As they approached, Everly couldn't help but notice the harbor seals sleeping on the edge of the dock, and one in particular seemed to raise its head when they approached and watch her get onto the boat.

"Ready, Dylan?" Pike said. Everly recognized Pike as one of the older cast members of the show.

"Yep, I think everybody is coming out today," Dylan said.

"Wait up!" a feminine voice yelled giddily, and footsteps

ran down the dock. Everly recognized Starla, and she was hand in hand with Ian. "We're coming too."

Dylan glanced at Ian but didn't give an impression. "Okay, let's go!"

It was a pontoon boat, and Everly recognized Pike, one of the stagehands, Rob, and another server named Cleo. Starla had moved to the front of the ship, and when Ian sat down, she claimed his lap, wrapping her arms around his neck.

"Where are we going?" Everly asked.

"Wherever the wind takes us." Dylan wrapped his arm around Everly, and he hugged her shoulder. She was cold and didn't mind the friendly warmth. Except that across from her, she saw Ian's gaze was boring a hole into Dylan's arm.

"Actually, that's not true," Dylan said. "We're going to Howler's Cove." He removed his arm and went to the steering wheel.

Everly tried to remember a location in Echo Bay called Howler's Cove and knew it didn't exist.

"I remember you mentioning it but have never heard of it."

"It's because it's hidden. You can only get there at certain times of the month."

"Really?" Everly asked, her curiosity piqued.

She tried not to glance at Ian, who was again engrossed with Starla. He seemed to know how to turn on the charm, gazing at her adoringly as his arm wrapped around her thigh, keeping her close. Everly averted her gaze and focused on Dylan, talking to Pike, steering the boat as they sailed across the open sea. The wind blew Everly's hair into a tangled mess, but she didn't mind. She was too captivated by the stunning beauty of the rocky cliffs and the colorful array of sediment that had formed over hundreds of years. Pike expertly navigated through the darkness, following the coast north and into an inlet between the high rocky walls. The lanterns from the boat cast a warm glow against the cliff, and a waterfall cascaded down the ledge and into the sea, creating a breathtaking scene.

"It's beautiful." Everly gasped when she saw it.

"It is," Dylan agreed. "It's one of our favorite places to come and hang out. There aren't any houses for miles." The pontoon pulled up to the cliffside and dropped an anchor, and now they floated along the wall.

The crew that had been here before began to turn on lanterns, making the night glow, reflecting a million shadows dancing across the wall. Even more surprising was when they dropped a weighted buoy with a rope into the water and began to undress down into their swim trunks.

"What's going on?" Everly asked. "I didn't know we needed swimsuits."

"I told you. We're going to Howler's Cove. Just lose the sweatshirt. You'll be fine." Dylan grinned and pulled his shirt over his head, revealing a well-muscled chest. He dropped his shirt next to his shoes. He grabbed a headlamp, put it on his head, and went to the boat's edge.

"What are you doing?" Everly asked, alarmed.

"Come on, Eve. Don't be scared." He pointed to the rest of the cast, who had also changed into their swimwear. Even Starla pulled off her top to show a red bikini. She grabbed a headlamp, put it on, and dove gracefully off the boat's edge into the water, following the line down.

Everly leaned over the edge and watched as Rob dove

after Starla, and then they headed toward the cliff, their headlamps lighting the way before disappearing into the cliff.

"There's an underwater cave," she said.

Dylan nodded. "It's full of secrets. Come on. Don't be scared." He handed her a headlamp and then went to the boat's edge. Everyone had already dove in except for Everly and Ian. "I won't make you. You can stay here; we will return in a few hours. Or you can take the plunge." He gave her a wink. "What do you say, Eve?"

A splash alerted her that Ian had already jumped into the water; she could see his sure, strong strokes as his light went through the darkness.

Everly's heart began to race. *Back in the water? So soon.* She had just barely survived her last encounter. But Dylan wasn't pressuring her. He went to the edge, and he smiled at her. "See you on the other side." He dove.

Everly sat on the boat alone, feeling the darkness around creeping in. The ocean, with its vastness, felt cold and uninviting. Gathering her nerve, she kicked off her shoes, pulled off her sweatshirt, put on her headlamp, and plunged into the icy depths.

CHAPTER 12

THE WATER WAS SO COLD THAT IT FELT LIKE NEEDLES piercing her skin. She quickly swam up to the surface, gasping for air. Everly knew it was a mistake to jump in. Fear and panic began to take over her as she felt helpless and alone in the ocean. Suddenly, a loud splash interrupted her thoughts, and she turned to see what was making the noise. Her headlamp illuminated the waves, but she couldn't see anything. She felt like something was with her in the dark, murky depths.

Taking a deep breath, she kicked her feet and followed the lead line toward the cliff. As she moved, she could feel the temperature of the water changing, getting warmer as she approached a cave. She kicked and swam with determination, and when she thought she would hit a rock, she found open air instead. Swimming toward the brightening light ahead, she emerged from the water to find a secret beach. It was a sight she never expected to see, and it left her speechless.

Pike had already started a fire and added logs to the mini

bonfire. When she came out of the water, she was greeted by Dylan. "You made it!" He hugged and picked her up, spinning her around playfully before gently setting her back down in the sand.

"You left me?" Everly said in disbelief.

"It's a test. To prove your worth. Congrats, you passed." Dylan gave her arm a reassuring squeeze.

As Everly brushed the hair out of her face, she couldn't help but feel amazed by the beautiful scenery around her. They were in a natural bowl-shaped area, surrounded by towering cliffs that rose to forty feet on either side. Above them was an open night sky that twinkled with stars. Within their little sanctuary were trees, bushes, and a well-stocked cooler that promised refreshment and sustenance for the night ahead.

It was evident that the group had been here often because the beach was filled with lawn chairs, hammocks strung between trees, and towels hung up on makeshift clothing lines, making it look like a cozy and welcoming spot.

Starla was already drying herself with a towel before moving to the fire to get warm.

"Welcome to Howler's Cove," Dylan said.

"And why exactly is it called Howler's Cove?" Everly asked.

"Because of this." He tilted his head back and barked. It echoed off the walls and into the air, creating a haunting howl.

"How did you find this place? It's not one of the local tourist spots." Everly's teeth began to chatter, and she shivered.

"And it wouldn't be. It's too dangerous because of the

riptide. You can only access this channel at night and in the early morning. Plus, we like it. It's like our safe space." Dylan grabbed Everly's hand and pulled her over to the fire. He wrapped a towel around her shoulders, rubbing them furiously to help her dry off faster.

"But why did you bring me here?" Everly asked suspiciously, her mind always in a state of caution.

With a charming smile, Dylan replied, "Because I wanted to impress you." He gestured toward the private beach, and Everly was genuinely impressed. "Am I doing a good job?" he asked with a hint of playfulness. Everly couldn't help but smile back at him and nod in agreement.

As they headed away from the water, she saw Ian and Starla claim a hammock, snuggling together as they gently swung back and forth. However, Everly's mind began to race, wondering if Dylan was only interested in her physical appearance. She found herself becoming self-conscious as she pulled her towel across her tank top, covering herself up. Despite her insecurities, she followed Dylan inland to a secluded area with more private hammocks.

Pike stoked the fire, grabbed a small shovel and ax, and headed further into the trees, probably to find more firewood and dig up dead trees.

"Here." Dylan opened a red hammock and helped Everly sit comfortably inside it, and she felt herself fall back into it, letting her legs hang off the side as she rocked gently.

"May I?" he asked permission to sit next to her.

Everly nodded, and Dylan settled beside her, his thigh pressing into hers. They watched the fire crackle, the embers flying into the night like fireflies.

"So tell me about yourself," Everly asked.

Dylan swung his leg, keeping them gently rocking. "There's not much to tell."

"How did you get involved with the pirate show?"

"It's a family business. I didn't know if you knew that. About one-third of the cast is related to either Marnie or Captain Roy. I grew up on the ship. It gets a bit lame, performing night after night. But having a place like this to escape to has been worth it. And having someone to share it with makes it even more special because I see it through your eyes."

He turned to face her, his gold eyes twinkling with playful mirth. "I've never taken anyone here before."

Everly laughed. "Lies."

Dylan's eyes crinkled. "Okay, I've never taken someone here that I've been so attracted to."

"You don't even know me," Everly answered.

"I don't have to know you to know that I want to get to know you better." His voice dropped, and so did his eyes, his attempt at seduction.

"Oh, I'm not falling for those lines. I should get back." Everly moved to stand up, but he reached out for her. "No, don't," he said fearfully.

"You can't make me stay here." Everly pulled her arm out of his and made her way to the water's edge.

"No, Eve. Don't get into the water," Dylan warned.

She looked back at Dylan and saw the terror in his eyes. His body shook, but his gaze was fixated on the water's edge. She couldn't resist but turn her head to see what had scared him so much.

Then she noticed the water had turned murky, and something seemed to be moving under the surface. Her heart pounded in her chest, and she took a step back. Her feet slipped in the sand at the water's edge. Her foot slid into the ocean.

Dylan grabbed her arm, yanking her up and away from the water just as a massive surge rose from the depths, the wave seeming to reach out before it crashed into the sandy bank.

Everly clung to Dylan, trembling in fear as she watched the water retreat with the tide.

"What was that?" she asked.

Dylan wrapped his hands around her, holding her close to him. Everly let him, comforted by his closeness, her eyes staring at the water.

Ian had also rushed forward, and she could see him wanting to pry her from Dylan's grasp, but she warned him away with a slight shake.

"Nothing," Starla said, coming to the water's edge. She turned her gaze to Everly. "Just the tide," she said flippantly, grabbed Ian's hand, and pulled him back to the hammock. "It has a mind of its own."

Ian gave her a nod, and Everly swallowed down her fear. Obviously, these people knew more about the tide than they let on, and if they wanted to solve the cursed tide, they needed to not isolate themselves. If they wanted to pretend the tide didn't just try and swallow Everly whole, then she could also pretend.

There was no way she would approach that water again, so Everly reluctantly retreated farther inland. She didn't fuss this time when Dylan gave her a blanket and wrapped her up in the hammock.

She listened as he crawled into it with her and told her

stories. Great fishing expeditions; the time he broke his foot during a stunt gone wrong. Everly couldn't pull her eyes away from the cove and the dark water. She couldn't stop her trembling and didn't even mind when Dylan wrapped his arm around her and pulled her into his arms. Every time she started to shiver, he hugged her.

He still stayed in his shorts as the night went on, not once even seeming to mind the cold wind. Everly could feel her eyes getting heavy, and it seemed like none of the crew were entering the water or planning on leaving.

Everly yawned, and he pulled her into his chest. "It's okay. You can sleep, sweet Eve. I will watch over you," he whispered.

When morning came, Everly was warm snuggled against a hot pad. Except it wasn't a hot pad. Sometime in the night, she had turned sideways and was snuggled against Dylan's body in the hammock. His skin was hot, radiating enough heat that she didn't need the blanket. The hammock had curled up and wrapped around them like a cocoon.

She opened her eyes and looked up into the warmest golden eyes that gazed down at her with delight. Dylan's arms were wrapped around Everly, his leg thrown over hers.

She blinked, unable to say anything in the compromising position they were in. Well, she was clothed. He was half-clothed and didn't even seem to mind. He stretched out his arms above his head.

"Morning." He leaned forward and nuzzled her with his forehead playfully. Nothing about his interaction was romantic but more friendly, like a puppy. He didn't act possessive but protective.

He kicked his foot out of the hammock and swung it back and forth. He reached out a hand and brushed a strand of hair from her face. "You started to shiver at night, so I hope you don't mind. I decided to help keep you warm."

"How, are you not cold? Don't you need a blanket?"

"I don't need one. I naturally run hot." He grinned, popped his head out of the hammock, and looked about. "We're the last ones up."

"We are?" Everly felt her cheeks burn and tried to get out of the hammock.

"No, not like that," he warned.

"Oh!" She turned over and felt the hammock swing. Everly fell out onto the sand, bringing Dylan down with her.

He was able to catch himself somewhat. His arms landed on either side of her head, and he got a knee into the sand before he crushed her.

He laughed the whole time, and Everly looked up into those joyous eyes. He was grinning, making a silent huffing noise, and then looked at the beach. He brought his finger to his mouth to signal silence and then pointed at the water's edge.

Everly, head in the sand, turned to see a group of harbor seals sleeping on a giant rock about ten feet out in the cove, basking in the morning sun. She sucked in her breath at the sight of them.

"They're gorgeous," she whispered.

Dylan was no longer looking at the seals but gazing at Everly as she was amazed by their beauty. "Yes. I agree. Gorgeous."

She turned to meet his gaze, and his eyes flickered down to her lips briefly, but then he was up, flying through the air, pulled by an invisible string.

Ian grabbed Dylan and pulled him off her, and with his immense strength, he flung Dylan into the ocean.

"Whoa!" Dylan hit the water and didn't come back up right away.

"Ia—uh, Duke! What did you do that for?" she cried out and rushed to the water, searching the depths for any sign of Dylan.

"He was getting too friendly," Ian grumbled. His hair was sticking up all over the place. Everly couldn't help but point out the red lipstick all over his cheek in the same shade that Starla wore.

"I don't think that it's your place to say how friendly people can get." She tapped Ian's cheek. He swore under his breath and tried to wipe it away but smeared the lipstick further across his face.

When Ian had tossed Dylan into the water, it was near the harbor seal area. Everly saw one slip into the water, and she held her breath. *Would it attack Dylan? Was he too close to their home?*

Dylan popped up out of the water and flung his hair back. The water droplets flew off his head like a shampoo commercial. He stood and walked toward them, his muscles evident in the sunlight.

Everly felt her mouth open.

"You're drooling," Ian grumbled.

"Shut up and hand me a napkin," Everly muttered, trying to hit Ian where it hurt in an attempt to silence him.

Her remark did precisely what she thought it would do.

Ian cursed and turned away. Dylan ran up to her on the beach and dropped onto his knees. His never-ending grin was still firmly in place.

"Are you okay?" Everly asked, feeling worried.

"Yeah, that was fun." Dylan didn't seem the least bit perturbed by Ian's antics.

A seal broke the surface as he spoke and hopped over to Dylan.

"Dylan!" Everly warned as the giant mammal bowled into him.

Dylan cried out and fell to the ground, but in seconds, he flipped the seal over and ran back into the water, diving with ease.

Starla called out, and she ran into the water after Dylan.

Everly sat there in awe as the crew took to the water one after another and swam with ease. They were breaking the surface and then diving back down. She watched as the five teenagers played with the harbor seals. Not afraid of them.

Ian came to stand next to Everly.

"Have you figured it out yet," he said softly.

"Have you?" she asked, unsure if he was testing her.

"I did last night when that one kissed me." He pointed to Starla. She couldn't believe he didn't even know her name. "I could smell it on her."

"Smell what?"

"The sea. She smells like the ocean."

Everly turned her head to study the movement in the way Dylan swam. His playfulness, the way his eyes looked at her. "They're grimm?" she said, surprised at how slowly she figured it out. *Did a bit of flirting destroy her grimm radar? Or was it that she didn't sense any harm from them?*

144

"Yep, just not sure what kind." Ian's hands twitched, and she could tell he wanted a weapon.

"Why can't we see their true form?"

"I don't know. It's weird that neither of us sensed it before this."

"Are we safe? Do you think they know what *we* are?" Everly said. "Or you specifically?"

Ian shrugged. "I don't think so. Otherwise, they might have attacked us." He quickly corrected himself. "No, not me. They wouldn't have gotten the jump on me. You're the one who fell asleep."

"You didn't?"

"I don't have a death wish. I stayed awake all night, watching them and the water. There was something sinister in the waves. I could feel it."

Everly shivered. "Yes, and I think Starla and Dylan know more than they let on."

"What do you think I've been doing?" he grumbled. "Once I overheard that Dylan planned to take you to his secret place, I had to work my charm on Starla to get an invite. That girl kisses like a starfish."

Everly couldn't hold back a snort. "I don't know. You looked to be enjoying it. It couldn't be that bad."

Ian's eyebrows rose, and he had a sly smile. "Let's just say I took one for the team. I couldn't let you go off on your own. You always end up in trouble."

"Thank you," Everly said, unsure if she believed him.

"Don't mention it. Really. But did you find anything about the coin?" Ian asked as the group slowly made their way to them.

Everly forgot that she hadn't told him she gave it to Skit-

tles. "Not yet; I left it with a cast member who would identify it."

"Why would you do that?"

"I had a good feeling about him."

"Whatever."

———

The swim back through the tunnel was not as scary in the
morning light, and soon, they left Howler's Cove behind.

Everly tried to use her sight to see beyond Dylan's
human side to find the grimm hidden beneath. But there
wasn't a glimmer or hint as to what he was. It had left both
Ian and her stumped. And whatever Dylan and his friends
were, they were peaceful grimms.

She wanted to press him, address him full-on, but she
didn't.

Back on the boat, Pike was showing something to Dylan.
Their shoulders were pressed together, and they were whis-
pering. "Found it last night further inland. All that's left.
The rest is gone."

When Everly came close, Pike tucked something red the
size of his fist into his pocket, and they grew quiet, secretive.

When they docked, Dylan stood up first and helped her
onto the dock. "Thanks for coming with me." His cheeks
grew warm.

"Thanks for inviting me. I hope you'll bring me again,"
Everly said, trying her best to flirt but hoping her face didn't
do some weird scrunchy thing.

"Yeah, I would love—" Dylan's head swerved, and his
eyes widened. "Eve, get back." He got on the dock and

pushed Everly away, trying to shield her. She tried to turn and look over her shoulder.

"No, don't," he cautioned. His face was grim.

"Dylan, what?" She pulled her arm out of his grasp.

Disregarding the warning, Ian bravely walked toward the edge of the dock and peered into the water. Everly followed and gasped when she saw the body with a striped shirt and red hat floating, his lifeless brown eyes staring into space.

"Skittles," she breathed out.

CHAPTER 13

ANOTHER DAY, ANOTHER DEAD BODY.

Skittles, the gift shop employee Everly had met only yesterday, had been found dead floating in the harbor only a few hundred feet from the *Jolly Dodger*. The harbor patrol had already removed the body from the water, and the Echo Bay medical examiner and local detective were examining it to investigate the cause of death.

As the investigation process unfolded, Everly remained near the ambulance, observing the police as they questioned the members of their group. Being relatively unknown to the authorities, she didn't face the same scrutiny as Dylan and Starla. Despite this, Everly couldn't shake off the unease from being involved in such an intense investigation.

As the chaos unfolded, she cleverly feigned shock and kept one of the EMTs occupied with her requests for a Mylar blanket and water while staying close enough to overhear the investigation details.

Detective Howard was about the same age as her father had been, had red hair, and wore sunglasses as he faced the glaring sun, trying to gather every clue that could help him solve the case. "What are your thoughts, Dr. Peter?"

"Foam," Dr. Peter answered, pointing. "See the bubbles near his mouth? It means he drowned." The medical examiner, Dr. Peter, was tall, with broad shoulders, short black hair, and piercing blue eyes hidden behind silver spectacles. "He hasn't been dead long—a few hours at most. Rigor mortis has set in. I can't get an accurate liver temp for the time of death because he was in the water."

"The crew of the *Jolly Dodger* said they saw him last night around 10:30 p.m. when he was closing up the gift shop. So we can estimate between then and 6:00 a.m. when the call came in." The detective was writing in his notebook.

Dr. Peter rubbed his chin. "Truthfully, his body should have sunk and wouldn't have washed up to shore for at least a few days. I don't know if we would have found him, except that he became caught in the fishing net."

"Does he have the marks?" the detective asked.

A long silence passed between them. "You know he does. As do all the others."

The detective cursed under his breath. "Show me."

Dr. Peter unzipped the body bag further, and Everly tried to lean over and look, but the doctor's back blocked the view.

"Another victim," Dr. Peter admitted.

"What else could these marks be? A sick calling card?"

"Look, Howard. I don't know if we can keep calling these accidents. There are too many similarities, especially to the victims from years ago. We should warn the people."

Detective Howard's face turned dark. "You will keep

your mouth shut. We can't let it get out that the deranged killer is back. Do you understand me?"

Dr. Peter's mouth turned down into an angry line. Everly could see his knuckles turn white as he gripped the edge of the body bag.

Howard nodded and continued as if nothing strange passed between them. "Was there anything found on him? Anything in his possession?" Howard cleared his throat and pointed to the pockets.

Dr. Peter pointed to the evidence tray. "Just a few coins, a receipt illegible from the water, and his wallet."

The detective put on a latex glove and went through the belongings, searching and not finding anything interesting.

"Detective Howard, I think you need to rethink my warning. These aren't just accidents."

"Stop, not now—five more days. Suppose we can get through the next five days. We can have peace again."

"That's not how it works, and you know it. We can't ignore—"

"You mean, *you've* ignored," Howard threatened. "You were the one who figured out the link years ago. These markings. Yet, you never brought your findings to light."

"Let me remind you that bodies recovered from water present unique challenges. Even though livor mortis is often present after death, initial findings can change depending on factors like water temperature, bloating, and even ocean currents, which can affect the body in various ways. Understanding what may have happened can take time and additional investigation. That is my fault... I should have—"

"That's all the public will hear. That it's your fault."

Howard clicked his pen and flipped his detective book shut. "Keep me updated following the autopsy."

"One more thing." Dr. Peter zipped up the body bag, turned, and was surprised to see Everly so close to them. She pretended to be fixated on the water and shivered, not making eye contact. His eyes narrowed, and he gestured for Howard to move to the front of the ambulance, where they could talk privately.

As soon as they were out of earshot, Everly bit her lip and stared at the body bag. Should she dare?

It wasn't her first time seeing a dead body. She'd seen plenty with her father and grandfather. Or mostly lots of photos of the recently dead.

Ian was standing fifteen feet away from her with Starla. He pretended to console her, but his icy gaze watched Everly. When she gestured with her head to the gurney, silently asking permission, Ian gave her a nod.

Adrenaline rushed through her as she slipped off the bumper of the ambulance and quickly moved to the body bag. Her hands trembled as she unzipped the black plastic cover, refusing to gaze at the face. She purposely cast her eyes to his torso.

His skin was white and pasty, and there were faint red welts along his arms and one along his abdomen.

Her brows furrowed as she tried to figure out what it was. Cementing the image to memory, she zipped up the bag and stepped back.

"What are you doing?" A voice startled her.

Everly turned as Dr. Peter stood beside her, his lips pinched into an angry line. Everly turned on the waterworks.

She covered her mouth with her hands, scrunched up her eyes, and began to cry.

"I just wanted to say goodbye to Skittles. He was so kind to me." Everly patted his belly awkwardly. Out of the corner of her eye, she saw Ian shake his head and cringe at her acting.

She didn't think Dr. Peter was buying her acting chops, but it didn't matter because the EMT came and lifted the gurney into the back of the ambulance, and Dr. Peter had to turn and give them instructions. Everly slipped away.

But when he turned, over his shoulder, up at the top of the marina, she saw someone try to break through the police tape but was kept at bay by the officers.

Hunter.

"Let me through; I can't find my friends," Hunter demanded, pushing his way forward again to be physically stopped. She could see the panic in his eyes. "I need to know *who* you found." He must not have seen her or Ian standing in the crowd and assumed the worst.

"Stop, or I will be forced to arrest you!" an officer warned.

"Hunter!" Everly called out, waving.

Once Hunter saw her, his panic subsided, but not the anger she saw boiling beneath his exterior. He became calm. Too calm.

Everly dropped the Mylar blanket, ran up the walkway, and crossed the police tape. He reached for her but then caught himself. He stepped back, tucking his hands into his pockets.

"You didn't come back." Hunter's voice was stern. He turned and looked away from her.

"I just got caught up with the cast, and we went to a beach and stayed overnight. You won't believe what I learned."

"You didn't come back last night," he repeated, and she heard the pain, the uncertainty, and realized how much he was struggling with not knowing what happened to her. She moved to stand before him and looked up into his green eyes filled with worry.

"Hunter, I'm fine."

As soon as his hands flew out of his pockets, he wrapped her in a warm embrace. She could feel his heartbeat and smell the cologne he was wearing. However, the hug was short-lived as he quickly turned his attention toward Ian, abruptly ending the tender moment.

"Hey." Ian came and stood next to Everly.

"You didn't report in, Ian." Hunter's voice turned to one of warning. Like a captain reprimanding his troops. The complete opposite of how he treated her just moments ago.

"Forgot." Ian shrugged and pushed past Hunter, knocking his shoulder into his on purpose. He started to walk down the street and head to their home. "So sue me."

"You are supposed to report to your GTL," Hunter said.

"Yeah, I've heard that all before, but I was busy." Ian turned to confront Hunter.

"Doing what?"

"Watching her get all cozy with a grimm." Ian pointed to Everly, and she felt her heart fall out of her chest. "I had to double up the charm to get invited to their secret beach rendezvous. She would have ended up grimm bait if it wasn't for me."

"That's not how it happened." Everly turned on Ian.

"Isn't it?" Ian said. "I'm in the middle of warm-ups and hear Dylan brag about how he plans to take you to their secret beach rendezvous. After more investigation, I learned that they're grimms. And you were going with them freely."

Everly was ticked. "Investigations? You mean make-out sessions. Plus, you were the one that dove into the water first, leaving me on the boat alone."

"You did what?" Hunter turned and pushed Ian. "You left her?"

"Relax, I would have been able to take them on," Ian answered. "Except she followed me."

There was something wrong with Ian, with this whole scenario. She didn't understand what was happening. Ian was acting strange.

Hunter waved his hands through the air. "Enough, head back. It's time to go."

"Go?" Everly said, momentarily forgetting their agenda. "Where are we going?"

"Crypthaven," Hunter said.

CHAPTER 14

As they piled in the van and drove along the coastline, Everly's gaze was transfixed upon a rugged lighthouse visible from a distance. The towering height and robust construction of the lighthouse filled her with awe. Built from large, rugged stones, the lighthouse's lower portion was sturdy and reliable, while the upper section was painted in a pristine white that contrasted beautifully with the blue sky. The living quarters were attached to the lighthouse's foundation, featuring a door and several windows that allowed ample light. The exterior of the living quarters had a small balcony wrapped around the structure, providing a stunning view of the surrounding landscape.

Everly couldn't help but wonder aloud in amazement, "Is this it?"

Hunter drove the van and pulled it into the lone parking space.

"This is Crypthaven," Kat said. "Or, more specifically, somewhere over in that general direction." She pointed over a large hill about a half mile from the lighthouse. "It's nothing but ruins after the fire and has been marked as a safety hazard, but according to what I could glean from Ms. Bellcamp, the grievers used a secret entrance near the lighthouse to get into the school."

Aimee hopped out of the front passenger seat and used her hands to shade her eyes as she scanned the rocky shoreline. "I see a footpath!"

Ian opened the locker inside the van and began to pull out weapons. He handed Everly a never blade. She had used one before when dealing with a rogue fairy that bit.

Cass was back to hanging near Ian like a lost sheep.

Hunter came around back and rolled up the back door, helping Kat and Everly down.

"What are we expecting to encounter?" Everly asked as she grabbed a smaller knife and put it in her belt.

"Anything. Don't forget. Every griever school was also a prison for grimms. We don't know what escaped the night of the fire or what's taken up residence within the ruins or tunnels," Hunter said.

Kat was about to join them on their hunt, but she pivoted when she heard about possible grimms. "Okay, yeah, I'm all for exploring libraries, but hunting dark tunnels? Nope, this sib is staying in the van." She closed the door on herself, and Everly was perplexed until she heard her voice over the radio in Hunter's hand. "Ready when you are."

Hunter smirked. "Just keep focused on us and not your PvP record."

"Hey, I can definitely do both," Kat said while furious clicking came over the radio. It seemed she had just joined an online battle.

"Let's go find the entrance." Hunter sighed deeply and

gestured for his team to follow him down the footpath. The trail wound around the lighthouse and descended to the rocky shore, eventually leading to a stony cliff that towered above the beach. Hunter and his team spotted a smaller path covered in overgrown rocks and grass as they approached the coast.

Curiosity getting the best of her, Everly explored the smaller path and found herself directly under the front of the cliff where the lighthouse was perched. She gazed up at the white stone building, then ran her hands over the brick, feeling the smoothness of the newer material that contrasted with the rough, weathered stone surrounding it.

"I think I found it!" Everly yelled, and Ian was the first to make his way around to the hidden path. He, too, ran his hands along the wall.

"There's definitely something behind this." He tried pulling it out with immense strength, but it wouldn't budge.

"Let me help." Hunter inserted a knife and tried to pry it open.

Hunter and Ian continued to work on opening the hidden passageway, but it was locked.

"Kat, you got anything?" Hunter buzzed over the radio.

"Let me see it."

He dialed her on his phone and turned the Facetime camera on so she could solve their problem.

"The door must weigh at least three hundred pounds. So, a hydraulic system must be used to open and close it. You are looking for a lever or a switch."

Hunter shut off the phone and gestured for everyone to fan out and search. They looked funny as all five walked along the wall, rubbing, pushing, or hitting every stone, looking for a secret lever.

"It's not here," Ian grumbled.

"Did Ms. Bellcamp tell you how to get into the passageway?" Hunter held up the radio and asked Kat.

"Well, not exactly. She didn't seem happy when I mentioned needing access to Crypthaven's library. In fact, she got very tight-lipped, and I think if she knew we were going to come here, she would ban us. So what she doesn't know can't hurt her," Kat said in a singsong.

"And what we don't know *can* hurt us," Ian grumbled.

"Let's go inside." Hunter pointed to the lighthouse.

All the main lighthouse doors were locked and windows boarded up. Ian was about to grab a hammer from the van when Everly stepped forward.

"I got this." She dropped to her knees and pulled her lockpicking kit out of her crossbody bag, inserting the pick and tension wrench and working them until she felt the pressure and release. The door unlocked and swung slowly inward, revealing the interior.

The living quarters themselves were cozy, with wooden floors and walls polished to a warm glow. There was a small kitchenette with a stove and refrigerator and a simple table and chairs for dining. An old, overstuffed chair sat beside a tall bookcase filled with books. A narrow staircase led up to what she assumed to be the bedroom. Another door led to the stairwell that went right up to the lighthouse.

"I thought there would be someone here. Like an old man in a rain jacket smoking a pipe," Aimee said. She came inside and ran a finger along the dusty bookshelves.

"Most lighthouses are automated now," Hunter answered. "They don't need to be monitored."

"Well, I don't see anything." Cass moved about the room and gazed out the window toward the ocean.

Everly bit her lip and scanned the room. *What was she missing?* They had already scanned the cliff and only found a walking path that ended into a dead end. Kat said it needed a hydraulic system and probably a lever.

Everly moved to Hunter and held out her hand for the radio. He handed it to her, and she pushed the button.

"Kat, what can you tell us about the lighthouse keeper? Before it became automated."

"Got it. Gimme one parsec." Everly could hear her fingers flying across the keys. "The Mann family have been the caretakers since the lighthouse was built, even after it became automated. The last descendant still lived there until..." She paused, and the radio went silent. "October 17, the night Crytphaven was attacked. It says the lone care-taker, Boswell Mann, known as Boz, disappeared and hasn't been heard from since."

"So the caretaker disappeared when the school was attacked by grimms," Everly repeated as she looked at the small living area with a new perspective.

"Think like the subject." She could hear her father's voice in her head. *"Put yourself in their shoes, Everly."*

She walked in a circle and looked closer at the photos on the wall. They showed an old lighthouse keeper with joyful eyes and a bright purple-and-red scarf, but then the image shimmered, and the beard shifted into fur and the mouth into a beak.

As she muttered the word "grimm" under her breath, she

tried to remain calm and think about the situation practically. If the lighthouse keeper was a grimm, he likely knew about the secret entrance to Crypthaven and was probably its protector. It wasn't uncommon for grimms to be protectors of doorways, gates, roads, and bridges, so she could assume that this lighthouse keeper was more than just a simple caretaker. She attempted to pick up the picture frame to get a better look, but it was secured firmly to the bookshelf with screws.

"Strange, it won't budge," Everly said.

"Why would anyone secure an old photo? We secure things down on our yacht, but this is a lighthouse. It's not going anywhere," Aimee said.

"You have a yacht too?" Kat said over the radio.

Aimee shrugged.

"Then it has a purpose." Everly leaned in closer to the photograph, her eyes scanning the details in search of any clues. As she studied the picture, she noticed the keeper in the background, his hand extended and pointing to the left. Without hesitation, Everly followed the direction of the keeper's hand until she came across an old swordfish lamp bolted to the floor. The swordfish was wrapped around the lamp's base, with its nose and tail pointing toward a wall. Intrigued, Everly traced the line of sight with her finger until she reached an old anchor wall decoration. The anchor hung sideways, with the tip aimed directly at a lighthouse photograph, leaving Everly wondering if there was a hidden connection between the two objects.

"I already searched that," Aimee said.

Everly followed the anchor, ran her hands along the lighthouse frame, and felt the hinge. She pulled it, and it didn't budge. "But there's a hinge. You can barely feel it. There has to be a trigger to unlock this frame."

Hunter searched the bookshelf, Ian started pulling the pots out of the kitchen cabinets, and Aimee went back to searching for other photo frames. Cass floated around. Her curiosity made her touch everything, and she bumped the lampstand of the swordfish, causing it to turn ever so slightly.

"That's it." Everly pointed. "Cass, turn it more."

Cass pushed her white hair behind her ear and carefully spun the swordfish 360 degrees, but nothing happened. The base was still stuck to the table.

"This is getting ridiculous," Aimee said. "It doesn't do anything."

Ian went and tried spinning the swordfish lamp the other way, and it continued to spin back and forth, and they couldn't unlock the picture on the wall.

"What are these markings?" Cass asked, pointing to the side of the table and along the edge.

Ian leaned down. "It's just a decorative pattern."

Hunter kneeled on the other side of the table and ran his fingers over the deep wells. "There's something familiar about this pattern. It's deeper every five marks."

Everly sucked in her breath. Hunter was right. She had seen that pattern before as well. Every single day at high school, on her locker. "It's a combination lock," she said excitedly. "Look, it's deeper here. This must be zero; then it's a deeper hash every five. We need to find the combination. Look around. There are clues here. We need to find them."

They spent the next ten minutes looking. Everly could tell when the other grievers began to lose steam, but not her. She could feel the adrenaline spiking, the need to solve it.

She knew what it was like, that need. She had seen her father spend hours in his back office trying to solve a case. He would come in with red-rimmed eyes and wrinkled clothes from sleeping in them.

"There's nothing here," Hunter said.

"Well, then, it has to be something obvious. Like what year was the lighthouse built?"

Hunter radioed in the question to Kat and came back with a date. "Same as the school, February 1, 1870."

"Seventy is too high for the dial. Try 2-1-18," Everly said.

Hunter moved to stand at the swordfish and used the long bill as his pointer. He had to duck under the bill as he spun it all around to reset it. "I got to admit. This feels pretty stupid."

"It looks like you are dancing with the fish." Cass cackled out loud. Her childlike joy filled the room, and when everyone looked at Hunter, holding it and rocking it back and forth, it did kind of look like they were slow dancing.

"Maybe you should get her number," Ian taunted.

"Shut up," Hunter said as the final number was hit and a click on the far wall indicated the picture frame had opened.

Everly was already waiting by it and swung it open when she heard the click. Behind the frame was a single lever.

"Good, it's not another combination lock," Hunter said.

"What, are you tired of seducing the swordfish already? I mean, I bet she wonders why you won't call her back." Ian slapped his knee, and Hunter took a fake swing at his shoulder.

Everly ignored the bickering and pulled on the lever.

"Wait!" Hunter said.

But it was too late. The whole lighthouse began to grumble and groan as gears that hadn't been used in years started to grind. She could feel the vibration under her feet, and then it slowly stopped.

She couldn't hold back her grin. "It's open."

CHAPTER 15

THEY FOUND THEMSELVES OUTSIDE THE LIGHTHOUSE, peering into the ominous tunnel the switch had revealed. Ian leaned in and shined his flashlight into the narrow passageway. The steps leading into the darkness seemed to go on forever, and no one was willing to take the first step. The group stood there, frozen in anticipation, wondering what lay ahead in the unknown depths of the tunnel.

"Why does it smell like rotten eggs?" Aimee asked, backing away and pinching her nose.

"That's the algae as it decomposes. It releases hydrogen sulfide," Hunter said. "The tunnel must lead to the ocean at some point." All eyes turned to Hunter in surprise. "What?" He tried to shrug it off. "I like science."

"Hot, athletic, and smart." Aimee grinned, reaching to ruffle his hair, but he ducked, avoiding her touch.

"What's the plan?" Everly asked. But no sooner had she spoken the words than she was roughly shoved aside as Ian moved past her.

Ian didn't even wait for instructions; he was the first to enter the tunnel. He was taking the lead.

"Hey, wait," Hunter ordered, but Ian didn't listen. Everly wondered if there was anyone that Ian listened to. She doubted it.

Cass was on Ian's heels. She gave a small wave of glee before strolling into the darkness without a care in the world. She probably thought she was on a date.

Hunter gestured to Everly to go next, followed by Aimee, and he took up the rear.

The tunnel was cool, with rough stone walls that were slightly damp. There would be a pool of water every few steps, making it slippery. The farther into the tunnel they traveled, the more muted the waves became and were replaced by the sound of soft drops of water.

After a while, the steps leveled off. Cass suddenly stopped, and Everly bumped into her back.

"What's the problem?" She looked around Cass's shoulder to see Ian paused at a crossroads. The tunnel split into two different paths.

Ian turned, looked over Cass's shoulder, and made eye contact with Everly. It was like he knew he could trust her.

"What do you smell?" she asked, knowing he could use his werewolf senses.

"No good. They both smell the same. All I'm getting is kelp from both tunnels."

Everly frowned and slid past Cass to stand shoulder to shoulder with him. "You shouldn't be. The one on the right should head back to the ocean; the one on the left should head inland toward the school. It shouldn't smell of kelp unless you are smelling something—"

A roar filled the tunnel, and Everly was slammed in the chest, propelled backward into the passageway, and hit the wall. She gasped in pain and blinked as bright spots flickered across her vision. The flashlight had dropped to the ground and spun, reflecting off the walls and illuminating a scary creature that stood ten feet tall. His eyes were burning red, and his body was covered in fur. When he screamed, a mouth with no teeth and a beaked nose were revealed.

Hunter leaped over Everly and stood before her, his hands on his never weapon. He swung and hit the creature, and there was a cry of pain, but then his meaty hand swung out and hit Hunter square in the chest; he fell, colliding with Aimee and Cass, who rushed forward to try and protect Ian. But all the grievers were on the ground in the tight tunnel, making fighting difficult.

Ian was first to recover; he had slunk into the second tunnel, and when the grimm moved forward to attack, he jumped on his back and wrapped his hands around the grimm's throat with his weapon. Someone kicked the flashlight, and it spun again and lit up the creature a second time. Everly saw a flash of purple and red.

Everly got up and waved her hands. "Stop, Ian! Don't you recognize him? It's the lighthouse keeper. Boswell."

Ian didn't halt his attack. "He let them in," Ian growled, his fury evident. "You saw that combination lock. Only he could know it. He let the grimms in; it's his fault the school fell, and everyone died."

The roar of fury slowly died down to a whine. The grimm now identified as Boswell slumped to the ground. Loud moans and sniffles followed.

"He's right." Boswell's voice was deep and regretful. "It

was my fault. I was their protector, and I failed them." In his human form, Boswell had lost weight, and his beard had grown down to his knees. He wore the knitted purple-and-red scarf from the photo, but it had been worn thin. His hands were bruised and covered in dirt as if he had been digging. "They came in droves from the ocean, and I didn't close the door in time. They waited at the water's edge for the grievers to return and swarmed the lighthouse. I didn't know until it was too late. I couldn't close the door. I couldn't close the door." Those thick hands covered up his face in grief.

He rocked back and forth, wailing and crying. "So much death, and it's all my fault."

Everly looked over at Hunter and Ian, who both stood there with shocked looks on their faces. Everly gestured for Ian to do something, and Ian shook his head.

"I don't trust him. It's an act." He grabbed his knife and didn't move.

Everly glanced at Hunter, and he shrugged. "I don't do well with crying."

Aimee shook her head before she was even asked. "He smells."

Everly moved forward to comfort Boswell, but Hunter grabbed her elbow. "Wait."

Cass had already moved to kneel before the grimm. Her small white hand reached out and patted him gently on the head. "It's okay to cry. The sky always cries, and what follows are beautiful flowers." She leaned forward and hugged him. The cave felt like it shrank as the giant grimm moved and brought up his hands to pull her into his grasp. For a moment, Everly thought he would eat the small changeling, but a few seconds later, he safely deposited her on the ground next to them.

"Why do you come here?" Boswell wiped at his face, smearing more dirt onto his already smudged face.

"We need to get to the secret library."

"It's buried," Boswell answered, his eyes flickering to the left. "After the attack came, the school collapsed in on itself. A protective measure to hide their secrets." He fidgeted. "There's nothing here anymore. Nothing but memories."

Everly noticed his lack of eye contact and fidgeting. "That's not true." She pointed out the clay on his clothes and hands. "You're here. You've been living here underground for seven years."

"Yes." Boswell nodded. "I failed as a keeper of the lighthouse and the gate. I'm no longer worthy of living in luxury as I once did."

"I wouldn't necessarily call this the lap of lux—" Aimee started but was silenced by Everly's elbow to the rib.

"We are not here to plunder the library but seek answers," Everly said. "We think that what happened here years ago has a link to what is killing people in Echo Bay."

"The grimm tide," Boswell said, his bright blue eyes filling with tears. "The killer tide, the tide's song."

"Yes," Everly encouraged. "You could help us stop it."

"You can't stop it," Boswell muttered, panicking. His head fell back in fear. "It's too powerful. But if we hide, wait it out, we will be safe."

"The grimm tide has already killed two nights in a row, and you are here cowering in a tunnel when there are students right here, grievers like those at Crypthaven, ready to fight. All you have to do is let us into the library," Everly said.

"I told you it's gone." He shuffled his weight and wouldn't look her in the eyes.

"You lie," Everly said, pointing to his hands. "You're hiding something."

Boswell's head snapped up fast, his hand disappearing into the folds of his long jacket, hiding the evidence. "How did you know?" His voice was weak.

"Everly can sniff out lies like nobody." Hunter crossed his arms and tried to intimidate Boswell. "So, will you help the grievers of Gravemark out? We want to do our best to help stop whatever this thing is that is killing innocent people."

"They're never innocent," Boswell mumbled incoherently.

"What was that?" Hunter asked.

"No one is innocent," he said, and the mood dropped. Everly felt a chill in the air. "Follow me. I will take you to the library, but you may not like what you find."

As his massive body turned, scraping against the tunnel's walls and ripping his tattered jacket a little more, Everly couldn't help but feel sorry for the grimm. It was as if he was living like a sardine in a can. They started following him toward the left passageway that led to the school. Everly felt a sense of satisfaction when her assumptions proved to be correct. As they climbed the stairs, she knew they were heading through the mountain to the other side where the school was situated.

Eventually, they reached an area where the tunnel had collapsed, and she could see deep claw marks where Boz had dug out each of the boulders and moved them to create a new, never-before-traveled passageway. The air started to get fresher, and the deep chill began to wash away, replaced by hope.

The makeshift tunnel opened into a much older one, passing through a cement archway into a large room with a domed rock ceiling. The dirt floor turned to tile, and torches lined the wall, creating a warm and welcoming glow. Everly noticed a giant pile of straw and a blanket tucked in a corner, which she assumed to be Boswell's bed. However, the table next to his bed caught her attention. Stacks of books were placed on it, piquing her curiosity.

"Here is what you are looking for," Boswell said solemnly. He pointed to a rock wall that had collapsed, and she could see areas that had been dug out and then the condition of the room. It felt more like a dungeon than a library.

Boswell had been digging tunnels, finding relics one by one, and bringing them here.

"Most of them were too damaged to salvage, but this is what I could save." He gestured with a large, clawed hand to the tables and stacks of books.

Everly walked over to the table and picked up the first book, examining the pages closely. She couldn't understand a word of the language it was written in, and the same was true of the second book. Ian had done the same, but when he flipped through the pages, his frustration grew to the point where he slammed the books on the table.

"What is the point of these books?" he exclaimed. "They're completely useless!"

Boswell raised an eyebrow. "Useless? These books are

not useless nor meant to be hidden away and buried underground. It should be available for everyone to access and learn from."

"Then what...?" Ian said in frustration. "Our history is now lost because you chose to save—"

"It's his history," Aimee said, picking up another book, her voice filled with revelation. "The secret library has the books of grimm. I wonder if it is the same at Gravemark."

Boswell moved to the side of the room as if ashamed of what he had been doing. "But I don't think you will find the answers here, dear children." He shuffled away into the tunnel.

Something was wrong. Everly could feel it in her bones —the room. Something about the layout felt familiar but foreign at the same time. Her eyes went over the room, scanning it, and then noticed a familiar pattern on the floor. Her head snapped up, and she mentally calculated the size of the room. They weren't in the secret library at all.

"It's an oubliette," Everly muttered under her breath. Then she yelled out a warning, "It's an oubliette." Just then, a clang rang out. Boswell stood outside the tunnel and must have activated a switch. "No!" Everly rushed forward just as a gate came down, trapping them inside the room. Everly grasped the bars and pleaded with the grimm on the other side. "What are you doing? Let us out!"

"I can't," Boz said. "It's come back. I must protect you all. It will leave soon, and I will return to let you out."

"That's like five days from now!" Ian yelled. "It will be too late. More people will die."

"But *you* will live." Boswell turned and slowly backed away down the hall; his form faded into the tunnel's darkness. "That is a sacrifice I am willing to make. Them for you."

"No, wait!" Aimee called. "You can't expect us to sleep here!"

Silence followed as Boswell disappeared into the darkness beyond.

"Aah!" Ian cried out as he yanked on the bars, trying to lift the gate. Even with his superhuman strength, he couldn't budge it.

"Kat?" Hunter used the radio to signal Kat, but all he got back was static.

"We're too deep underground for the radio signal," Aimee said, pulling out her cell. "No bars either."

Ian hadn't given up on their escape; he continued to slam himself against the bars, and he screamed in frustration. Everly briefly wondered why he was so desperate to escape, and then she remembered the silver cage. Ms. Bellcamp would lock him up every month so he wouldn't hurt anyone when the werewolf curse took over. This was probably déjà vu all over for him.

Hunter moved through the room, opening up trunks and boxes, searching for tools to help them escape. "I found some food, at least," he said, pulling out some rations and gallons of water. "So we won't starve or die of dehydration."

"No, just humiliation." Aimee sat on the chair by the table and dropped her head onto her hand. "I can't believe we fell into a trap so easily. We are going to be the laughingstocks of Gravemark. We should have killed the grimm when we had the chance."

Cass's face paled, and she started to tremble; she moved and disappeared behind Ian. "He was probably the one who attacked Crypthaven and blamed it on the stupid tide. I bet you there isn't a tide, just a lone guardian ogre thing with hygiene issues," Aimee continued.

Everly could understand Aimee's frustration. She, too, felt anxious and trapped, but she didn't feel the same threat from the grimm as the others. Her father said she needed to trust her instinct, and her instinct said Boswell was harmless.

She moved to sit in the second chair, pulled out a blue leather book, and flipped through it. The characters on the page were unlike any she had seen, a collection of circles and triangles with flared tails. It was beautiful to look at but beyond her understanding. One by one, she picked up a book and flipped through the pages, adding it to another pile. How would she figure out how to stop the grimm tide?

"I should have noticed it sooner." Hunter sighed, pointing at the floor and the markings in the cement. They were half filled in with dirt and covered with straw. "Every school has an oubliette. It would need to be accessible to the grievers."

"It's not your fault," Ian said, using his foot to push the straw aside to see more of the symbols that marked the hidden oubliette—a chamber underneath the ground that held all the grimm creatures in eternal sleep. It was a prison for grimms. Now, it was a prison for them. "I didn't notice either. The tunnels converged, and we ended up in another seam, and he did a good job of hiding the oubliette."

"Do you think he meant to trap us here?" Everly asked.

"Why else would he take us here?" Aimee scoffed.

"Well, I mean, he is living here. I don't know why a grimm would want to live over the entrance to the oubliette.

Not to mention all the books. What do you think he was researching?"

"Probably ways to open the oubliette and wake the monsters from their sleep," Aimee added.

Everly didn't think so. There was something about the way Boswell had organized the books. There was still one collapsed wall that had come from the floor above. It seemed a bit risky to try and scale the giant dirt mountain leading up to the ceiling. She could see bits of furniture and books buried under the rock and cement, but if Boswell hadn't felt it was worth digging out, then it probably wasn't important.

Everly continued to walk the room, looking for another way out. She lifted all the rugs, brushed the straw and dirt aside, and came to the same conclusion Hunter and Ian had.

An oubliette was meant to keep people in, not let people out. Luckily, they were in the chamber above the oubliette and not inside the oubliette itself. Otherwise, there might be no hope at all.

Everly shivered and moved to stare out into the tunnel.

They sat in the semidarkness for what seemed like hours. Everly had to agree with Aimee that she didn't want to sleep near Boswell's bed. She chose a spot with her back to the wall where it seemed to be a little warmer area of the cave. She dropped her forehead onto her bent knees and tried to get some rest.

Soon, one of the torches started to flicker out, then a second one, leaving only one more torch. "Is anyone else getting cold?" Aimee said, her teeth chattering. She was rubbing the sides of her upper arms to get warm. "I didn't realize how much heat those torches gave off until they were gone."

"It will be fine," Hunter said. "I've got one more torch, and if we need to, we could burn the table, but it will be risky with all the straw." He picked up the gallon of water, took the lid off, and gave a cursory sniff before handing it to Aimee. "Small sips. We must stay hydrated until Kat rescues us."

"Do you really expect an emo sib to come and rescue us?" Aimee's eyes shot up in disbelief. "I bet you she's just playing games on her computer and avoiding all the heavy griever work."

"She'll be here," Everly said, her teeth chattering as she stared at the heavy iron gate.

When the last torch went out, sending them into darkness, Ian put his flashlight on the table and turned it on, so its beam was aimed at the ceiling. He took out his flask and took a sip. He grimaced as he swallowed and then put it back in his jacket.

A horrible thought flashed through Everly's mind. *What if something happened to Kat? What if we aren't rescued and trapped inside with Ian? What happens when he runs out of wolfsbane before the next full moon? When is the next full moon?* Everly was calculating the days when Ian came and sat beside her on the floor.

She nervously looked away, trying to hide her guilt at mentally accusing him of something he hadn't even done... yet.

"We should stick together," Ian said. Everly raised her eyebrow at him, and he quickly added, "For warmth."

"That's a great idea." Cass came and sat right on Ian's lap and spread across Everly's, forcing her legs down. Cass became a blanket, lying across the two of them. As much as

Everly wanted to yell at the girl, she was putting off so much body heat she was like a mini furnace.

"You're so warm." Everly sighed and looked down at Cass, whose head was lying in the crook of her legs. Her dark, exotic eyes seemed catlike, but her pupils were so prominent in the lack of light that she probably could see just fine. Her white hair shimmered like starlight, and Everly felt herself subconsciously begin to run her fingers through it.

Cass closed her eyes and sighed contentedly. "All changelings are warm." She yawned and snuggled in further. "That's nice," she said softly. "My mother used to do that."

Everly's hand paused momentarily as she remembered what Cass had said about her parents. Grievers captured them and put them in the Gravemark oubliette, so she was alone—a foundling— and their school was known for taking in orphans. She continued to stroke Cass's hair.

Soon, Hunter came and chose the spot right next to Everly. He even adjusted Cass so her head was in his lap, leaving Aimee standing awkwardly, trying to decide whether or not to join their little puppy pile.

She didn't. She continued to sit on the chair. Shivering. "Come on over here," Ian coaxed, trying to give her a charming smile.

"No." She turned her back on him.

Everly could feel the tension in the room. Once Hunter had chosen to sit next to her, it left Aimee as the last one. A blast of wind came through, and she shivered again.

"Come on. Don't be stubborn; just sit next to us," Ian commanded.

"Come." Cass held up her hands straight into the air. "I'm warm."

Still, Aimee didn't move.

It was when Hunter said her name. "Aimee." It was a whisper, pleading with her to see reason. She turned to him, her eyes filled with tears that could have gone unnoticed in the dark, except that she wiped them away. Aimee came and sat next to Hunter but left a good eight inches between them. It was getting colder, and Everly gave Hunter a wide-eyed look that meant *help her!*

She could see his hesitation; he didn't want to start up something. At the same time, he needed to take charge as the leader. She nodded toward Aimee, giving him permission.

Hunter lifted his arm, put it around Aimee's shoulder, and pulled her into their group. "We're a family," Hunter whispered into Aimee's hair as she gave way and curled up into his side. "We take care of each other, no matter what."

Aimee nodded and laid her head against Hunter's chest. Her eyes flickered to Everly's, and for a split second, there was no animosity there. Cass got up and shifted a third time to spread out across all their laps. She was so tiny, but the heat emanating from her was like a fireball, warmer than any fireplace. When Everly looked with her sight, she did glow.

Cass reached up her hands and began to play with Aimee's necklace. She started to hum a song. It was ethereal, haunting, and quite sad.

The five sat locked in a warm huddle, serenaded by a changeling. Everly was sure it was quite a sight.

Then, soft humming turned into words, and Cass sang in another language. They listened in awe, unable to speak.

Cass's voice rose higher than a soprano but still remained as soft as a whisper.

Everly heard movement outside in the tunnels, and she caught the barest glimpse of a purple-and-red scarf and knew their guard, Boswell, must have heard Cass's singing and came to investigate. But he only stayed for a few seconds before she saw him move away, back into the tunnels.

Everly let Cass's song lull her into a safe sleep. Hunter's hand sought hers in the darkness. Everly clasped his fingers between hers, not letting them escape. He brushed his thumb across her hand, and instantly, she could feel the heat rising in her blushing cheeks.

CHAPTER 16

"Okay, you guys. It's not cool that I have to drag myself out of my warm van, abandoning Kingmaker27 during a boss raid, to come rescue you, only to find you all sleeping."

Everly snapped awake as a flashlight flickered across her face. She blinked against the light as it moved over, and the beam hung on Hunter like a spotlight.

"Okay, team leader. Explain yourself," Kat interrogated Hunter. "You went radio silent."

Everly lifted her hands and covered her eyes as the beam raked across her face again, and she started to see spots. "Kat, a grimm locked us inside. We need to find a lever or switch."

"Oh, sorry, my bad. Just thought you were all slacking on the job."

As the flashlight moved away from their faces, its beam illuminated the area around the gate. Kat was fully geared up in protective clothing from head to toe. Despite her small stature, she had donned a full protective vest, bat, and helmet, making her look like a catcher ready for a Little

League game. The only problem was that the protective gear was too big for her, and she had no one to help her resize the straps, causing it to dangle off her body. Nonetheless, she had mustered up the courage to leave the safety of her van and find them. The thought of her going into the tunnel alone sent shivers down Everly's spine, and she couldn't imagine the courage it must have taken her to do so. It was already scary enough when they were a group of five.

Cass sprang up with an abundance of energy while Everly struggled to get up due to the hours she had spent lying on the floor, causing her body to feel stiff. Ian extended his hand and pulled her up with such force that she was propelled toward him, causing her to lose her balance. His hands quickly wrapped around her waist, steadying her and pulling her closer to him.

"Sorry." She tried to move away, but Ian didn't release her.

"Wait," he whispered.

Everly looked up and met his gaze. It was the first time they had looked at each other in what felt like forever. Were his eyes always this blue? She felt herself staring. He was staring just as intently.

Everly swallowed and opened her mouth to say something.

Ian reached out a hand toward her face. Everly's pulse began to race. "You have a piece of straw in your hair." He pulled a yellow strand of straw out and flicked it into the air. Then he released her.

Immediately, she felt the lack of body heat from Cass and the group, and she shivered.

Hunter and Aimee had gone to the gate and tried to

direct and boss Kat around. "You sure there's nothing on the wall on the left?" Hunter asked.

"I'm telling you, there's nothing here." She flashed her flashlight all over the wall. "There's no lever to trigger this gate."

Cass raised her hands over her head in a very fae-like stretch. It was like she was moving joints, which was impossible for the human body.

"Let me." As Cass moved toward the gate, she turned her body and somehow slipped through the impossibly thin space between the bars. She reached forward and turned a torch on the wall, and the lever clicked. The gate began to roll back up.

"Are you telling me you knew where the lever was and could have let us out at any time?" Hunter said in barely contained frustration.

"Uh-huh," Cass said, giving another yawn. "But I was sleepy, and no one asked me to do it. The big grimm said we had to stay here for five nights. I was obeying his orders."

"Why, you little!" Aimee's fingers had curled into angry claws, and she seemed ready to pounce on the girl. Ian stepped in front of her and held up his hands.

"No harm done. We escaped, right?"

"No thanks to her!" Aimee screeched, pointing at Cass. "We could have been out of here hours ago." Then she turned on Kat. "And why didn't you come to our rescue sooner?"

Kat held up her hands. "I'm not a griever, remember. I'm just a sib. I'm not made for hand-to-hand combat."

"Whatever," Aimee snarled. "Let's just grab the books

and get out of here." She stormed through the gate and turned to wait for the rest to follow.

Hunter opened the griever bag filled with weapons and began to stuff in some books. "There's too many. We can't possibly bring all of them."

Everly hung back, surveying the room layout and where Boswell had placed and organized the books. "Not those. Or the ones on the far wall."

"Why not?" Hunter asked.

"Boswell was obsessed with the attack on Crypthaven. He feels guilt over not protecting the students. Why else would he have spent seven years digging through the ruins of the library? He was looking for answers as well. He would have put books that weren't important farthest from his reach." She moved through the stacks and pointed at the pile on the table and the one by his bed. "The most important books he would keep closest to him at all times."

Everly gestured to the one nearest to his bed. "We just need to take those and the ones on the table." She picked up the blue leather book. "There are tons of wax stains on this one, which means he was poring over it for a long time. Burning the candle wax until he fell asleep, and it spilled over onto the books."

"Who is going to translate them?"

She didn't think of anything at first, but then Everly replayed the scene in her mind of each of them picking up a book and looking inside. Everyone had a confused expression on their face except for one of them.

Cass's eyes had hung on the words on the page until she looked up and saw everyone tossing their books aside, so in solidarity, she did too.

"Cass can read them, can't you?" Everly turned, clasping her hands sweetly before her.

"What?" she breathed in surprise. "I can't read. I don't know what you're talking about."

"You can read. I saw you," Everly said. "You were fascinated with a book with a gold emblem on the spine. But lo and behold, that book isn't here anymore."

"I don't understand what you mean?" She swallowed, stepping further back.

"You took it." Everly moved forward, cornering her. She held out her hand.

Cass shook her head.

"Cass," Ian warned.

The girl dropped her head and pulled out the journal. It was small, about four inches by three inches, and she placed it in Everly's hand.

Everly opened the book and saw it was the same script as the other books. "It's okay, I'm not mad. All these books belong to you." Everly handed the book back to her. "Take whatever you want. Just help us so no more people die."

Cass's eyes filled with tears, and she clutched the book. "Oh yes, I will help."

"It's settled, so we can go."

Everyone turned to load up their gear to head out of the oubliette. Everly paused at the entrance. "Do you hear that?"

No one answered, so she walked back into the oubliette. There was a sound just like before. She moved toward the collapsed part of the library. Something had been reburied here. Everly used her shoe, brushed away the dirt, and revealed a bit of gold. She reached down and yanked out a golden bracelet. More treasure. She slid it on her wrist and raced back to catch up with the team.

Everly pointed toward the exit, and they barely made it through the tunnels to the crossroads when they were once again confronted by Boswell.

They heard his heavy breathing before they saw him. He was brushing against the side of the cave too, and they could listen to pebbles fall.

"Lightkeeper, that's enough. We're not scared of the consequences of the grimm tide. You can't hide us in here. We need to protect people," Hunter said bravely.

Everly squinted into the darkness. The skin on her arms rose in alarm. Her senses were tingling.

"That's not the lightkeeper," Everly whispered, seeing the flashlight reflecting off dark scales. It glistened and then ducked back into the shadows. "It's something else."

"Grievers." Hunter's voice deepened in a warning. He slowly dropped the bag full of books and pulled out his weapon.

Behind Everly, Ian and Aimee did the same. Each one of them had pulled out an iron weapon. Aimee had a pair of sais; Ian had a never blade. Kat lifted her baseball bat. Her heterochromia eyes flashed in fear. Cass hissed and backed up to the wall. Everly looked down the tunnel and reached for her own never blade. This wasn't the same aura coming from the lightkeeper. She could almost feel the grimm's anger wafting toward her.

Then, suddenly, a long cry filled the air, bouncing off the walls and echoing all around them. Everly winced and instinctively covered her ears; the sound was too painful. Aimee and Kat followed suit, but Hunter and Ian remained unfazed, their eyes fixed on something deep within the tunnel. The two boys stepped forward, and the cry came again, wrenching and piercing. Everly winced in agony, but the boys seemed immune to the sound. It was a strange and eerie experience that left the group feeling uneasy.

"What was that?" Everly turned to Aimee with a confused look.

When she turned back, Hunter and Ian were gone.

CHAPTER 17

"Where did Hunter go?" Aimee breathed out in a scared whisper.

Everly picked up the dropped flashlight and shined it down the tunnel that stretched toward the sea, but it was empty. The other tunnel led toward the lighthouse.

"Come on." Everly gestured with the light, taking the lead and heading down the one away from safety.

"You can't be serious," Aimee hissed, grabbing Everly's arm and the flashlight out of her hand.

"Our team is in trouble. We don't leave them behind," Everly answered, feeling irritation toward Aimee.

"No," Aimee sneered. "I mean, you can't be serious in thinking I'm going to let *you* take the lead." She pushed Everly back behind her. "I'm the senior griever. It's my job to protect the rest of you." Her face had gone cold, her gaze deadly, and she tightened her grip on her sais.

Everly saw Aimee in a new light. Not the rich girlfriend who dated Hunter Abernathy, but the seasoned griever, who had done her fair share of reapings.

Aimee dropped her backpack into the tunnel. She kept one of the sais by her leg and the other in front as she used the flashlight to guide her steps deeper.

The ground became rocky, the smell of the ocean stronger as they continued.

"Did any of you get an eye on it?" Aimee asked.

"Scales," Everly said. "I saw black scales."

Kat licked her lips and began to recite off different creatures with scales. "Mermaids, gorgons, naga, grindylow, scylla, leviathan, hydra, dragon, cirein-cròin. Oh, Lord, I hope it's not a cirein-cròin." The tunnel began to climb upward.

"What's a cirein-cròin?" Everly asked.

"Only the largest sea monster that can eat seven whales and then shape-shift into a small silver fish. How do we even go about catching that? It's not like Aimee's family has a boat rigged for monster-size harpooning," Kat rattled on.

"Okay, Google, we get it," Aimee snapped, trying to get Kat to calm down.

Kat could only stay quiet for a few seconds before her nerves made her talk again. "Why do you think it kidnapped the guys?" Kat murmured from behind Everly. She kept turning at every sound to scan the tunnel behind them. "Is it going to eat them?"

"I don't think they were taken," Everly said. "I think they left on their own accord. That sound we heard. It was painful to us, but it didn't affect them."

Aimee nodded. "It's a level-three lure, all right," Aimee said as she stepped around a corner, and the cave opened up to a high cliff.

"Careful," Cass yelled as a creature darted from another hidden tunnel and confronted them.

A siren.

According to her mother's journals, a siren was described as the unpleasant, deadlier cousin of the mermaid but could walk on land at will. Their song was not just a lure but, when sung, also a potent spell.

This siren had a fully scaled humanlike body, long dark hair covering her torso, and long daggerlike nails. Her eyes were wide, black.

The siren cocked her head and looked at the four of them sideways. Her mouth opened, and she screeched, very much like an eagle. Her hands opened wide, and she advanced on them.

Aimee stepped forward, her sais on either side. "I'll take care of her. You get the guys?"

"Yeah, sure. Where are they?" Kat's head spun as she searched the cave for them.

Everly's gaze went right to the cliff. Her heart was pounding as she rushed forward, ducking under the clawed hand of the siren as it swung at her head. Aimee grunted as she blocked the siren's foot kicking out at her and stabbed her sai into the top of it.

A loud, painful screech echoed through the cave.

Everly reached the cliff's edge and looked down, her stomach dropping at the distance; it must be at least a sixty-foot drop. Sharp rocks lined the bottom, and the waves were cresting and crashing into them before pulling out to sea. She didn't see any sign of Hunter or Ian having leaped to their death.

Just then, Everly felt hands grasp her shoulder and fling

her away. She stumbled and landed on her back. She struggled to move and looked up as Ian leaped to land on her. His hands went for her throat, his pupils wide and unseeing.

Everly gasped as his grip tightened around her neck, his thumbs squeezing. She kicked and flailed with her legs, trying to buck him off, but it was useless. He was stronger than her. She reached over his palms and grabbed the insides, pulling them outward to relieve some of the pressure, and she got in a single breath. But it wasn't enough. She was quickly overpowered again.

Kat screamed as Hunter stalked her around the other side of the cave. Kat dodged left and then right. When Hunter lunged, she jumped right over him and came out of it rolling.

"Ian," Everly gasped as tears slid out the corners of her eyes. "It's me," she tried to plead with him.

He didn't seem to hear her pleas.

"No!"

Aimee fought bravely; her shoulder was covered with bloody cuts from the fight with the siren, but she was tired.

Cass lunged out of the tunnel and jumped on the siren's back, her claw fingers digging at the siren's face, giving Aimee the chance to escape.

"Cass," Aimee said in surprise at the changeling's determination. But Cass wasn't letting it get the better of her.

"Those my friends," Cass hissed. Her mouth struggled to form the words over the sharp, needlelike teeth.

Aimee raced to Everly's rescue. Aimee jumped and knocked Ian to the side, but it was only a quick reprieve. Aimee yelped when he turned and grabbed her around the throat and lifted her in the air, pressing her against the wall.

Aimee's sneakers were swinging in the air as she struggled to find purchase. He thrust her once, twice against the wall, and she collapsed.

Everly coughed, rolled over, and saw they were losing the fight. Hunter hit Kat, and she was thrown against the wall and went limp.

A cry of fear followed as the more powerful siren violently flung Cass across the cave, and she slid, her hands scraping the floor for purchase as she went over the side of the cliff.

"NO!" Everly gasped.

The siren turned toward them. "Where is it? Give it back."

"Return what?" Everly asked.

The siren's mouth opened to sing again, and Hunter was moving toward her as well. Ian grabbed her shoulders and slammed her once against the floor. She saw stars.

Tears poured out of Everly's eyes. This was it. They were all dead, and she was about to be killed by her mentor. Ian gripped her throat again, and his fingers tightened.

"Ian," Everly pleaded. Bright lights flickered in her vision, and she knew she was losing consciousness. "It's okay. I forgive you."

"No!" the siren screamed and physically ripped Ian away from Everly, flinging him off like he was a sack of potatoes. She stood over Everly, her chest heaving, her eyes on the golden bracelet.

Aimee struggled to her feet, reaching for her sai, and approached the siren. Cass had clawed back up to the cliff's edge and pulled herself to safety.

"Give or die," the siren's voice whined loudly. She

leaned down, the fingers inching along Everly's skin, and paused to touch the gold.

Just then, a roar came out of nowhere, and Boswell barreled into the siren.

She screamed in surprise and dug her claws into his chest, but the great beast of a grimm didn't stop his momentum. "You! I remember that voice. You caused the finfolk to attack us." He roared as he lifted her bodily above him, her claws raking across his arms as she tried to fight her way free.

"I need it!" she hissed. "Death comes." Her claws stabbed Boswell over and over. And when he got to the cliff's edge, he jumped, taking them both toward the sea.

A clatter of metal hit the floor, and Everly saw Aimee release her sai. She fell to the ground; her shoulders started to shake as she sobbed. Whatever spell the siren had woven over Hunter and Ian dissipated when she fell.

Both looked around the cave in confusion. Hunter's eyes dilated, and she could once again see his beautiful green eyes, and then they widened in terror when he saw all of them bleeding and Everly coughing and grabbing her throat.

Everly still had tears blurring her vision, but she moved away from Hunter and toward the cliff. "Where—" She coughed, pointing with a trembling finger toward the water. "Boswell?"

Cass looked over the edge, and she shook her head. "I don't see him. The sea could have washed him away."

Hunter kneeled and reached to touch Everly's neck. "Here, let me," he said.

"No," Everly snapped, waving him back. "No, get back. Aimee and Kat, watch them. In case the spell isn't completely worn off."

"Gladly." Aimee took the second sai and grabbed Hunter by the back of the collar of his shirt.

Kat grabbed Ian's collar and yanked a little too hard. She took a second dagger from Aimee and seemed to have too much fun jabbing Ian in the back with it for retribution.

"What is going on?" Ian said, rubbing his head.

"Just playing a game called, 'I stab you, and you whine.'"

CHAPTER 18

THE RIDE BACK TO ECHO BAY WAS FILLED WITH A HEAVY silence that hung in the air. Ian was behind the wheel, and though Hunter and Ian tried to apologize, their efforts fell flat on the ears of their companions. No one felt like being pleasant, and the tension in the car was palpable.

Everly did her best to dress and clean Aimee's wounds following her instructions. But the roads were twisty, and it was hard to put ointment on. Most were superficial cuts except for two on her upper shoulder and back from the siren's claws.

"Oh, crud." Aimee sighed. "I think I'm going to need stitches. She used her teeth to wrap the bandage around her arm. "Kat?" she called out.

"On it." Kat was reviewing the listings on her computer. "There are a few private doctors in Echo Bay that make house calls."

"What about Dr. Owens? Is he still in town? He's a family friend of my parents."

Kat was working her magic; Everly watched as she did

a directory search for the house number, and then she hacked into the utility company for the address to check for spikes.

"Nope, the electric, gas, and water bills have dropped."

Aimee cursed under her breath.

Kat bit her lip. "Oh, here's one with a medical degree."

"Get him," Aimee said, dropping her head back onto the bench seat and closing her eyes. "I'll pay whatever he asks."

"Aimee." Hunter leaned into the back from the front passenger seat. "I'm sorry," he said. "I didn't expect to be so easily controlled or put under a siren spell. This is all my fault."

Aimee turned her head and sniffed. Her beautiful face wrinkled up as she began to cry. Hunter slipped from the front passenger seat and came and sat between Aimee and Everly.

Aimee immediately wrapped her hands around his shoulders and began to sob. Everly could feel herself become invisible as Aimee clung to him.

Everly met Kat's gaze, who rolled her eyes and mouthed, "So dramatic." Cass was up on the top bunk eating a Twizzler and sucking it like a straw.

Recovered from the ordeal, Cass was enthralled with the new candy and not even paying attention to the reconciliation happening six inches from Everly.

Hunter pulled back. Aimee's gaze met hers over his shoulder, and she saw the barest hint of a smile. It was like a crocodile that had once again lured an unsuspecting, sweet male into her clutches. Everly even wondered if those tears were real.

That was the problem with Hunter. He was a noble

knight. He was always putting everyone else first and putting their burdens on himself.

Everly stared down at her lap and began to roll the unused bandages back up. She was feeling selfish in her anger toward Aimee and Hunter's relationship. They had been dating off and on for years. Of course, they would have an easy connection.

By the time they pulled into the driveway, Kat was shouting instructions. "Okay, I'm tracking the doctor's phone. He is going to be at our house in ten minutes. So that means alibi, people. Cass, you go into my room and stay there with Ian. I'll grab all the computers and get rid of the evidence. We can't make it seem like there are all these teens here without supervision. Aimee, how did you get the cuts?"

"Wakeboarding. I hit the reef. I've done it enough times in the past."

"Okay, then!" Kat clapped her hands. "It's go time."

Everyone jumped out of the van and ran into the house. Aimee went to the hall closet, grabbed her wakeboard, splashed water from the kitchen sink, and dumped it by the front door.

"Beach towels?" Everly asked.

"Upstairs hall closet," Aimee directed. "I need to change into a swimsuit."

Everly ran upstairs, grabbed a towel, ran it under the water, took it outside, and tossed it off the balcony into the sand. After she shook it out enough, she returned to see that Aimee changed into a skimpy bikini.

"It was the only one that didn't cover up my shoulder blade," Aimee explained weakly. She had even jumped in the shower, having removed the earlier bandages.

"Almost here," Kat yelled, her voice muffled from the spare room.

Everly was just about to head into the room when Hunter came out of the bathroom in his board shorts.

She froze in the hall, looking up at his tanned washboard abs. He, too, looked like he had just come out of the shower. Hunter was running his hands through his wet hair to make it look like he had just come out of the ocean, but to her, it was like he was walking off a runway.

The towel in her hands dropped to the floor and so did her mouth. She couldn't look at him as her cheeks grew red. She craned her neck to look at the awkward photo of a crane on a beach.

"E." Hunter moved to stand in front of her. "What is this?" His warm hand touched her shoulder. "Let me see." He lifted up her chin, leaned close, and saw the red marks on her neck. His green eyes met hers, and she looked away again. Everly couldn't handle the guilt she saw there. His hand was still on her face. His fingertips brushed against her throat, and she flinched from the memory, not the pain.

His hand moved from her neck to brush hair from her face. She met his eyes, and instinctively her hand moved to keep him from coming any closer. Doing that meant she was laying her palm on his chest, though. She could feel his muscles tense and his heart's faint beat that seemed to pick up at her touch. He leaned in closer.

"Everly." His voice was husky. "Did I—" He swallowed. "Did I do this?"

"No," she breathed out. "It wasn't you."

His face crumbled into a look of relief, and she reached her unoccupied hand out to touch his arm. He placed his hand over hers, and when he met her gaze, his eyes were glassy with unshed tears. "I'm sorry I couldn't protect y—"

The doorbell rang, interrupting them.

Everly picked up the wet towel and handed it to Hunter before she ducked into the bedroom and pressed against the door, her hand over her heart as if she could contain the wild beating that was pounding loudly. Except, she wasn't alone. She looked over at Kat, who was sitting cross-legged on the bed with her laptop in her lap. Her pink hair wasn't brushed but contained under a knit beanie.

Cass bounced on the other bed, and Ian stood at the foot. His eyes burned in fury as he stared at her. Everly swallowed and turned to look back at the door, realizing that their whole conversation happened right where everyone could see.

Everly tucked that stray blonde hair behind her ear and moved to sit.

"Lights," Ian ordered.

She flicked the light off just as she heard the front door open and Hunter greet the doctor. "Hi, right this way. We decided to go out wakeboarding, and then Aimee got caught in a current and hit a reef."

"You should have gone to the hospital." A muffled voice spoke from the other side of the door. Everly could track him as he moved through the house. His voice echoed, so he must have entered the dining area.

"I know," Aimee said. "But my parents are doctors, and we always know that private care is best. Especially you, Dr. Peter."

"Dr. Peter," Everly whispered, her head turning to Kat with a questioning look. Everly crawled over to the bed and leaned over to look at the laptop. "What is his specialty?"

"Oh, well, um?" Kat tugged on her knit hat. "That might have escaped my attention. I was only looking for medical degrees."

When she pulled up his photo, it was as Everly feared. "He is also Echo Bay's medical examiner."

"So...?" Kat said with wide eyes as if she wasn't catching the connection.

"He's a trained pathologist. He will know that a coral reef didn't cause the wound."

"Oh, yeah, well, I didn't think about that," Kat muttered. "There aren't a lot of doctors in this town this time of year. Even the hospital is understaffed."

"Too late now," Ian said, ripping open another bag of licorice and handing it to Cass to keep her occupied. The changeling was getting bored being cooped up in the room. "They're just going to have to act their way out of this one."

Everly crawled back to the door, sitting on the floor, pressing her ear to the wood, trying to catch every word.

It was mainly chitchat. Hunter talked about the weather and boats, and then Dr. Peter asked them the dreaded question. "What are you doing out here so late in the season?"

"It's our gap year," Aimee said. "We've decided to travel before picking a college, and I've always loved Echo Bay. It's just so safe here."

There was a slight cough in reply. Everly wasn't sure who the one who coughed was—Dr. Peter or Hunter.

Everly kept looking at her watch, waiting for the hour to tick by, and then noticed the time with a sinking stomach. She had missed her work shift. Even if she snuck out the door right now, she would still miss the show's beginning.

She held her watch to Ian and saw his reaction too. She

looked to the window and wondered if they could squeeze out it.

He read her thoughts and shook his head. "It's not worth it."

Everly wanted to argue, but she heard the front door open and close. She waited, counting to sixty, before she got up. She didn't go outside but went to the window that overlooked the ocean. The sun had set, and the colorful fog and light show accompanied the first act of the pirate show.

She watched a streak of blue laser dance through the sky, followed by a firework exploding and dropping into the sea. When her eyes followed its trail, they met another pair of eyes standing out on the sand.

Dr. Peter. He hadn't left but stood just outside her window, his gaze fixed on hers.

They stood frozen. *Does he recognize me from this morning? Probably not. Would he suspect me since I was there when they discovered the body and then when he had to stitch up Aimee?*

Her heart sped up, and her mouth went dry. Dr. Peter turned and walked through the sand back to the street parking, where he got into his blue Tesla. The lights went on, and he slowly drove off. Everly sighed in relief, but it didn't last long, as they were no closer to finding the answer to the grimm tide.

"Cass, about those books?" Everly turned back to see that Cass had fallen asleep in an awkward position. Her head was dangling off the bed, a red strand of licorice hanging from her lips, and the soft sound of snoring followed.

Everly pulled the candy from the changeling's mouth and put it on the nightstand before heading out to the living room to look into Hunter and Aimee's solemn and uncomfortable faces.

"What?" Everly asked, feeling a sense of unease.

"He knows we lied," Aimee said. "After he was done, he questioned me again how I got the injury. If it were the coral, there would be tons of minuscule scratches, not just these three big ones. I'm so stupid."

"Relax, it doesn't mean anything," Hunter said, touching her shoulder and trying to comfort her. "Teenagers lie all the time."

"But not to him. He's the medical examiner from this morning."

"That was *him*?" Aimee pointed at the door in disbelief. "Kat! How could you?"

"Already apologized once. Twice is asking a bit much, you know," Kat said as she brought her laptop out to join the rest of them in the living room. "But, um, guys. We need to apologize to someone else," she said, turning her computer screen around. Ms. Bellcamp's furious and pinched face filled up the desktop. Her blonde hair was slicked back with a headband; she had on a white button-up blazer.

"What were you thinking?" Ms. Bellcamp didn't yell, but her voice was shrill. "Crypthaven is off-limits. It's so dangerous in the tunnels. You could have been killed. This was so irresponsible of you. That's it. I'm coming back there tonight."

Typically, Everly was used to seeing Ms. Bellcamp with her cool and calm demeanor. She never expected her to be so frazzled at the prospect of them having gone to the school.

"Everything went fine," Hunter assured his teacher,

using every single bit of Abernathy charm. "We were able to find the access to the tunnel through the lighthouse.

"Yeah, and they got locked in the oubliette, but I rescued them." Kat jumped into the Facetime call.

"You were locked up?" Ms. Bellcamp's voice rose to a shriek. "In the oubliette?" Kat winced at the inflection of her advisor's voice and then shrank back to hide behind Hunter.

"We even met the lighthouse keeper."

"Boz?" her voice softened. "Is he still alive?"

Hunter stood there calmly, facing the screen, not in the least bit intimidated by the interrogation. "There was a slight misunderstanding with Boswell. First, we thought he was our enemy, but then he saved us from a siren attack?"

"Is everyone okay? Are there any lasting effects from the siren's song? Do you need a doctor?" Ms. Bellcamp continued to worry over them, asking a million questions like an overprotective mom.

"I shouldn't have agreed to let you go to Echo Bay." Ms. Bellcamp's brows relaxed, and she became curious. Her fingers steepled together, and she leaned in. "The books in the secret library are all untranslated. We've only been able to read the four main grimm languages. Draconian, ancient dryad, runic, and ogregarian."

"Cass can read this one," Hunter said, holding a blue bound book.

"Cass?" Her blonde eyebrows rose in surprise. "The changeling. What do they say?"

"Still working on that."

Ms. Bellcamp nodded. "I see; well, continue with your work. I hope you can finally solve this case, and maybe it will help Boswell come to terms with what happened."

"That's right," Everly said. "You are one of the few that survived the attack. He is blaming himself for everyone else's death."

"I know that feeling well. Survivor guilt never goes away."

When they signed off on the call, it was almost 10:30 p.m.

Hunter folded the laptop and turned to look at his team, who were all beaten up and sore. Everly and Kat had ice packs on their necks. Aimee took some painkillers and was curled on the couch with a blanket.

"What do we do now?" Ian stood with his hands on his hips, looking out the sliding glass door as another rocket hit the sky and exploded in a blast of white. "We missed the show and might have lost our jobs in the process."

Hunter sat on the arm of the couch. "Let's go over what we've discovered so far."

Aimee held out her fingers and began to tick them off. "One, some of the cast of the pirate show are grimm. Two, Everly found a gold coin. And three, our attempt to get into the Crypthaven secret library got us almost killed and useless grimm history books. Four, there's a siren there that seems to be able to control people. I understand the other team's frustration and why no one has solved this in a hundred years. No one knows what we are hunting."

"The siren was after this." Everly held up her hand to expose the gold bangle.

"Where did you get that?"

"In the oubliette. Boswell had buried it. I think the siren wanted this."

"What about that gold coin?" Hunter said. "Do you still have it, Everly?"

Everly froze. "No. I gave it to Skittles. He thought it was part of the Lennox treasure, and he was going to study it, but then he—" Her hand covered her mouth. "He died. I don't know if he had the coin on him or not. And then the siren wanted this bangle. She said death would follow. Maybe the treasure is cursed."

"The treasure is cursed? Get that thing out of here or so help me!" Kat jumped up and pointed out of the house.

"We don't know for sure," Hunter said.

"Well, let's not find out, shall we." Kat got up and opened the slider door. "Come on, just toss it outside."

The room grew silent as it slowly filled with tension. The last vestiges of the pirate show's final fireworks fell from the sky, reflecting across the glass slider and painting the room in an ominous red.

Red like the stone in an antique necklace that a particular server wore. The same one in the Polaroid Skittles proudly showed her.

"I think I know how to find out if treasure is cursed. We either find out if the others that died had the treasure on them, or we interrogate someone who we know has found a piece of the treasure."

"Who?" Hunter asked.

"Starla." Everly pointed to her chest. "That antique necklace she wears is a confirmed piece of the Lennox treasure. I recognize it from Skittles's photos. I also know that Pike and Cleo were digging in Howler's Cove. They may have found treasure too."

"What about Nicky Delucca?" Kat asked.

"We'll have to find out, along with the other victims. We need to find out what was on them when they died. But for now." Everly pointed to the ship. "Our best bet at figuring out the connection between the grimm tide and this treasure is about to slip away to Howler's Cove."

Ian grinned. "I'm up for a little interrogation."

"Don't you mean kissing?" Kat teased.

Hunter met each of his team members' eyes, assessing them and their ice packs and bandages before going to Aimee, who didn't seem comfortable about another encounter with grimms already. She couldn't look at him. "You're hurt, Aimee. You don't have to go," Hunter said, letting her off the hook.

Aimee nodded, and her eyes became glassy. She wiped at her nose with her sleeve and sniffed. "Thanks for that. But what kind of griever would I be if I just sat back and let others get into trouble without someone to bail them out." She stood, went to the closet, and picked up her sais. Her brown hair was pulled back into a short ponytail, and she looked young and vulnerable. She took a deep breath, and in that second, she steadied herself, and her eyes became hard. "Let's do this."

CHAPTER 19

THEY TOOK THE JET BOAT TO HOWLER'S COVE, CUT THE engine, and floated to the other pontoon boat tied up. Ian directed their group, keeping an eye on his watch so that they wouldn't accidentally show up at the same time the other group did.

Silently, they cut through the water and anchored their boat. One by one, Hunter handed everyone a headlamp; this time, they wore black neoprene bodysuits. Everly felt weird braiding her hair and donning a belt that would hold her weapons. They looked like a special ops team.

Kat had bundled up and was wearing multiple layers of clothing. Her fuchsia hair poked out from under a knit hat. She was going to spend the night on the boat, protecting it. She had a flare gun, harpoon, and other weapons.

Aimee was going over last-minute instructions with Cass. "We don't know what is on the other side of that cliff. Stay back, stay hidden, like you did in the cave. Don't show yourself until we need help. Got it?"

Hunter crossed over to the pontoon boat and searched it for weapons. "Nothing," Hunter called back.

Out of nowhere, an enormous wave slammed into the boat, sending everyone into a frenzy as they clung onto the sides and seats to prevent falling overboard. The impact was so strong that Everly couldn't help but cry out in fear, wondering where the wave had come from and what could have caused it.

As the water settled, Aimee noticed a distinct V-shaped trail left in the wave's wake. "That's not normal."

Ian leaned over the side of the boat and looked intently at the dark depths. After a few intense minutes, he slipped into the water and headed toward the marker. Everly followed him, surprised that the water was warmer than she expected. Aimee and Hunter joined them, and they all treaded water outside the drop line.

Cass floated next to them, her white hair spreading through the dark water like fluorescent tentacles. The group was left to wonder what caused the massive wave and hope that nothing else would happen to disrupt their journey.

"Lead the way, Ian." Hunter gestured with his chin.

"Just remember that I don't know what kind of grimm they are. They smell of the sea, but my griever senses couldn't pick up anything else. So be ready for anything."

"Heard," Aimee said.

"Take a deep breath, it's a long swim." Ian rose out of the water, took a deep breath, and dove down, his flippers helping him cut through the water. They followed. It wasn't as scary the third time passing through the tunnel, and when they came up on the other side, she expected to see a roaring bonfire and Dylan, Starla, Cleo, Pike, and Rob playing music, eating, and having fun.

Nothing prepared her for the gruesome scene before her and the still body lying in the sand, hair covering her face, arms bent at an awkward angle, like a rag doll tossed to the ground.

Everly's heart raced as she stared at the body.

"Ian," she called, her voice trembling. As they approached the body, it became apparent that it was a female cast member, but it was difficult to tell precisely who due to the darkness. Everly shined her flashlight on the body and saw an antique necklace hanging at an odd angle over her shoulder, which confirmed that it was Starla.

Everly inhaled and swung the flashlight in an arc, surveying the beach in complete disarray. The hammocks were ripped from the trees, the lawn chairs were broken and scattered, and some were found in the water. The coolers were knocked over, and there were dark stains on the sand that she feared were blood pools. The scene was chaotic and unsettling.

"Is she...?" Everly asked, afraid to approach the body.

Ian leaned down and checked for a pulse. His shoulders slumped, and Everly could see him struggling with Starla's death. "She's still warm. We must have just missed the killer."

"Spread out!" Hunter barked and rushed out of the water. "It could still be here!"

Everly raced onto the beach, her eyes wide as she searched the shadows.

Cass made a hissing sound and slunk into the shadows. Aimee turned to face the water, her sais ready. Ian's eyes went right to the tree line. "Grimm!" he breathed out and pointed.

Everly's heart raced as she focused on the branches, waiting to see what would come rushing out to attack. A branch snapped; Everly's hand tightened around the blade and prepared to defend herself, but something was nagging her about the whole scene.

"It's coming," Hunter whispered.

The branches moved, and Dylan stumbled out of the trees. His face was covered in scratches, his arm hung limply at his side, and his eyes were white with terror. He stumbled and fell to his knees in the sand.

"Eve," he mumbled, reaching for Everly. "Run." He fell over onto his side.

Ignoring Dylan's plea to run away, Everly ran to him.

"No, don't," Hunter ordered, but she ignored Hunter's warning. Everly landed in the cold sand, grabbing Dylan's hands as she tried to assess his injuries.

"Dylan." Everly touched his cheek. "What happened?"

"The curse. It's true. We thought it couldn't reach us here. I'm sorry." His amber eyes squeezed shut, and she saw tears squeeze out of the corners.

"Where are the others?" Everly asked, referring to Cleo, Pike, and Rob.

He shook his head, his hands trembling. "I don't know where Pike is. Cleo and Rob didn't come. Starla shouldn't have taken it. We should have put it back."

"Dylan, tell me who did this. What happened to Starla?"

Dylan let out a long, anguished sob as a dark shadow passed over him, and he recoiled in fear. Ian leaned down and grabbed his shirt, lifting him in the air, his feet dangling, unable to find purchase in the sand.

"What are you?" Ian growled out.

Dylan's eyes went wide, and he shook his head. "What do you mean?"

"I mean, what type of grimm are you? I can smell it on you." Ian dropped Dylan to the ground, and he collapsed.

"Grimm?" Dylan looked over at Everly for help. "I don't know what he's talking about, Eve."

"Creatures that pretend to be humans," Everly answered.

"I don't know what that is." Dylan's voice trembled, giving off all the tells of someone speaking the truth.

Ian pulled a knife from his belt and taunted Dylan with it by tossing it and catching it by the hilt. "Well, pirate, I'm not in the mood to play games, but I am willing to show you how good I am with a real knife. This one's not rubber."

"W-wait!" Dylan tried to scramble away from Ian. "You're all crazy?"

Another tug in Everly's gut told her that something was wrong. He was reacting like a human.

"Maybe we have it wrong?" Everly said, turning to Hunter. "Is it possible he doesn't know he's a grimm?"

Hunter frowned. "It could be. We only have Ian's word that he is grimm?"

All eyes, including Dylan's, went to Ian accusingly.

"Why do you say he's grimm?" Aimee asked.

"They all smell like the ocean." Ian rubbed the back of his head. "Especially when I kissed Starla. It was as if my senses were firing like a beacon."

"Maybe your wolf senses went a little haywire?" Aimee suggested.

"No, I'm right." Ian became defensive, but his voice rose, and Everly could hear he lacked conviction. "I think." He put the knife back in his hip sheath. When the group became silent, he stormed off toward the beach and stared at the giant rock where the harbor seals had slept the other day.

Dylan still lay on the ground, wide-eyed and fearful. Hunter moved first, reaching a hand and pulling him to his feet. "Aimee will take a look at your wounds."

Aimee nodded and pulled Dylan to the other side of the beach, away from Starla's body.

"What do we do?" Everly asked.

"We call it in," Hunter said. "There's been a murder, and we still don't know what happened."

"Murders." Cass's higher-pitched voice pierced the night, and she came from farther inland. She appeared like a ghost of the darkness, her pale hair and skin making her seem ethereal and almost see-through. "There's another one." She turned to point into the trees. "That way."

As soon as Cass said more, Dylan's voice rose in pitch, and he began to wail. Aimee held onto him to try and comfort him.

Everly followed Cass into the darkness and came upon the still form of Pike. He was the strongest in the pirate show, but his body was beaten and bruised. Whatever did this had to be stronger than the show's bodybuilder.

"What else did you find?" Hunter asked Cass.

"Nothing. There's nothing else here. Just the boy." Cass pointed toward the beach. "Whatever killed them is gone. But I will check again." She slipped into the shadows

Everly lifted her flashlight and studied the body for signs of how he was murdered. Again, there were red puffy marks along his body and a giant circular one.

"Looks like the marks from cupping therapy," Hunter said. Everly jumped in surprise. Hunter had followed her so silently. "You know, where a therapist uses cups and suction to help treat pain, migraines, or even boost immune systems."

"I don't think that's what this is, though," she said. "Skittles had the same mark on his body as well, and according to Dr. Peter, this isn't the first victim to have these marks. I think—" She moved her flashlight over Pike, and that's when she saw a shimmer in the sand next to his body.

Everly leaned down and brushed the sand away to uncover a gemstone the size of her hand.

"Is that a ruby?" Hunter breathed out. "It's huge."

Everly took a dry twig and pushed the gem out of the sand. She took the flashlight and shined it through the ruby. A deep red color painted the sand. "It's real, not glass. Glass wouldn't reflect like this."

"Where would he get a ruby?" Hunter asked.

"Probably the same place as Starla got that antique necklace she's wearing. I bet you they found Lennox's treasure."

Hunter turned his flashlight and scanned the nearby area. "We must leave because it will be too hard to find at night. Aimee is caring for Dylan, and we need to get back."

"What about Pike and Starla?" Everly asked, refusing to budge. She was hurting. "We can't leave them."

"We have to let the police handle this, Everly."

"But I knew them, if only for a few days, and this feels wrong. Like I'm abandoning them?" This time, she couldn't hide her tears of frustration. "This is my fault. If only I had gotten here sooner. Returned and questioned them. They would still be... alive."

"Shh." Hunter pulled Everly into his arms; she buried her face into his chest and let the tears fall. "Or you'd be dead too. Listen to me, Everly. You are not invincible, and this is not your fault."

"But I—"

"You can't think that way." He stepped back and used his thumb to wipe away her tears gently. "It's okay to grieve for your friends, but you are not responsible for what happened tonight. If it wasn't for you, we wouldn't have even found this cove. Now, we are one step closer to figuring out the grimm tide."

Everly sniffed and nodded. It took her a minute to gather her thoughts and wipe her eyes. When she thought Hunter wasn't looking, she leaned down and took the ruby—carefully tucking it into her wet suit.

Then she walked past Starla and stared at the antique necklace. *Was this the source?* Everly didn't know what came over her, but she reached down and slipped it over her head, tucking it next to the ruby. There was something about these pieces that kept showing up. She was beginning to believe that the treasure was cursed.

When they came over to Dylan, Aimee had a syringe and measured out a medication dose. "What are you doing?" Everly demanded.

"I'm giving him a sedative." Aimee checked the dosage and moved over to Dylan. "I've questioned him, and he told us everything he can about what attacked him. Which is not much. He only remembers hearing Starla and Pike scream. Cass and Ian swept the island, and he's safe. We have to leave, and we can't have him remembering we were ever here. We have to protect our team." Aimee injected Dylan in the arm.

"Wait." Everly leaned down and quickly asked him before he lost all consciousness, "The treasure. You found it?"

His head bobbed. "Buried in Howler's Cove."

"Who all found it? I saw Skittles's Polaroids. I know it's Lennox's treasure."

Dylan's head rolled back. "Pike, Starla, and Cleo. However, Cleo gave her piece to a boy she liked. I was too scared of the curse to take any treasure."

"I think that makes you the lucky one," Hunter added.

"Where is the treasure now, Dylan?"

"Gone. We came back to get it yesterday. It was gone. All Pike found was that ruby in the sand." Tears filled his eyes. "I wish we never found it. It's brought us nothing but bad luck." His voice became choked up with emotions, and she thought he would tell her more, but then he relaxed and sighed. His eyes fluttered, and he fell into a deep sleep.

Everly sighed in frustration and glared at Aimee.

"Oops!" Aimee shrugged and packed away her med kit.

Hunter was already knee-deep in the water; he was speaking into a radio, telling Kat to try and send in their exact coordinates to the harbor police.

Ian seemed out of sorts. Ever since he realized that Dylan was not grimm and neither were Starla and the others, it appeared he had lost some confidence.

"Let's go!" Hunter dove under the water first. Ian followed him.

Everly didn't even remember getting into the water, but

she felt like as soon as she did, eyes were on her, watching her every move. Even when she got into the jet boat, she couldn't shake that feeling, and they drove away up the coast. And as they did, they could see the flashing lights of the harbor patrol coming.

Everly closed her eyes, leaned forward, and let herself cry. Cass came, laid her head on Everly's shoulder, and started patting her awkwardly. She couldn't even remember changing clothes or falling into her bed when they returned to the house. She was so exhausted. But as she drifted off to sleep, she remembered hearing a song—a melody.

CHAPTER 20

It was almost noon when Everly awoke to the smell of fresh coffee. She rolled out of bed, stared at the pristine white ceiling, and rubbed her dry and crusted eyes. Her body ached; she was bruised, not to mention emotionally drained. Her soul felt like a dried-up well, and there wasn't a drop of happiness to be found.

In the bed beside her was Kat, dreaming away in her Batman sleep shirt, plaid pants, and a purple sleep mask with headphones. Kat had used the headphones after her first night sharing a room with Everly and commented on her nightmares. Everly tried apologizing, but Kat just pulled out her headphones and said, "I got you covered, girl. I once had to share a room with Deenah, and this can block out anyone's snoring—and even your night terrors."

The headphones must be working because Kat's mouth was slightly ajar, and she was drooling on her pillow. If only Everly could sleep that hard. But sibs never saw the things that grievers did, because everyone wanted to protect them. They didn't always see the blood.

Knowing she looked like a zombie, Everly treaded out of the bedroom and into the kitchen.

Ian was pouring a fresh coffee, and she stopped to stare. He wasn't wearing a shirt, and long, faded, silvery scars covered his muscled back.

Was it from a battle with a grimm? But they didn't look recent. So it had to have been years ago. Maybe—

"It's from that night my parents were killed. Or so I thought." His voice was gravelly in the morning from disuse. He took a sip of coffee. Ian didn't even turn around to acknowledge her standing there. *Did he hear her?*

"How did you know—"

"You forgot already that I'm werewolf cursed. I can hear you breathing three rooms over." He slowly turned around to lean against the counter. Ian was wearing dark jeans; his blue eyes were cloudy, and his blond hair was ruffled as if he spent the evening tossing and turning. He held a cup of coffee in his strong hands and was staring into its darkness like it was the pit of despair. "I can recognize you by your scent." His fingers tightened on the cup. He brought those tortured eyes up to meet hers.

Immediately, fear came over her. *Did she smell?* What would she possibly smell like to a wolf-cursed human? She pulled at her sweatshirt and gave it a cursory sniff.

"Oh, uh, what do I—" She started awkwardly, but Ian cut her off.

"Honey and—" He came closer, inhaling her. "—vanilla."

Everly froze, unable to look up into those ice-blue eyes. "It's my shampoo."

"It's distinctive. You're one of the few girls who don't mask your natural scent with unnecessary perfumes."

She looked up and was trapped by Ian's gaze. This time, she saw him. It wasn't the cold face of Ian that was constantly barking at her or insulting her. This was a different side of him. One that scared her even more. It was the wolf side of Ian that was possessive and somewhat unnerving.

Everly stood in the kitchen, still in her shorts and over-sized hoodie that she slept in. She was frozen as if she was caught in the gaze of a predator.

"Is this what you came for?" he asked, voice dripping with the double entendre.

"W-what?" Her heart started to beat faster in her chest.

Ian leaned even closer to her, his lips parted. His eyes flicked down toward the coffee cup he offered. "Coffee? Isn't this why you came into the kitchen dressed like a hobo?"

"I'm not dressed like a hobo," Everly grumbled, grabbing the coffee out of his hand. "It's called comfy chic." She took a sip and immediately gagged. "Black?"

"Cream hides the flavor and scent of the natural coffee bean." He held a second cup of coffee and brought it up to his mouth to take a drink. "I thought I already told you how much I despise things that hide one's natural scent."

Everly took the mug, went to the counter, pulled out a packet of sugar, and ripped it open, dumping it in the cup, followed by a few tablespoons of half-and-half. "Well, some-times bitter things are easier to tolerate with a bit of sweet-ness." Her words were firm and packed with a hit directed at Ian.

He chuckled and took another sip of his coffee. When Everly turned back around, his face went dark again, and she realized that her hooded sweatshirt collar had dropped so that her neck was exposed, and the bruises were more distinguishable now.

"Everly, I don't know what happened in that tunnel. I can't explain what came over me. But you have to believe me, I have no recollection of anything other than escaping the oubliette. I didn't even know I hurt you."

Everly played with the sugar packet as she listened to Ian's apology.

She wanted to forgive him, and she did, but she was wary. He had been controlled, and he hurt her. *Who is to say it couldn't happen again?*

"You're forgiven," she said quickly, taking a drink to hide her true feelings.

Ian was watching her struggle to drink and swallow. "But you don't trust me."

She put the cup back on the counter and pulled her sleeves over her hands. "I was hurt," Everly said, playing with the cuffs. "By someone we thought—*I* thought—I could trust."

"You can trust me," Ian said. He slammed his palm onto the counter, making the liquid in the coffee cup vibrate. "I can't be held responsible for a spell used against me. That wasn't us. I wouldn't have hurt you." He took a step toward her, and she backed up subconsciously.

"But you did—hurt me.."

Ian froze, hurt by her reaction.

"You're not scared of Hunter," he said bitterly. "You want to calm his fears."

Everly inwardly groaned. He must have seen their whole exchange the night before in the hall. "Maybe, I would be fearful, if he attacked me as well. But I've also known Hunter for years. His sister and I are best friends."

"Right," Ian scoffed. "Because they're so perfect." He was being sarcastic, but he was right. The Abernathys had hidden the truth from her. Both of them had, but so did her father and grandmother.

"I didn't say that."

"You didn't have to. I see the way you watch Hunter when you think no one is looking. You worship the ground he walks on."

"I do not." Everly was getting angry.

"You do," Ian said. "It's pathetic to moon after a guy so much when he doesn't feel the same way you do."

Everly's heart was hammering in her chest. Why did this conversation hurt so much? *What is going on? Why is he being so mean again?* She thought she had kept her feelings hidden, but obviously not. It was pretty darn evident that even Ian had spotted it.

Tears burned in her eyes, and she saw the blur in the corner of her vision. She looked up and saw Hunter standing behind Ian in the hall. *How long has he been standing there? Did he hear Ian's statement?*

Then, a sickening realization hit her when she looked into Ian's cold eyes. Ian knew Hunter was just outside the kitchen. That's why he attacked her like this. Ian could smell him coming, which meant everything Ian had said was done on purpose to embarrass her.

Everly carefully placed the coffee cup on the counter, her hands remarkably steady despite the emotions rolling and bubbling up inside her. She held her head high and walked past Ian, not making eye contact with Hunter as she retreated into her bedroom.

She took a deep breath, reached for her toothbrush and clothes, and headed into the bathroom to change. As she returned to the hall, she could hear Hunter and Ian arguing.

"What's your problem?" Hunter asked. "Why can't you be nice to her?"

"Nice? I'm nice," Ian scoffed.

"Yeah, right. You tolerate Everly."

"Well, she's letting her feelings get in the way of the mission."

"She is..." Hunter's voice dropped to a whisper. "Or you are?"

"She's not thinking clearly. Hunter, she needs to go back to Gravemark. Right now."

"She's proven herself time and time again," Hunter interjected. "When are you going to stop being an idiot?"

"It seems like our roles have somehow reversed." Ian chuckled sourly. "I'm the one who wants to protect her, and you're the one putting her in danger."

"What do you mean?"

"You saw what happened to those kids and that Pike guy. He was huge. A bodybuilder. And he was crushed by something out there, all because they found that cursed treasure. I know that you put it together as well. You just haven't admitted we have a problem. Do you see her wrist? Everly found a piece of that treasure at Crypthaven. What if Crypthaven happened to have gathered much more than a bracelet in one spot? You have to understand the significance of that curse. That is probably what drew the finfolk and siren there. They wanted that treasure. That is what destroyed the school."

Everly looked down at her wrist; sure enough, she had slept with the bracelet on and had the necklace and ruby on her nightstand.

"We don't know that is the way they're targeted."

Ian jabbed his finger into the counter to make a point. "She gave that first coin to that guy named after a candy bar."

"Skittles," Hunter corrected.

"I bet you he had the coin on him when he died." Ian leaned close to him and whispered, "Dylan said the treasure wants to be found, and Everly has come across two pieces of it now."

Hunter exhaled and ran his hands through his hair as he realized what Ian was saying. She saw Hunter's face go white. "And she's carrying it around with her everywhere she goes. If it's true that treasure is like a homing beacon for death..."

"She's in danger," Ian said.

"Guys!" Aimee's voice came from the living room. "The Howler's Cove incident made the news. They're holding Dylan in custody. They are charging him with the murders."

"What?" Ian and Hunter exclaimed at once.

"That wasn't supposed to happen." Hunter rushed out to the living room and stood staring at the screen as the rest of the report came on.

The room grew silent as everyone crowded around the TV to watch the disheartening news. The news van was once again on the dock, and they were catching a video of the harbor police coming in with the bodies.

Detective Howard was there, as well as Dr. Peter and

hundreds of citizens of Echo Bay. Multiple deaths of teens tended to draw more attention than others.

The townspeople and everyone else were getting fed up with the deaths. Young and old alike were yelling, waving signs that said, "Echo Bay is cursed. Keep our children safe." They were chanting and screaming. Some people called for the police chief to remove himself from office.

The camera drew close, and the medical examiner held up his hand, covering the lens. He was getting impatient, and then a pushy news reporter got past the barricade and approached Detective Howard.

"You can no longer call this just a coincidence. We've had four deaths in three days. That is more than we have had in years. What is going on? What aren't you telling us? Should we be worried? Is this another repeat of what happened seven years ago, with senseless deaths that ended when that whole private school burned down? We need answers!"

Detective Howard moved to the camera, his face stoic. "I can assure you that we have a perpetrator in custody." Dylan's face appeared on camera. The news clip began to describe the others found in Howler's Cove.

Kat shook her head. "I don't think he is capable of killing his friends."

Ian grumbled, "He could. They smell like grimm; I'm never wrong."

The TV camera moved across the screen and, in the background, caught an image of the *Jolly Dodger* again.

"Oh!" Cass got excited and held up the blue journal she'd been reading. "It's just like in my book!"

"You read it?" Ian asked in surprise.

"It's a love story about a mermaid who fell deeply in love with a dashing pirate. He was the king of his kind—brave, fearless, and conquered all the seas. The mermaid loved him so much she gave up her true love, the sea, to be with him."

"This sounds a lot like *The Little Mermaid.*" Kat tapped her notebook but took down everything Cass translated.

"Shh!" Aimee waved at Kat to be quiet. "I want to hear the rest. Go on, Cass."

Cass picked up the book, running her finger down the words, paraphrasing the story. "However, the mermaid was betrayed, for the pirate could not love anyone but his treasure. Heartbroken and angry, the mermaid cursed the pirate's treasure. Whoever possessed the treasure would die a terrible death. It was a warning to all those who valued material possessions over love. The mermaid hoped that the pirate would give up the treasure and choose her one day. Instead, the pirate hid his treasure to escape a gruesome death, but doing so weakened him."

"That sounds a lot like the pirate show," Ian said. "I know we didn't work there long, but a cursed treasure, pirates, and all the victims were either involved with the show or were last seen in the vicinity of the ship hours before their deaths."

Aimee frowned. "Why didn't we make this connection?"

"Because it's weak," Kat said.

Ian grumbled, "I did."

Hunter looked at Everly. "What do you think? What does your intuition say?"

Everly felt sick at accusing Dylan or anyone who worked on the *Jolly Dodger*. "I think we're wrong. I don't think Dylan and Starla are grimm. I think that Ian is mistaken."

Immediately, Ian tensed. He glared at her, and she mouthed, "I'm sorry." Ian got up and moved into the kitchen, putting another wall between them.

"But I think Marnie and Roy Marksman should be questioned. Dylan said that most of the crew is related to each other, and Captain Marksman has been in Echo Bay for several generations. We should find out any background information we have on Marnie. She was the one who rewrote the show, including the cursed treasure."

Kat sat at the keyboard. "What's her full name?"

Everly shrugged and looked at Hunter.

"You guys are so worthless. I'll scrub the data from their website. She probably has some kind of producer credit, and if she wrote the show or made all the costumes, there will be articles about her. Just give me two." She clicked her mouse twice. "And bam! Okay, Marnie Markle. Birth date? There's nothing on her. No W-2s. No credit cards. It's like she doesn't exist."

"Let's see her," Hunter said.

Kat spun the camera and showed a headshot of the woman with her wild, wavy waist-length hair, beads, and bangles. She was wearing her purple top and sparkly dangling earrings. "Now, that is a mermaid if I ever saw one. Look at those green nails! Are those real or painted?"

Marnie was the epitome of a real-life mermaid.

The team grew excited and began to plan how to go about cornering and interviewing the suspect. They would need to wait until the police cleared the docks, and the pirate show had been canceled until further notice because of all the deaths and controversy.

Is this how it was? Identifying a grimm and knowing

they would capture her and lock her away in the oubliette. It was like giving out a death sentence to someone you had met and was nice to you.

Everly's heart wasn't in it. She ducked into the bathroom. She locked the door and turned the water in the shower on, drowning out any more of their conversation.

She stood outside the stall, letting the steam cover the mirror until she wiped away the condensation and stared at herself. Her hair was in a messy bun; her skin seemed even more pale. She pulled at the collar of her sweatshirt. There were still red marks. She would try to cover them up with makeup so it wouldn't stress out the boys anymore. She sighed and looked at the dark circles under her eyes.

But what about the treasure? Ian couldn't be right. Could he? And if it was true, she wasn't just carrying one piece of that cursed treasure. She was holding onto three. But there wasn't a way to prove it. Skittles wasn't found with a piece of treasure that they knew of, and then what about Nicky? If the treasure was the link, she needed to prove they all had a piece.

After her shower, she had a renewed determination. Everly braided her hair and pulled on another oversized gray sweatshirt, her favorite whitewashed jeans, and Adidas sneakers. She grabbed a new burner cell off the nightstand along with the necklace, ruby, and her crossbody bag and headed out.

Aimee and Kat were sitting on the couch pointing at the TV and watching every newscast repeatedly. Cass was slathering her frozen waffles with syrup, and Ian ate a bagel. No one noticed when she left, closing the front door with a click.

Her footsteps were quick, sure, and she didn't waver in her direction as she walked the fifteen minutes to Saint Vinnie's Hospital. Across the street was the Echo Bay Police Station.

Everly stood across the street under a tree and studied the layout of both buildings. Each precinct was different in how they handled their cases. In some counties, their medical examiners worked out of the precinct, county courthouse, hospital, or—in the case of her grandfather—their homes. When her grandfather retired, the records were moved to the local hospital.

Echo Bay's police station had plenty of clear signage, and next door was the hospital. Everly had to make a decision: try to see evidence of cold cases when she didn't have an in at the police station or go with the hospital. She entered a nearby grocery store, bought flowers, and headed to the hospital. She was walking in sync with another family, holding the door open.

"How can I help you?" an elderly gentleman behind the check-in desk asked. He wore a volunteer name tag, and it was a cheap plastic kind that was swapped out. In shaking handwriting, she could see his name was Bill.

"Hi, I'm here to visit my uncle Jerome," Everly said.

"Oh, I thought all his family came by already." Bill's face lit up.

Everly could feel a moment of panic build up. Of course, the man probably knew everyone in town and their relations. "Yeah, I don't get to see him often. So when I heard about the accident..."

Bill's chin wobbled as he nodded his head in understanding. "Yes, it was tragic to lose Nicky." He leaned forward and, with two fingers, typed in Jerome's last name. "Room 420."

"Thank you." Everly turned.

"Wait. You need to sign in and get a name tag." His arthritic hands held up a red pen. Everly took the pen and wrote Janelle Miller.

She placed the sticker on her shirt and followed Bill's directions toward the elevator. Her heart was in her throat as she approached the fourth floor, and her feet felt like leaden weights as she walked down the hall and stopped at room 420. The door was slightly ajar, and Everly tiptoed inside to see a man sleeping in the bed. The curtains were drawn closed.

He was scruffy, with suntanned skin and weathered wrinkles, indicating a life at sea. A heart monitor was hooked up to him, and a slight beep punctuated the silent room. The scent of cleanser was familiar, as well as the sterile room. It made her think of her father's last moments.

Everly pushed down her emotions and headed toward the built-in wardrobe. Kneeling, she opened the door and saw a box filled with Jerome's belongings. A slightly fishy smell came from the boots sitting next to the box.

Movement from the bed made her freeze as a slight snore came from its inhabitant. Everly waited until he settled and his breathing became deep and even.

She didn't know what had possessed her to come and search his things, but all she had was a hunch. A gut feeling. She lifted the cardboard lid and looked at the neatly folded clothes. On the top was a ziplock bag containing his cell phone. Very carefully, Everly opened the bag and took out the cell. It was an older model flip phone similar to what she had been given for the reaping assignment.

She pulled out the pants and ran her hands along the pockets, turning them inside out, finding a pocketknife, a receipt, and lint. She did the same with his overalls, finding a tobacco tin and comb. Then she shook out the pants until a small coin fell out and rolled along the floor. She picked it up. It was just a gold dollar.

The snoring had stopped. The room was silent.

Everly saw the barest reflection in the TV screen before she was flung backward onto the floor. The coin fell from her grasp.

Crazed dark eyes loomed over her, and Everly felt a cold blade pressed against her throat.

CHAPTER 21

"WHAT DO YOU WANT FROM ME?" A GRAVELLY VOICE asked.

Everly stared into the wild and panicked eyes of Jerome. He was still in his hospital robe and had snuck out of the bed. He had taken the butter knife from his breakfast tray to threaten her. But behind the crazy man, she saw the fear.

"You're just a bit of a girl," he muttered to himself, but then his head shook. "Doesn't matter. They can look like anything." The knife pressed further into her throat.

"Who?" Everly said, lying very still, her hands held palms up to show she didn't mean harm.

"The creature." His lips pulled back as he hissed the word, spit covering his lips.

There was a commotion as the door burst open, and Hunter entered; he saw Everly on the floor and acted, bowling Jerome over. There was a loud scuffle and kicking. Everly raced for the door and shut it as Hunter slammed Jerome's hand against the tile over and over until he released the knife, and it clattered to the floor.

Hunter was sitting on the man, one hand on the front of his robe, the second on the empty wrist.

"Don't move!" Hunter warned, his hand squeezing the front of the shirt. He lifted Jerome off the ground and then shoved his back onto the floor—a threat of what he would do if the man moved.

Jerome nodded, his face white with fear, and his eyes moved to Everly, pleading with her to intervene.

"Everly?" Hunter breathed out her name, asking if she was okay.

"I'm all right. He didn't hurt me. I was the one who startled him. He was reacting." Everly reached out to touch Hunter's shoulder. She could feel his tense muscles through the shirt. "It's okay. I don't think he wants to hurt me."

"He had a knife to your throat," Hunter muttered.

"And just yesterday, you and Ian tried to kill me; not everything is as it seems." She hated to remind him, but she needed him to take it easy on Jerome. There was something about him. An instinct that told her that he didn't want to harm her.

Hunter released Jerome and moved to stand over him, placing himself directly in front of Everly in case the old man tried anything. Everly rolled her eyes and tried to move to speak to Jerome, but Hunter wasn't having it. He pushed her behind him again.

"Hunter, please," Everly said. She could feel his turmoil; his body shook with fury, but he stepped aside.

"It's okay." Everly tried to soothe the trembling man. "He's not going to harm you." Hunter tensed, and Jerome winced in fear. Everly decided she needed to clarify. "No, that's a lie," she corrected. "He will hurt you if you make a move that is threatening toward me. Do you understand?"

"Yes." Jerome got to his feet, using the hospital bed as support; he moved to the far side of the room. He was keeping the bed between them.

"We have questions about the night that Nicky disappeared. Did you see what happened?"

Jerome gazed out the window. "The sea came for him. Like a fish, his foot got hooked on a line that pulled him to his doom."

"You mentioned a creature. What did it look like?"

Jerome's eyes narrowed, and he recoiled slightly, the memory scaring even him. "Death," his voice rattled. "It was like staring into the face of death itself. It came out of the water, eyes black like an unholy beast, body covered in scales, long hair; it was going to kill me." He moved back, rocking back onto his heels. A deep sob came from his throat.

"But it didn't," Everly observed. "Why not?"

Everly slowly moved closer, giving him plenty of room and reading his body language.

"Tell me," Everly said.

Jerome shook his head. He sniffed and wiped at his runny nose. "No, I can't. You'll think I'm crazy."

"I won't," Everly said. "I'm here to help."

"He's not." Jerome nodded with his head toward Hunter, and Everly had to agree with that assessment. Hunter was a ball of barely contained fury. She couldn't imagine the amount of self-control it was taking for him not to beat the answers out of the old man.

Everly bit her bottom lip and debated how much to reveal.

Jerome shook his head again. "Please, go away." His voice was raising in pitch. Everly worried that a nurse would hear them and come to investigate. She moved further away from Jerome.

"Until you come clean about what you know, that boy's death... is your fault."

A soft wailing came from the back of Jerome's throat, and he rocked himself. "He dropped it when the ocean took his life, but I was going to give it back."

"Give what back?" Everly pressed, moving in, refusing to leave until she had the final clue. She was so close to getting the answers that she forgot how reckless she could be.

"This," Jerome sighed, unfurling his thick hands to reveal a single gold coin smaller than Everly had found. "I picked it up off the dock; the creature wanted it but couldn't find it. I kept it safe."

This was it. Everly felt a surge of excitement rise when she saw the glint of gold. She took the gold coin from his hand, and it shifted. She saw the same wing image on it from the Polaroid. It was a coin Cleo gave to Nicky. He did have a piece of treasure on him when he died.

"No. No. No." His voice turned into a whine. "It's not safe."

"If you want to prevent another senseless death, then you need to tell me." Everly used every ounce of authority in her voice.

"Why would you help us?" Jerome said. "When you only want to destroy us?"

"Destroy?" Everly frowned. A flutter at the window drew her attention, and she again saw Corvis. He was tapping the window with his beak. *Where had he gone the last few days? Why did he suddenly return now?*

When Everly turned back to Jerome, she saw it. There was a shimmer, and his skin shifted, revealing that two long tusks grew beneath his thick mustache. His eyes were a dark brown, and she saw the scared grimm looking back at her—a walrus-type creature.

"You're a grimm?" Everly said, eyes widening.

"And you're both grievers," Jerome said, reaching for the fork on the table. He swept it up, and she brought up her arm as he made a stabbing motion, causing their forearms to connect. Even though he was bigger, he had been bedridden for days, and Everly was able to quickly disarm the older man and push him back onto the bed. Hunter was there, slamming his palm into the man's chest. A knife appeared almost out of thin air, but Everly knew it was probably from a wrist sheath. Jerome's eyes were wide as they followed the tip of the knife Hunter held close to his heart.

"Stop it!" Everly growled. "Behave." This time, she wasn't sure if she was warning Hunter or Jerome. "Right, now I need you to tell me about this tide." She flipped the fork around in her hand and could have used it to threaten Jerome, but instead, she put it on the plate and sat in the chair next to the bed.

Jerome gave Hunter a nervous look, and the knife didn't lower. "What do you want to know?"

"Everything. What is the tide?"

"I don't know. Only that it comes from the sea every seven years, and its victims are the ones who have a piece of the Lennox treasure." Jerome shook.

"Why don't you leave Echo Bay?"

"And go where? We can't survive on land. Our kind needs to be near water, and if we're near water, the treasure will always find its way to us. We try to teach our young to fear the curse, but they think they're invincible."

"Why can't everyone sense the treasures?" Everly asked.

"I don't know. I've heard the treasure calling every seven years since I was a kid; an even more haunting song always followed it, and death always followed that. But I've been able to resist the call. Others are deaf. My brother? Never heard a thing. I even thought Nicky would be safe, but then... somehow, he got a piece of that cursed treasure."

Jerome's face was sad, resolved, and he closed his eyes, refusing to speak again. Hunter sheathed his knife and headed out of the room first.

Everly waited by the door, watching the man, seeing the pain and loss of one of his friends flicker across his face as he started to cry again. She closed the door softly.

Hunter stood leaning against the hospital wall; his eyes were cast downward as he texted on his phone. Those green eyes slowly rose and met hers, and she could see the disappointment there.

"Thank you," she said softly, hanging her head. "For coming after me."

"You shouldn't have left without telling me," he reprimanded.

"How *did* you find me?" she asked.

"Ian told me you took off. Then I tracked your burner."

Everly resisted the urge to lift her shirt and smell herself subconsciously. Did he smell her leaving?

Hunter pushed off the wall. "You done? Or do you want

to interrogate more grimms and put your life in danger?" His shoulders were stiff, and the reprimand direct.

Hunter turned away, walking back toward the elevator, leaving her behind. He pushed the button on the elevator and waited for the doors to open, and then they stepped inside and turned around.

Everly wanted to explain. "I wanted to question the eyewitness," she said meekly. "I think we should talk to that Detective Howard. I want to know what items were found with the victims from seven years ago."

The door dinged as it hit the first floor, and they exited the hospital.

"Can I have it?" Hunter stopped on the sidewalk near a tree and held out his palm.

"Have what?" Everly pretended ignorance.

"The bracelet and whatever you took from him upstairs."

Everly didn't want to give it to him. It was her treasure. She recoiled at the thought of sharing it. How dare he? It was hers.

"Everly." Hunter's voice grew forceful.

She reached into her crossbody bag and carefully handed him the coin and bracelet, leaving the necklace and ruby inside her bag. "Here." She dropped them into his open palm.

"Corvis," Hunter called and waited for him to appear.

Everly's lips pinched together, knowing he wouldn't listen to Hunter. He was her omen. Her pride dropped like a bomb when she saw Corvis's black form on a branch near them. Hunter held up the coin.

"You heard what is going on with this treasure. I need you to take it to Ms. March and see if anyone at our school can determine if it is truly cursed. I know how fast you fly, and I need you to do this not for me but for Everly." Hunter turned pleading eyes toward her, asking her permission to command her omen.

"*Oh! Shiny!*" Corvis seemed highly pleased. "Sea rats are jealous. Is this what *you* want?" His dark head turned, and he looked at her out of the corner of his eye.

She sighed. It was a sound plan and something that she should have done earlier. "He's right," Everly mumbled. "We need help; take it to the school."

Corvis flapped his wings and dove, snatching the coin from Hunter's hand and flying away. He tucked the bracelet into his pocket and picked up his pace through the parking lot.

Everly's shorter legs had to work double time to catch up to him. She could tell by the hunch in his shoulders and his pace that he was mad but trying to hold it in.

"What's wrong?"

He stopped. "Wrong?" He let out a wry laugh. "You took off with a cursed bracelet without telling anyone." Hunter turned, his eyes boring into hers accusingly, waiting for her to deny it. "You have a target on your back, and you just..." He held his hands up. "Left."

"I don't need permission to leave the house," she responded, snapping at the pressure of his questioning.

"There are two rules we live and die by. Rule number one—" He held up a finger, his voice grave. "—always hunt in pairs."

Everly understood where his anger came from. "You're right. I screwed up. I shouldn't have gone alone."

He shook his head. His green eyes filled with remorse.

"Rule number two is that grimms can never be trusted. He had a knife to your throat."

"I didn't know he was a grimm."

"That's the point. Grimms can sense grievers the same way grievers can sense grimms. But sometimes we don't know. Just like Ian thought Starla and Dylan were grimms. You always go out with a partner and backup. What you did was completely irresponsible. You were reckless and put yourself in danger." Hunter grabbed her wrist.

She ripped her hand from his grasp. "You forget who my father was, that I am trained to defend myself."

"Oh, is that what it's called when I storm through a door and have to save you?"

"I had the situation under control."

Hunter's jaw clenched, making the muscle tic. "No, I think Ian was right. It was too soon for you to come on a mission. You keep thinking you have to do everything yourself. You broke our two cardinal rules, which means you're grounded."

She could tell Hunter was furious, but it was odd that she was being treated unfairly. Yes, she might have been presumptuous to question a man by herself, but she thought it was just an old man. She didn't expect it to be a grimm.

When they got to the parking lot, Hunter opened the door of his black Jeep and got inside. Everly followed suit and hopped into the passenger seat. That must be how he had found her so fast. He drove.

Hunter turned the ignition on and pulled out of the parking lot. He was silent as they headed through town. The tension between them was unnerving, and Everly felt like a child being given the silent treatment. She couldn't help but stare at the *Jolly Dodger* when they passed the docks.

"We know now who the tide is targeting," Everly said, trying to fill the silence. "It is the cursed treasure. We should go back and talk to Detective Howard and search their evidence from the cold cases seven years ago. Maybe, if we get enough treasure, we can lure the tide onto shore and attack it."

Hunter didn't say anything. When Aimee's house came into view, she expected him to slow down to pull into the private alley and drive, but he passed right by.

"We passed the house." Everly pointed to the disappearing beach house.

"I know," Hunter said.

"Where are we going?" Everly's head turned to study Hunter's face.

"I'm taking you back." He stared straight ahead at the road, his knuckles gripping the steering wheel.

"Back? You mean to the school?"

"You should never have been allowed to be a griever."

Everly's heart raced, and she could feel the anger building inside of her. "You don't get to make that decision."

He turned his handsome face toward her.

"Oh, but I do. I'm the team lead, and I can choose who is on my team. I've already notified Ms. Bellcamp of your dismissal. Ian is in charge of the team until I get back."

"No." Everly gripped the door handle as her heart fell into her stomach. "Why are you doing this? Why are you being so unfair?"

"I'm not being unfair. I'm being practical. You are not ready, and that stupid bracelet has made you a target. So I'm driving you far away from the ocean and this killer tide until it's gone. Do you hear me?"

Red. Everly was seeing red whenever she looked at Hunter. This was not the boy she had a crush on. This was a boy that was crushing her dreams. Ever since she learned that her family were grievers, she felt she had found her calling. Her father trained her for this, and she didn't want Hunter to take it away.

She knew better than to argue with Hunter. They knew how to push each other's buttons and get into fights. It's what they did best. Everly always picked a fight with Hunter so that she would find a reason not to like him; if they fought, they couldn't possibly fall in love. If they fought, it would keep a safe distance from her heart.

But this felt like a betrayal of the worst kind. Even Holland was allowed to go on reapings as a sib, and Holland could hardly find her way out of her walk-in closet. Granted, her wardrobe was huge and very much like a maze. Cass, the changeling who tricked all of them and lied to them, was still allowed on the grieving team. Okay, well, she had been attending all the same classes as Everly, and she was stronger and could shape-shift. So that made her valuable.

Everly wanted to fight back with words but could tell that Hunter was waiting for her attack. So she did the opposite. She held her tongue. It was painful to do, and she wanted to inwardly scream in frustration at the inconvenience, but she knew if she wanted any chance to change his mind, then it needed to happen when his guard was down. And to get his guard down, she would have to do the unexpected. Do the opposite. Be compliant.

Even though she was going to grind her back teeth into

sand by holding her tongue, and she could feel the beginning of a tension headache, she held fast.

She stared out the window, gripping the door handle as if it were the only anchor she could rely on. That and it kept her face hidden. It also held the burning tears that threatened to spill forth if she so much as looked at Hunter at bay.

She could do this. It was only—what? A few hours' drive. Oh goodness, she was going to die. There was no way she could make it without talking or biting his head off.

A half hour passed, and Hunter kept casting worried glances her way. But she just rested her forehead on her hand and stared straight ahead. She was enjoying watching him squirm.

"Everly?" he called.

She didn't even blink.

Hunter tried to lighten the mood by turning the radio on and playing with the station until one of her favorite songs came on. She didn't move an inch.

After another half hour, they pulled over at a gas station, and he got out to fill the tank. Unlike their last trip together, Everly didn't feel like buying him food. She stormed into the station, picked up road snacks and a drink, and got inside the car, slamming the door. Loudly.

When Hunter got inside, he glanced at the single drink and bag of pretzels and went to get his own. Everly quickly wiped at her tears with the sleeve of her shirt and held back her emotions when he came back.

He sat in the front seat and turned to look at her.

"Everly?"

She refused to answer. Instead, she let her anger build a wall between them. She turned her furious eyes on Hunter, and he swallowed. His lips parted, and he gazed at her with surprise.

"Your eyes look so b—" he complimented her, and she cut him off.

"Don't even. Just drive," she snapped.

He put the car into Reverse and drove. They sat in uncomfortable silence as Everly brainstormed all the conversations she could have with the headmistress, Ms. March, Ms. Bellcamp, and anyone else she could talk to, to avoid getting expelled. She didn't know what kind of power Hunter had or if he could remove her from the program, but it was a threat he had lorded over her since she first stepped foot into the school.

Some time had passed, and she had fallen asleep. It wasn't until they came up Memorial Way and the gravel road that she woke up. Seeing the headstones again made her feel even more in awe of the grievers' sacrifice. Hunter drove up to the front of the school and parked the car.

Everly flung open her door and jumped out, rushing for the steps and hopefully to get to the office to plead her case. Maybe if she was fast enough, she could get reinstated back to Echo Bay before Hunter left. Then, he would be forced to take her with him.

Hunter was out just as fast as Everly. He raced around the front of the car and reached for her arm.

"Everly, don't be mad."

"Don't tell me how to feel," Everly said.

Hunter winced at her bitterness. "True, you're right. I shouldn't have said that. I want you to know that I have reasons for my actions."

"I'm sure you do, but I don't have to agree with them."

"You don't have to agree. You just need to listen."

"Yeah." Everly smirked. "I've never been big on listening."

Hunter grinned, gently touching his chin where the slight scar was. The one she had accidentally given him while they were playing lacrosse. The competition between them became heated, and she wasn't paying attention to her stick and swiped too close to his face.

Seeing that scar made her frown, and her anger deflated like a balloon. She finally had the strength to ask, "Hunter, do you hate me that much?"

"What?" The question seemed to catch him off guard. "I don't hate you," he rushed out quickly.

"Then why do you insist on hiding me away?"

"I do it because I want to protect you."

"But I don't need protection," she said. "You're not my knight in shining armor. I'm not a princess that needs saving."

"I know that."

"Do you? Because you sure have a way of being overprotective. You don't act this way with Aimee and Holland."

"That's because Holland knows what she is getting into. She knows the risks. We both lost a lot to the grimms, and she deserves a chance to fight her own demons."

"You forget that you are talking to a legacy," Everly said. "My family have been grievers far longer than yours have."

"I've not forgotten." His voice grew soft. "Your family has lost just as much, if not more, to the life committed to being a griever. It's why I don't want to be the one to kill the last remaining Hart. It's even worse now that you have an omen. I don't want you to end up like Kerrigan."

Everly felt her walls crumbling when Hunter mentioned his older sister, Kerrigan, who had lost her omen in a fight, and it had driven her insane.

"Again, none of this is your responsibility or choice to make. It's mine. I accepted the invitation to Gravemark. I know the risks. I made the commitment. You have no right to take that away from me."

"I can if I know what's best for me."

"For you?" Now, this conversation wasn't making sense at all. When did it come back around to being about Hunter?

"Everly. I can't do my job with you on my team."

"That doesn't make sense."

Hunter frowned. "Do you not know how I feel about you?"

"Yeah, it's obvious that you have contempt for me. Why else are you doing this to me?"

"Contempt? Everly, I—" He turned and ran his hands through his hair in frustration. "You are by far the most irritating woman I have ever met."

Now, the tears were burning. His words were like fiery darts aimed at her heart.

She turned to go up the steps into the school. She needed to escape him—to run away.

She made it two steps before he grabbed her hand, spun her around, and kissed her. Everly was caught off guard, on the defensive, her hands pressed against his chest, but when his lips met hers, it destroyed the wall she had put up between them. Hunter proved to her with his kiss what he couldn't say with words.

Everly felt her knees go weak, and she felt his response by wrapping his hands around her waist to hold her. Her own tentative hands reached up to wrap around his neck. She was dreaming and did not ever want to wake up.

When Hunter broke the kiss, her breathing was as ragged as his. Their foreheads touched. "Everly, I don't hate you," he whispered. He leaned back, a smile playing at the corners of his mouth. "You drive me crazy in the best way possible. Whenever you're around, I can't stop thinking about you. You consume my thoughts, so I can't focus on anything else. It's like nothing else matters when we're together, and I can't help but put you first. You are my top priority. Which makes it dangerous for me."

Everly's heart raced at his confession. This was precisely what she had hoped for, wanted, and dreamed of. Hunter liked her, but then she listened to what he was saying.

"What do you mean? You and Aimee frequently go on reapings together."

Hunter shook his head. "Everly, Aimee doesn't affect me the same way you do. She's been my shield. If I was dating Aimee, then it was the perfect excuse not to pursue you. I've loved you since the night you gave me this scar. Your passion, your anger. The way your blue eyes shine when you're angry. I love everything about it. But I didn't want to bring you into my world. Not yet."

"Then why was it so terrible when I became a griever? We could share the same world." She pressed her hands against his chest and stared into his eyes, pleading, trying to understand.

"Because then I realized how dangerous my life was, and I want to keep the person I find most precious to me safe. How can you fault me for that?" His hands were gently stroking her arms.

Everly was grateful for Hunter's grip because she felt that her knees might buckle and she'd fall without it.

"I thought I made it obvious how I felt the night of the fire."

"You did?" Everly looked up at him, and he grimaced.

"Okay, geez. I guess it wasn't that memorable that you forgot already."

"No, I mean, I didn't know what to think at the time. You were dating Aimee."

His eyes fell toward the ground in shame. "I was. And that was my fault. I was overcome with emotion at the thought of losing you. I acted without thinking. But, Everly, please. I don't want to lose this... us... you. I need to complete this mission, and I can't do it with you there." Hunter came forward and wrapped his arms around her. His voice was muffled in her hair. "Please stay here. That cursed coin makes you a target, and I don't know if just removing it from you is enough to keep you safe." He stepped back, and his hand cupped her face. Those green eyes were filled with worry. "Please, I need you safe."

Everly couldn't speak. Her heart was doing somersaults. Of course, she wanted to please Hunter and protect him by listening but knew he was still putting himself in the line of danger.

"Can you do that?" he asked.

Her mind worked carefully through what he was asking of her. To stay safe? She could promise that.

Everly nodded.

Hunter sighed and leaned forward to give her the softest, gentlest kiss. Completely opposite of the one he gave her a few minutes ago.

"Wait for me," he begged.

When she didn't respond, he returned to his Jeep and got in. She knew he would be rushing back to Echo Bay.

Everly watched as Hunter drove off, still in a daze. She couldn't believe what had happened. She turned on her heel to head into the school and froze as she faced Holland.

Holland stood there just outside the door on the top step. Her dark hair shined in the sunlight. But it was her eyes that were sparkling with tears of frustration. Her mouth puckered in anger as she tried to hold back her bitterness.

"Holland," Everly called out, racing up the steps.

Holland's hand raised to cut her off. "Don't. I don't want to hear it." Her fingers began to tremble, and her first tear fell. "I trusted you."

"You can still trust me. It's not like that," Everly begged.

"You know how I feel about my friends *using* me to date my brother."

"I didn't use you. It just happened."

Holland shook her head. "Things don't just happen. How long?"

"What?" Everly could feel that she was losing control of the situation.

"How long have you liked my brother? Truthfully?"

Everly swallowed. She shifted her weight from foot to foot, not wanting to make eye contact. But she needed to tell her the truth. "Always." She met Holland's turbulent gaze. "I've always had a crush on Hunter but never acted on it."

"What was that I just saw?" Holland pointed toward the step where they had shared their second kiss. "And it sounds like you kissed when he was still dating Aimee. That makes you a cheater."

"No, wait. We didn't—" Everly tried to explain.

"I never expected this kind of behavior from you. But I should have known. You're just like everyone else," she spat out angrily.

Holland spun, her heels making loud noises as she stormed away. The front school door closed behind her as Everly tried to grasp the handle but missed.

It slammed in her face, and Everly could feel the finality of it. She might have gained a relationship with Hunter but lost her friendship with Holland.

CHAPTER 22

EVERLY TRIED TO FIND HOLLAND TO TALK IT THROUGH, but her best friend avoided her. She wasn't answering her phone or in her dorm room, and she couldn't find her in any of the common spaces.

As Everly ran down the steps, she turned the corner of the school and crashed into a tall, warm body.

"Whoa!" Hands reached out to steady her.

"Sorry," Everly blurted, looking up into a familiar face that startled her. It took her a few seconds to place him out of uniform.

"Officer Stevens?" Everly said, looking up at the tall man. He was twenty, the youngest graduate out of the Misty Creek Police Force, and tan, with golden brown eyes and sandy hair. He seemed even younger in his khaki pants, green shirt, denim jacket, and sneakers. It must be the uniform that aged him. "What are you doing here?"

"Oh, you don't have to call me Officer Stevens when I'm out of uniform. It's Josh."

She blinked, trying to register the handsome man before

her with a first name. "Josh?" she said in surprise. "You don't look like a Josh."

Josh nodded, and his cheeks reddened. "Joshua Reggie Stevens." He stood up straight and gave her a little salute. "At your service, and apparently... every student on the campus now."

"What do you mean?"

"Ever since the night of the fire, I've been seeing the strangest things. Then I got this—this letter." He looked around and pulled out a slightly crumpled letter with a wax seal. It was his invitation to Gravemark.

"Congratulations." Everly beamed up at him. "You're now one of us."

"You mean the oldest student at Gravemark?"

Everly grinned crookedly. "You're not that old."

Josh shrugged. "When I look around here, I feel ancient. I don't even know what I'm doing here. Ms. March said that I was more like an honorary student and that it happens sometimes where someone gains abilities later in life. She sat me down and explained what happened with Officer Mitchell and that he was working with a..." He struggled to say the word "werewolf." "It just doesn't seem real."

"It's very real. My dad was a griever."

His golden eyebrows rose. "That makes so much sense. He was so good at catching criminals. I didn't think it was because he could see these creatures."

"Well, he couldn't," Everly corrected. "He could when he was younger, but as you age, the gifts weaken. He used what he was taught here to fight in the outside world. Didn't Ms. March explain that to you?"

"She explained many things, but I think most of it went

out the door when I saw a giant talking tree." Josh rubbed the back of his head sheepishly and blushed again.

Everly laughed. "Oh, you mean Professor Stubbs. He's great. You'll learn a whole lot from him. What about your job?"

"That is what is so interesting. Apparently, I'm now employed by the school. Ms. March and the board spoke with the head of the police department and said that they needed extra security on campus but didn't want to hire a security company. They will pay half my salary if I live on campus."

"I didn't know they could do that."

"Me neither." He looked down at his feet. "With the department budget cuts, it seems a win-win. Safety for the school, extra grief classes on my downtime, and I will still work for the department."

"Griever classes," Everly corrected.

"Yeah, that." He grimaced. "I feel so lost and behind. I hope that you don't mind if I come to you with questions."

"No, I don't mind at all." Everly gave him a wave, and Josh continued up the stairs and headed toward one of the halls.

Everly continued with her search and still couldn't find Holland. She went to Ms. March's office and knocked on the door.

"Come in," a soft voice spoke from within. "Where is it? I know I had my brooch somewhere."

Everly entered the office and stood next to the chair. Her eyes glanced past the old doilies and fixated on the short woman on the other side of the desk who was searching the floor for her brooch. Today, she wore a two-piece lemon-colored dress and jacket set and pointed-toe pumps.

"What is it, Everly?" Ms. March asked breathlessly as she dropped back into her chair.

Everly reached into her bag and pulled out the brooch that Corvis flew out to Echo Bay. She placed it on the desk, and Ms. March became excited. "Oh, where did you find it?"

"In the hall," Everly lied.

"Oh, well. What can I do for you today?"

"I request to go back into the field immediately. I know that Hunter reported that I disobeyed orders and brought me back, but I am close to solving the grimm tide."

Everly spent the next quarter hour reviewing everything she had discovered. The entrance to Crypthaven, Boswell, and the grimm in the cave. The gold coin, Skittles's death, the bracelet, the story of the treasure. As she spoke, her gaze drifted to the desk, and sitting on a black velvet pouch was the gold coin.

"A coin that looks just like that." Everly pointed at it in confusion.

"It is." Ms. March pulled the velvet bag a little closer to her, and the coin came with it. "Corvis is incredibly fast. I had hoped to have answers already for Hunter, but I don't." She picked up the coin, put it into the velvet bag, and held it to Everly. "I think it would be best to take this to Mr. Halsey next. See if our resident grimm can make head or tail of it. He does have an affinity for hoarding knowledge."

"But about my request?" Everly asked as she took the bag and felt the coin beneath the fabric layers.

"It's denied. You're needed here."

"But I didn't do anything wrong. I should be with the team."

Ms. March's eyes narrowed. "You are not part of the original griever team chosen to go. I only sent you there to get you out of the media attention, which has died down since you've gone. Your team lead has written to me, and I agree. You are not needed. There are only a few more days, and the grimm tide will disappear for another seven years. I think you've done all you can."

"This is not fair." Everly sat in the chair and leaned forward earnestly. "I can help."

"I don't understand why you think this is up for discussion. This is an order. We have three of the best grievers at Echo Bay, plus our best sib researcher. Believe it or not, cases can be solved without a Hart always interfering."

The wind was knocked out of Everly's sails so fast she could feel her heart sink into the floor. Her head dropped toward the ground, and she felt utterly useless. Despite her earlier elation at being kissed, it was now overshadowed by her anger at Hunter deciding her fate as a griever and taking her off the team. But then, there was Ms. March's frustration. It seemed that there was a hidden grudge against the Harts. She thought they always got in the way. Maybe it wasn't so great being a legacy after all.

"I understand," Everly said bitterly. She stood, the chair scraping against the floor as she left the office, velvet bag in hand.

———

"It is indeed something," Mr. Halsey said, sitting in his overstuffed chair, tilting the gold coin right and left as he looked at the inscriptions. "Where did you say you got this, and you think it has something to do with the grimm tide?"

Everly was sitting on a stool next to Mr. Halsey and very carefully pouring a teapot of water into the offered cup. It was interesting that she never even saw Mr. Halsey heat the pot. He just placed his hand on the side of the ceramic kettle, and a few seconds later, it began to steam. He gestured for Everly to help herself to the tea tins, and she plopped one in her cup and began to stir.

"In a cave. It wanted to be found, led me right to it."

"I see." Mr. Halsey played with the curl of his mustache in the same way a villain of a cartoon would. She wondered briefly what a sight it would be to see Mr. Halsey in his grimm form. How big would he be? Would he be terrifying?

"Do you recognize it?" Everly asked.

"Not I," Mr. Halsey said, "but I may be able to get word to one of my brethren, for they are the type that obsesses over burying their treasure, whereas I prefer to hoard knowledge. Most pirates of the ages were not human but sea dragons."

"Sea dragons!" Everly almost spit out the tea she was drinking.

Mr. Halsey raised a bushy eyebrow, and Everly very carefully put the cup onto the saucer before she spilled it on his fancy rug.

"Why is that so hard to believe? Our kind have roamed the earth for centuries, and sea dragons are notorious for hoarding treasure."

"Our kind. That means you're a dragon?" she said in awe, then looked at his hoard of books and pipe he constantly smoked. She could see the wispy trails and imagine the dragon beneath his human exterior. "It all makes sense."

"Of course, it makes sense. Why do you think pirates were so feared? Because sea dragons had a real craving for human flesh and treasure. They ruled the seas until the sirens came."

"The sirens?" Everly asked, leaning forward eagerly.

"Yes, the sea dragons are always male. And, of course, the merfolk didn't take to the pirates treading their waters, killing and stealing. They drew too much attention. So I guess that this is from a sea dragon's hoard."

"There's a myth that it belongs to the pirate Lennox."

"Lennox." Mr. Halsey shook his head. "I don't recognize that name. I will have to get word out to my brethren and see if someone is willing to come and speak to me."

"You would do that?"

Mr. Halsey seemed uneasy. "It's not that simple. Just because we're related does not mean that we tolerate each other. Sea dragons are not the most gracious of guests. No manners whatsoever." He shook his head in disgust and took a sip of his tea, and there was a slight rumble of appreciation in his throat. "That's good." He smiled, and beneath his mustache, she thought she saw the barest glimmer of a sharp tooth.

"Now, tell me about Crypthaven's library; what kind of books were there?"

Everly spoke about the journals that Boswell had dug up and found. The whole time, Mr. Halsey's face seemed alight with pleasure.

———

The nightmares returned in force. This time, she was at the edge of the ocean, and it was near sunset. Her feet sank into the cold sand, the tide was low, and she could see shells and sea glass twinkling up at her, taunting her to pick up a piece. Everly picked up a shell, but it shattered in her hand, stabbing her palm. Blood ran freely down her fingertips and dropped into the white sand. Everywhere the blood dropped, a spiral of red fingertips flowed out and crawled toward the ocean. Soon, the blue of the sea turned red with blood... her blood.

Everly sat up, gasping. Her hand flailed as she hit it against the nightstand, knocking over her ceramic lamp. It crashed to the floor and broke. The pieces on the floor mimicked the broken shell from her dream.

She swung her legs out and gingerly placed them on the floor, careful not to step on any broken pieces. Something was nagging her. A piece of the puzzle that she couldn't quite figure out. It was like all the puzzle's edges were lined up, but the middle was fuzzy.

Glancing at the alarm told her it was close to eleven. *There isn't any chance that Mr. Halsey will still be up, is there?* She decided to take a stab at the dark. Maybe she would go to the library and read. Everly grabbed her boots, shoving her sockless feet inside, grabbed a pullover hoodie, and headed out of the dorms.

Crossing the campus at night felt weird as she made her way to the library. It was a singular building that was once an old church and had catacombs below. Or at least that's what the brochure said.

She hesitated at the library doors. *Indeed, they'll be locked.* Her hand grasped the iron handle, and she pulled.

The door opened. All the lights were off except for a warm glow from the back of the library, or Mr. Halsey's reading nook.

The library was eerie at night as she passed the stacks. The moonlight cast shadows between the shelves, making the harmless books seem to reach for her as she walked by. When she came to Mr. Halsey's favorite area, the overstuffed chair sat empty. Even the roaring fire had died out to the barest of coals, a table lamp casting the only glow. The ordinarily hot room had a chill, and Everly couldn't help but shiver at the lack of heat.

"Mr. Halsey?" she called out and listened. Mr. Halsey had his own apartment in Liberty Hall but was never in residence, so she assumed he preferred his second home. The library.

There were always piles of books next to the chair, on the table, and stacked neatly on the floor. The floor was bare.

Where did he go?

She was about to abandon her insane quest and head out of the library when a soft scratching echo came from the fireplace.

Everly froze.

The noise came again, and she crept to the fireplace and kneeled down to see a metal floor plate bolted to the grate. She looked around the fireplace, grabbed one of the poker sticks, and found that it fit right into a unique circular latch on the grate that Everly pulled.

The grate and the metal plate swung over the floor, revealing steps beneath the library. The library used to be an old church, so this could be another entrance to the catacombs.

"Oh, no." Everly looked down into the darkness. She could still hear the scratching coming from below. Should she follow the noise alone? What was there to be afraid of? She was on campus protected by grievers... that was also a prison for grimms.

Everly moved to the desk at the front of the library and opened the drawers, searching until she found a flashlight. Grabbing the flashlight and a pair of scissors to be safe, she returned, stepped into the fireplace, and headed down the steps.

When she had descended about fifteen feet, she felt the temperature drop, and a cool breeze brushed past her face. There must be a tunnel that goes outside to fresh air, Everly thought.

She lifted the flashlight and walked slowly, listening every few feet for the whispers. They grew louder, and then the tunnel opened into a giant cave, and torches lit up the walls around the ground, flickering, creating dancing flame patterns off the rocky surface. But the monstrous shadow that appeared before her made her pause.

The silhouette of a giant dragon raising his neck flickered on the wall. Wings fluttered, and she could feel the air sweep across her face. Her heart raced as she knelt behind a boulder and looked over her hiding space at the grand spectacle of a real-life fire-breathing dragon.

A thickly muscled neck lifted a giant head with red scales and horns. As the light flickered across the scales, she could see them shift from red to orange, and the tips of the dragon's spikes, tail, claws, and horns were all black as if dipped into an inkwell. Long white whiskers curled from under the dragon's nostrils, and Everly could see the human bits of Mr. Halsey shine through in the color of the eyes and the shape of the mustache.

She was about to step out and greet her grimm teacher when Mr. Halsey hissed a warning and sent a blast of hot air toward her. She ducked, and then seconds later, a flame flickered across the stone, and she hid behind. The rock behind her back grew warm as the fire burned across it.

Her heart raced. *What happened? Did he see me? Did he not recognize me if he was in his dragon form?*

"How dare you enter my sanctuary without a proper greeting?" Mr. Halsey's dragon voice was deep and rumbled through the earth. His great claws and scales scratched across the stone as he moved into the room. She had heard this earlier, leading her to the deep cave.

Everly wanted to apologize profusely. She didn't mean to disturb the dragon. She was about to speak up and say so when someone else beat her to it.

A burbling sound of water came, followed by splashing, then a chittering noise. It was clicks and whistles in a language she couldn't understand. No semblance of English was spoken.

Mr. Halsey growled in warning, "Not the old tongue, Seveyrn."

Everly bit her lips and gathered her courage to lie on the floor and creep along the ground until she could see who he was talking to.

A sudden movement caught her attention as she gazed into the cave's depths. There was a crystal pool in the middle of the cave, and a dark shadow was moving within it. Then it crawled out. Surprisingly, it was another dragon. This one was lizard-like in appearance, with a stunning blue color. It had shorter arms and no wings but had great fins protruding from the side of its head. Its angular mouth gave it the appearance of an eel, which was fascinating and unsettling to her.

"Melechial." The sea dragon, Sevryn, spoke Mr. Halsey's true name. "I've come as you've requested. What need you of me to summon one such as I?"

Melechial? Everly let the name roll over her tongue. It was a much better fitting name for a dragon than Mr. Halsey. This name seemed right, ancient, and powerful.

"Speak truth," Melechial commanded. His foreclaw reached out, the dark claws angling for the sea dragon's neck in warning. He unfurled the other claw to reveal the gold coin. "What of this? Is this of your hoard?"

Sevryn swung his mighty head to study the coin. "It's not mine, oh fire-breather. But I do recognize the scent. It is of Lucerne's cursed hoard. Lucerne hasn't been seen in a century."

"Where is the great sea demon hiding, for one such as him does not leave without a trace?"

"I know not where our king has gone."

A rock slid down the path, and Everly looked up to see a confused Josh. He stood in the open, staring wide-eyed at the two dragons in the cave.

Everly crawled frantically, grabbed Josh's arm, and yanked him out of sight.

"Dragons," he breathed out, his face going pale. "Drag—" He didn't get to finish as Everly clapped her hand over his mouth, silencing him. The dragons' voices dropped to hisses and growls as they slipped back into what Melechial called the old tongue.

"What are you doing here?" she whispered, pressing Josh against the rock wall.

He tried to speak, but her hand was still covering his mouth. Slowly, one finger at a time, Everly released pressure from his lips.

"I followed you," Josh whispered. "I was doing my rounds and saw you leave the school. I never expected to find you down here—much less dragons."

She wanted to chastise and ask him more questions, but the dragons switched back to a language she could understand.

"The tide then," Melechial said, changing his questioning. "What causes it?"

"The moon's ebb and flow control the tide. Even one as great as you must surely understand its power," Sevryn said coyly.

Melechial loomed in the cave and curved his neck over the sea dragon, showing his dominance and domain. He hissed a warning, "No, the one that kills. Surely, you've heard of such a thing?"

Sevryn recoiled slightly, showing discomfort in the line of questioning. "Whispers, oh great one. Only whispers among the fish, but we know that fish are nothing more than tasty morsels with little brains."

"My patience runs thin with your games."

"I dare not interfere, for it is not my tale to tell." Sevryn tried to retreat back into the water, but Melechial roared, his claw pinning the much smaller dragon to the bottom of the pool of water. Sevryn hissed and snapped at Melechial's torso, but he quickly realized how overpowered he was. He lay sideways, his mouth agape as he breathed heavily.

"You pirate," Melechial threatened. "You may not get involved now, but you will be there to swoop in and steal the spoils. So speak, or you may never leave this cave alive."

Sevryn hissed and tried to escape the much larger Melechial to no avail before he finally acquiesced. "Nothing more than rumors. You surely have no interest in rumors."

"Try me," Melechial growled.

"King Lucerne angered the siren. In retaliation, she cursed his precious hoard, and now, something hunts our king. A creature so terrifying he has forced our sea king to go into hiding."

"You know more than that. What is it?" Melechial growled and flexed his claws, digging one into Sevryn's neck. Sevryn pulled out of Melechial's grip and slithered back into the water with a loud splash.

Everly had thought he was gone for good, except the water parted, and a snout appeared. "Beware the hoard," Sevryn spoke out in warning. "For the Kraeken follows."

Sevryn dove back into the water and disappeared beneath the depths.

Everly and Josh stayed hidden, counting the seconds, debating whether to sneak away or stay.

"You can come out now, Everly." Melechial's voice echoed in the cavern. "As well as the other human with you."

Josh shook his head, not wanting to obey.

Everly gave him a reassuring look and then stood up.

"It's hazardous to one's health to enter a dragon's lair uninvited." Melechial had moved silently and was only two feet away. His great head rose over the rock, and his golden eyes met hers.

"I know, but I seem to be a magnet for danger."

She swore there was the faintest raising of his lip. *Was he laughing at her?* The heat of his breath brushed across Everly's skin, and she shivered. He shook his head like a dog shaking off water, and then his body shimmered; in seconds, his dragon form was gone, and leaning casually against the rock she had moments ago been cowering behind was Mr. Halsey.

He was in a dark vest with black pants and shoes. He ran his hand through his mustache and tucked the gold coin into his vest pocket.

"What are your thoughts?" Mr. Halsey asked.

"I think you're magnificent," Everly blurted out. "I mean, I've never seen a dragon up close."

"Nor should you ever want to. Most dragons, even sea dragons, still hunger for human flesh. I'm one of the few that can resist the temptation, but I must warn you. The temptation is one hundred times harder to resist in my dragon form."

"Is it because you think more like a human when you're in a human form?" Josh had regained his courage and joined in the conversation. He still held onto the rock for stability, but he seemed to have gotten over the shock of a dragon and then seeing it transform before him.

"Yes, very astute. When we are in our natural form, it is harder to control our very natural desires, and the sea dragons are scavengers of the ocean; they will eat anything alive or dead."

"You knew I was here?" Everly asked.

"As soon as you stepped into my den, I could smell you." He tapped his nose, and his mustache twitched. "You smelled like a medium rare steak."

Everly stilled. Fear and awe twisted in her stomach at the revelation. Josh took a step back in self-preservation.

"But I have more control than others of my kind," Mr. Halsey added, but it didn't encourage Josh, who took another step back. "Come, let's head back up to my warm library."

Mr. Halsey ushered them back up the way they came. He followed behind, casting wary looks over his shoulder and back down to the pool of water. Everly wondered how deep that water vein went? It must lead out to a main waterway that fed into the ocean, for how else could the sea dragon travel this far inland? But if Sevryn could make it this far, could a siren? Suddenly, Everly didn't feel as safe as she did before.

"Are you ever wrong?" Everly asked. "I mean, your sense of smell. Do you ever mistake humans for grimms or vice versa?"

"Hmm, no. Although, certain items can mask a scent."

This gave Everly something to ponder as they made it back through the grate, and Mr. Halsey closed the secret entrance to his lair. He turned to look at both of them. "I don't think I need to remind either of you that you mustn't speak of what you saw or how you should never go back down there again. Next time, I can't guarantee that you won't end up dinner because you never know who I may be entertaining." Mr. Halsey moved to sit back in his high-back chair. His fingers steepled together as he gave Josh a severe look filled with warning and hunger.

Josh shuddered. "Heard, loud and clear."

Everly nodded but pressed on. She couldn't help but continue with her investigation. "What did you learn?" Everly asked.

"Not much more than you. It does seem that a siren is involved; I have a feeling that Sevryn knows more than he is letting on."

"What of the gold coin? He said it was from Lucerne's hoard. Does Lucerne have a human name?"

"I assume so. Dragons are possessive creatures whose true names are as valuable as their hoards."

"I'm almost positive that it's Lennox," Everly said with assurance. "Is what Sevryn said about dragons never leaving their hoards true?"

"Yes, we become physically ill when we stray too far from it. Which is why sea dragons became pirates and privateers; they would take their hoards with them as they pillaged the sea and gathered more."

"But wouldn't the other dragons on the ship try and steal the treasure?" Everly asked.

Mr. Halsey laughed. "We don't tolerate our kind near us except for important gatherings. His crew would likely be humans who he could pick off one by one and eat, or very loyal grimm."

"That could mean Lennox could be close by, protecting his treasure." Everly began to pace.

"Or dead," Josh added.

Everly gave Mr. Halsey a look.

"It's possible; there are few creatures strong enough to kill a dragon other than another dragon."

Everly looked to Mr. Halsey and recited what he had taught her. "The older they are, the harder they are to find. They can mask their aura."

"That's correct; it doesn't matter how good your griever's

sight is. If an ancient doesn't want to be found, they won't be."

"Same for the siren, I bet." Everly leaned against the fireplace.

"No, not necessarily. Sirens are fickle; their control isn't as well as other grimms."

"What of the creature?" Everly asked.

"Luckily, Sevryn did tell us what we are dealing with." Mr. Halsey moved to a wall of drawers and began to pull them out one by one until he found a protective leather tube and handed it to Everly.

She fingered the ancient leather used to hold maps and protect them from the weather. She pulled off the top and very carefully removed an aged scroll.

"When you described the marks on the bodies, I could only think of one such creature, but I thought he was extinct. I didn't think he was alive anymore, but this proves he must be." Mr. Halsey followed behind her, a trail of smoke above his head.

Everly's hands trembled as she walked to the large table and spread out the scroll, careful not to damage it as she spread it. More than one canvas lay tucked inside the tube.

It was an inked drawing of a terrifying sea creature with tentacles, an oblong head, and a sharp, razor tooth–filled mouth. Above the image in sharp strokes was the text:

KRAKEN

Mr. Halsey picked up his pipe and lit it, drawing a long puff before tapping the scroll. "The Kraeken." The name rolled off his tongue. "Or as you humans always mispronounce and call him, Kraken." This time when he spoke the name, it sounded like "cracker." "He is a legendary sea monster known for his massive size. He has tentacles that can reach up to three hundred feet long without ever exposing his body. He can grip and drag down even the largest of ships. His skin is thick, almost impenetrable, and he has a huge, gaping mouth filled with razor-sharp teeth. That is what I fear hides within the tide."

"How do you kill it?" Everly felt hopeless at the possibility of trying to kill it.

"You don't," Mr. Halsey said. "It's suicide. Not even a dragon would tangle with the Kraken. And that is why I fear the grimm tide can never be conquered."

Josh stood there, eyes wide, trying to follow along with the case. She could see he struggled to understand exactly what they were discussing since he didn't know what the grimm tide was. He moved over to the scroll and rifled through the other bits of broken paper.

"That can't be." Everly shook her head in disbelief. "I don't believe you. Grievers wouldn't give up and let these senseless deaths happen every seven years. There has to be a way." She slammed her hand down on the table.

"There is none. That creature is ancient, older than all of us. Even older than me. To kill him would be a senseless tragedy." Mr. Halsey's voice grew firm.

She forgot that she was arguing with a grimm about how to kill another grimm. It would be like trying to talk someone into killing one of the founders of their country. Everly believed she had reached the end of her help from her grimm professor.

"But if a siren could bespell the Kraeken." Mr. Halsey tapped the image. "She was either truly powerful or truly crazy."

Everly's lips pressed into a thin line, and she left the library. Josh had shaken a bit of the parchment, tucked it into his jacket, and followed.

When Everly got outside, she stared up at the stars. What was she supposed to do now? Call the griever team? Tell them they had to kill a giant sea monster, but one that couldn't be killed?

"Hey." Josh pulled out the scrap parchment. "Not sure if you saw this, but I grabbed it for you."

Everly took her flashlight and shined it across the yellowed paper. Her breath caught in her throat when she saw an ink sketch of a battle between Lucerne, the great sea dragon, and the Kraken.

It was an incredibly detailed image of a dragon and the Kraken fighting. The dragon was immense—much more giant than Sevryn—with arrow-shaped scales, an angular face, and a long tail, while the Kraken was massive with innumerable tentacles that it used to wrap around the dragon. The two mythical beasts were locked in a fierce battle, with the dragon biting off one of the Kraken's tentacles. The sky in the background was dark and stormy, making the scene ominous. It was an epic battle, but a very detailed shape appeared repeatedly in the waves. It was a hidden image. One that Everly had seen before as a logo.

"I need to go home. Now!"

"Do you want me to come with you?" Josh stepped forward.

"No. I don't think you can. I have to go back. Back out on assignment, and you aren't cleared yet. Well, neither am I, but that's beside the point."

"What can I do to help?"

"Can you hot-wire my car? Holland took my car keys, and I need it."

Josh's eyebrows rose in surprise. "Oh, well, as a matter of fact, I can." He turned his knuckles and popped them. "Let's see this car."

Everly was grateful that Josh started her car and didn't ask any more questions. Instead, he reluctantly went back on patrol and let her speed home. Bursting through the door of her house at 1:00 a.m. would probably bring the wrath of her grandmother down on her, but she didn't have time to be quiet.

She raced up the stairs two at a time and through the attic door. Pulling the chain light, she lit the room up. Her aunt was sleeping in the bed, oblivious as always. Everly maneuvered through the piles of clothes and boxes to find the box of old records. She dumped them out until she found a familiar sleeve. One that had a weird spiral shell on the cover, which she thought was the record label name and image. Everly grabbed the "Tantric Echoes" record sleeve and turned it over, looking at the producer label. Produced in Echo Bay. Siren Productions LLC.

"Well, I'll be..." Everly held the image to the light, revealing the singer's photo.

It was an older black-and-white photo taken in the fifties, but the woman in the photo hadn't changed in over seventy years.

She reached into her crossbody bag and pulled out the articles her mother had gathered, some dating eighty years ago. She compared the photo to the record label. It was there, in the background, the same woman with long, wild hair, standing just out of focus as the police were investigating the murder of a teenager in Echo Bay.

Everly sucked in her breath. This was bad. She placed the mini record in her crossbody bag.

She needed to get ahold of Hunter.

CHAPTER 23

"Pick up. Pick up!" Everly called the Stillwell landline. It went unanswered.

Birdie came down the stairs in slippers and a pink bathrobe with her hair in curlers. "What's the matter, bug?" Birdie was on full attack alert, and Everly could see the giant revolver hidden in her robe pocket.

"I can't get ahold of the griever team. I've tried their burner phone numbers, and they go to voicemail. I don't think they have service." Everly quickly explained her suspicions.

"Go. I'll deal with getting ahold of the society and informing them of your intent to return to your team. Be careful, bug," Birdie warned and hugged her.

The drive seemed to take forever as she pressed her foot to the gas and sped back to Echo Bay. When she pulled into the driveway of the beach house at 3:00 a.m., it was dark.

Everly pounded on the door, but it was eerily silent. Resorting to her lockpick set, she quickly broke into the house and raced through the living room to find the bedrooms empty.

"Where is everyone?"

The phone was off the receiver. Had it been knocked over or purposefully left off? Everly looked around the empty room. She opened the hall closet and saw it was bare of weapons and griever bags, which meant they were probably out hunting.

Everly went over to Kat's computer, which was still open. She used the mouse to click on the last Facetime call.

It was to Ms. Bellcamp about two hours ago.

She clicked the Call button.

It rang, and Ms. Bellcamp appeared on the screen a few seconds later. The setting behind her was dark, but her teacher was awake and not in bed. Her blue eyes were confused. "Everly?" her teacher said in surprise. "It's the middle of the night. What do you need?"

"Do you know where the griever team is?"

"No, I haven't heard from them," Ms. Bellcamp answered. "Are you in Echo Bay? I recognize the living room. I thought you were sent back to Gravemark?" She moved, and there was dark paneling and a round window.

"I was. But I came back because I needed to get ahold of Hunter. Do you know how I can reach him?"

"Are you okay? Do I need to get you? Do you need help?" Ms. Bellcamp replied without answering her question.

Everly paused, thinking hard about how to phrase her following statement.

"Yes, Ms. Bellcamp. Because I know the secret of the grimm tide, and I plan to stop it once and for all."

"Wait! How—"

Everly ended the call, closed the computer screen, and pressed her fingers to her temple. *Focus, Everly. What to do next?*

She needed help, and there was only one other person she could think of who would be willing to help her. She needed Lennox—the sea dragon she believed to be hiding in plain sight. Opening Kat's laptop, she searched the online database and found Detective Howard's address.

Obsessed with the treasure, wanting to keep the deaths a secret, it had to be Detective Howard. She wrote down the address, and within minutes, she was at his basement-level apartment.

Everly pounded on Detective Howard's door and covered her nose as the smell of yesterday's overflowing garbage can tried to make her gag. The basement apartment looked like it had a sewage leak problem, but it was also close to the ocean. Death, scavengers. It had to be him.

Despite ignoring her knocks, Everly could hear the TV playing loudly. Someone had to be home. Everly moved up the stairs and went around to try and look through the basement window. She could see a recliner, an end table covered with empty beer cans, and a very passed-out drunk detective.

"Hey!" Everly pounded on the window and saw Detective Howard's foot move slightly. "Wake up!" Using her sleeve, she tried to wipe the dirt from the window to get a better look.

"He's not going to wake up." A deep voice spoke over her shoulder.

Everly jumped at the voice and fell back in surprise. Her hand went to her purse and the mace inside. The speaker was standing in the shadows and came and stood under the porch light, revealing Dr. Peter's familiar yet unexpected face. "I've given him enough sedative that he will sleep through whatever happens tonight. I don't want anyone else to fall victim to the tide."

"You?" Everly said in surprise. Up close, Dr. Peter didn't look like the lithe medical doctor; she could feel his dangerous aura in the darkness. "You're the dread pirate Lennox?" It made sense—obsessed with the dead and could cover the tracks of the creature hunting him. He was the first to inspect the body for treasure. "You took my coin off Skittles, didn't you?"

"Don't you mean my coin?" He just turned his head like a predator evaluating his prey; the light reflecting off his glasses made her breath catch as she saw his true form.

It was only a split second, but before her was a magnificent dragon with shimmering green iridescent scales. His body was long and serpentine, with sharp claws and a powerful tail made for propelling himself effortlessly through the water. The green dragon's head was adorned with a spiky horn crown, and his blue eyes glowed with an otherworldly light. His mouth curled back, revealing dangerous teeth.

Sevryn was like a minnow compared to the power and threat from the dragon before her.

"Please don't eat me," Everly muttered out loud without thinking.

The dragon's maw opened, and it hissed.

Everly recoiled, covering her face with her arms, feeling the hot breath, waiting for the death blow that never came. For that hiss was followed by a second and then a third.

When she opened her eyes, it was to see Dr. Peter standing before her laughing. "It's been a while since anyone has seen my true form. I've almost forgotten it."

"How can you forget that you are a great dragon?" Everly asked.

His face darkened. "Sometimes it is easier to run from my past than confront it, little griever."

Everly gathered her courage to speak out against him, knowing that by doing so, she may be killed. "You know what I am?"

"From the moment I saw you dockside. It was brave of you to look inside the body bag, but I had already taken the prize. Then, your friend's pathetic excuse after dealing with the siren. I can recognize her sent anywhere."

"You could have eaten us."

"Why would I eat you when you are here for the grimm tide, not me."

"You know what the tide is. You've known all along."

"The Kraken, why yes." Dr. Peter shuddered. "That may be the one thing I truly fear. He has destroyed my vessel, my lineage, and everyone that I've ever held dear."

"Then why don't you stop it?" Everly countered. "Surely, you can take on the Kraken?"

"You've not seen it then, or you wouldn't ask me to do the impossible. Every seven years, it slinks out of the bottom of the ocean and tries to kill me; I fought it, almost dying. Then, one year, I buried my treasure, thinking surely it was the year it would kill me. Two of my crew followed and saw where I buried it. They stole my treasure. The next day, the Kraken killed my quartermaster. The day after, my gunner. That's when I figured out how I could escape it. It didn't want me but whoever held my treasure." Dr. Peter's dropped his head. "It became easier and easier just to let others die in my stead."

"That's still murder!" Everly snapped at him.

Dr. Peter laughed a deep, hearty laugh. "And I'm still a pirate. Murder is my bread and butter."

Everly let out a breath. "That's why you became the medical examiner."

"I've lived for centuries and seen hundreds die at the hands of the ocean and her beasts. It was an easy job that fell right into my lap. It fed my hunger for death and other things." His voice trailed off, hinting at more sinister outcomes.

Everly felt her mouth go sour but refused to follow that thought.

"So you let innocents die."

"I wanted to tell the townspeople about the cursed treasure. I did, but you heard it, little griever. The human detective refused to let me warn anyone. He became greedy. His collection of my treasure has filled his top sock drawer for quite some time. It's only a matter of time before the Kraken comes for him."

"What about Dylan, Starla, and Pike at Howler's Cove? They were just teens!"

Dr. Peter sighed. "That was a terrible accident. It was a perfect hiding place. I really did try and bury it well. No matter how deep or far I send it, it always wants to be found."

"Is there no way to stop the tide?" Everly said.

"Can you stop the wind, the waves?

"We have to try. I—" Everly wanted to say more, but a distress flare rose into the night. "Someone needs help!"

As the flare fizzled out and plummeted toward the ground, it came to rest close to the shoreline, illuminating the rapidly receding waterline and revealing the eerie ocean floor in the pitch-black darkness.

"It's coming," Dr. Peter said with a solemn finality.

"Someone's in trouble." Everly started to run toward the flare but stopped to turn around and face the dragon, cowering behind a human's visage. "Maybe it's best if you stay here and hide. You've spent too long as a human; I don't think you'd be strong enough to help. I only see a pathetic medical doctor when I really need a pirate king."

CHAPTER 24

ANOTHER FLARE LIT THE SKY, AND EVERLY DIDN'T think she would make it in time. Her feet pounded on the dock as she ran up the ramp and onto the *Jolly Dodger*.

Marnie stood there, her hair blowing wildly in the wind, her patchwork dress falling off her shoulders, and her eyes filled with tears as she stared at the water pulling back. In her hand was the recently fired flare gun. She collapsed onto the deck, and Aimee and Kat stood near her. Cass was nowhere in sight.

Hunter and Ian stood on deck, swords in hand, and faced Captain Roy, who, despite the early hours, was still in full costume, with his black pants and red captain jacket. He must live in that coat. He was on his knees, a blade at his throat.

"We just had some questions for you," Hunter said.

"No, you are accusing me of killing my kin." Captain Roy's voice broke. "I'd never do that. I've built a life for them here."

Ian had the rest of the show's stunt crew tied to the deck

rails. She recognized Cleo and Rob, but the others were not familiar. Did they gather all the crew to interrogate them?

"Tell us, what are you? I know you're grimm." Ian was pacing in front of them, his nostrils flaring as he smelled them, demanding to know that he was right.

Hunter noticed Everly's arrival, and his blade dropped slightly from Captain Roy's throat. "Everly, what are you doing here?"

Roy took the moment's distraction and spun away from the blade, freeing himself. Once he did, the rest of the cast quickly freed themselves from the knots as if proving that they pretended to be captured to protect their captain. They grabbed swords that didn't look like props and came and encircled them.

Despite all the commotion, Marnie didn't move; she was focused on the outgoing wave.

"Marnie?" Everly approached the woman tentatively. There was something odd about her behavior. "Are you okay?"

Her face crumpled into one of remorse. "I should have told them the truth, protected them."

"Who?" Everly asked.

"They didn't know. Maybe, if they did, they could have survived, and now Dylan will pay the price."

"Marnie, what did you do?"

Marnie suddenly seemed older than her years, tired, burdened with a secret she had been keeping. "I discovered it by accident—Roy's coat on the rocks when I was a young teen. I didn't know what I had at first. But then, when I saw him come and put it on, he became a beautiful seal and went into the ocean. For hours, I watched him play in the waves, and then when the sun set, he came back out, removed his coat, and hid it among the rocks. I took it. And the next day, when he came to go back out to the sea, he couldn't find it. He searched desperately for hours among the rocks, and I could see his heart breaking. When I came out of hiding holding his coat, he looked at me, and I knew I couldn't return it. Not when I wanted him to stay with me forever."

"Nay, my love." Roy got up from his knees and came to her. "When our eyes met, I knew I could never leave you to go back to the sea. I let you have my coat."

She cried, tears flowing from her eyes. "Then our kids were born, and when they first shed their skin, I was scared they would love the sea more than me. So I stole their coats and locked them up. But it wasn't just our kids. We gave any selkie that came to our shore work and provided them life by the sea, doing what they loved, in exchange for their coats. We wanted to be human. We were a family."

"A great family." Roy's eyes were also filling with tears.

"I *knew* they were grimm," Ian added loudly, his chest puffed up.

"What does this have to do with that?" Aimee asked, pointing at the wall of water slowly building off the coast and threatening to come crashing down on them.

Marnie looked at the wall of death. "It was my fault for designing the show and romanticizing the legend of the treasure. If they knew what finding it meant, they could be safe."

"No one's going to be safe from that!" Hunter said.

"Please," Marnie begged Aimee. "I can right my wrong if you just let me. I can save them."

Aimee glanced at the group before nodding. Marnie

raced down the ramp and into the building that housed their costumes.

"She's gone," Ian grumbled.

"No, not my Marnie," Captain Roy spoke proudly. "She will come back for us."

With the wall of water growing, there was a loud noise, and the wind was building with it.

"Hunter," Everly yelled, pointing toward the ocean. "It's the Kraken and will kill anyone in possession of the cursed treasure."

His eyes widened, and he reached into his pocket and pulled out the bracelet.

Marnie was struggling to carry a heavy trunk up the ramp. One of the stage crew helped Marnie bring it to the deck. She took the key from around her neck and unlocked the trunk lid, flipping it back to reveal a trunk full of fur. She kneeled and ran her hands over them lovingly.

"It was how I kept the show going. It wasn't meant to be forever. The young ones lost their skins when they were babies. They forgot what they were. Wanted more. Knew something had been lost but not what," Marnie rushed out. "I can protect them now."

"What is she doing?" Hunter asked as Marnie carefully picked up a skin. A line of cast members gathered, each taking a skin from her. They slipped it on like a jacket, and Everly couldn't pull her eyes away as they shimmered and changed into giant harbor seals.

One barked at her and then dove into the ocean. They jumped off the ledge into the shallow water and escaped one by one.

Marnie was escorted by Roy, who was still in his

human form, to the side of the boat. He placed a loving arm around Marnie. "Ready for another adventure?" he asked sweetly.

"As long as I'm with you." They jumped into the water together.

"Hey!" Ian yelled and ran to the side to try to stop them. "Now what?" he yelled.

Roy was helping Marnie swim to safety. They were surrounded by seals, helping her float and get to land.

"We were wrong." Everly came over to stand in front of Hunter. Her eyes filled with worry. "Marnie's not a siren. Just a human who fell in love with a selkie. Nor are the selkies to blame for the tide. They are only victims of an unfortunate coincidence."

As they stood on the deck, the wave was a giant wall, and a flash of lightning lit the sky. In the depths, they could see a dark shadow.

"Who then?" Hunter asked. "Who is at fault?"

"Her!" Everly said, pointing to the figure at the helm dressed all in black, with black leggings, boots, and a jacket. Her short blonde hair was blowing straight back, whipping her pale face. Her eyes seemed filled with regret.

The grievers froze and stared at Everly like she was insane.

"That's not possible," Ian said. "We'd know. I mean, she's been with us for years."

"And before Gravemark, where was she?" Everly answered, spinning to try to convince the other students.

"Crypthaven." Kat's hand covered her mouth.

"She's the siren and the one who attacked us in the cave. She was trying to take treasure from us, to protect us."

Aimee grabbed her neck. "Protect? Yeah, right. She almost killed us."

Ms. Bellcamp's steps were unsure as she descended the stairs, her hand holding onto the railing for stability against the wind and a cutting rain that started. Each drop felt like a painful stab.

"It's true, all of it. I made a mistake. One I regret, and I've been trying to correct it for years." Her hands came up, and she covered her mouth to stop them from trembling. "It was my desire to be wanted, needed, and loved by another, and when he rejected me, I wanted to destroy him. I let my siren's fury grow so great that it grew into a curse when I sang. One that I am incapable of stopping."

"And Crypthaven?" Hunter yelled. "That was you?"

"The griever teams had amassed an enormous amount of treasure over the years, which unfortunately acted as a beacon for the Kraken. I wanted to protect them. I let my cousins, the finfolk, into Crypthaven via the tunnels. They were supposed to take the treasure and leave. However, their anger boiled over when they saw the oubliette and what had happened to the grimms. They were furious. My siren song, which I had hoped would bring peace, only fueled their rage; it backfired as it did with Hunter and Ian. It brought death. Ultimately, I have to take responsibility for what happened, and Crypthaven's fate lies in my hands."

The wind was as loud as a train, and Kat whistled between her fingers and pointed. "Everyone, great chat and all, but grab your butts and hold onto something."

They were so enthralled with the revelation that they didn't see how close that wall of water was coming. It seemed to have hung in the air for minutes, and all of a sudden, it was there crashing down on them.

Everly looked up and dove for the railing, wrapping her arms around it as the wave hit her full force and ripped at her body, threatening to crush her beneath its weight.

She couldn't breathe as she clung to the railing, locking her ankles and hoping it would be over and air would come soon. Buffeted by the waves, she held on but could feel her arms losing their grip.

Then the wave passed, and Everly let go and was swept to the other side of the boat, crashing into a wooden crate. She coughed, rolled over, and spit out water, and when she looked up, it was to see that most of the seating areas had been destroyed. All the rows of colored seating had broken off and been swept away, and tables and bench seats were up on the street level. Some had damaged a few cars, and one looked like it went right through a living room window.

The ship was no longer a dry dock, as it had fallen into the ocean. Everly worried about the hull; was it still seaworthy since it had been lifted out of the water for decades?

But then a shadow passed over her head. Everly had barely regained her balance when the ground grew dark.

"Watch out!" Ian slammed into Everly's side. He grabbed her and rolled them out of the way as a giant tentacle slammed into the decking right where she had stood moments ago. The ship slanted with the weight, and they slid right over the side. Ian grabbed the edge of the boat, his other hand gripping Everly's wrist as they dangled.

"Don't let go!" Everly looked down and saw that she

dangled not over the water but the dangerous sharp wreckage of the stage.

Ian groaned and tried to pull her up, but his grip was slipping.

"You think you could lose a few?" Ian gritted between clenched teeth.

"Really? Now's not the time to joke." Everly tried to dig her toes into the ship's side to help relieve the pressure on Ian's grip. "Maybe you should lift more weights." Everly pushed up, and Ian pulled until she could get her other arm onto the edge. He didn't stop. Ian pulled himself up and then reached to assist Everly. They saw the destruction just as they cleared the edge and rolled back onto the deck.

"I don't know how we stop that," Ian breathed out.

"Harpoon!" Everly said, pointing at the warehouse, where there were still six or seven different harpoons and various spears attached to the wall. "Do you remember where the gun is?"

Ian nodded. He jumped off the deck onto the only part of the dock that wasn't destroyed but was half submerged in water. He was fast, but would he be fast enough?

Hunter was lifting a crossbeam and pulling Aimee out of what used to house a trampoline. Cass had anchored herself to the ship with rope. Everly scanned the deck but couldn't find Kat's fuchsia-colored hair. "Where's Kat?"

"Here!" Ms. Bellcamp's voice came from the ocean. Everly's heart raced as she caught sight of the siren. The creature's black scales glistened under the water, and her once-blonde hair had transformed into a dark shade of green. Her razor-sharp teeth were visible as she wrapped her hands around Kat's neck.

"No! Don't hurt her!" Everly cried out, worried that she was going to kill her.

Instead, Ms. Bellcamp floated effortlessly, keeping Kat's head out of the water and resting on her shoulder. "I got her!" Ms. Bellcamp called out. "She's out cold."

Everly bit her lip and tried to figure out whether or not she could trust her.

"Give her back! Now!" Everly yelled.

Ms. Bellcamp flinched and swam forward, pushing Kat's body toward a rope ladder. Hunter raced down it and, very carefully, lifted Kat out of Ms. Bellcamp's arms. It wasn't the most accessible position to maneuver, and the siren used her immense strength to help push Kat almost to the top of the ladder.

Hunter was caught off guard and almost lost his grip on Kat. But Everly was there, pulling her up on the deck, just as another tentacle the size of a tree trunk came swinging right for Everly.

Everly rolled with Kat, trying to cushion her head, but the Kraken was targeting Everly. She pushed off and ran toward the bow, and the Kraken followed; another tentacle took a swipe at Everly, and she ducked.

"Make it stop!" Hunter yelled at Ms. Bellcamp.

"I can't. I've tried. Do you not understand? Whenever I sing, bad things happen. I only make it worse." Ms. Bellcamp crawled onto the deck. Her body was much taller and lither in her siren form. "That's how I got in this mess to begin with!"

"Try!" Hunter yelled back.

Ms. Bellcamp opened her mouth to sing. Everly covered her ears as a horrible noise came forth. The Kraken stopped;

his deadly tentacles hung in the air, swaying softly. She continued to sing, stepping forward, and Everly could hear the song change from a desire to a command, and that's where she lost control.

The Kraken bellowed, a great deep sound erupting from below the ship, and giant bubbles popped.

"He didn't like that," Ms. Bellcamp said nervously.

The ship moved under them as the Kraken began to lift them. Everly fell to her knees. "Try again!" Everly commanded.

Ms. Bellcamp trembled, and she sang again, her voice wavering. Unsure.

But the reply was a hundredfold as something else besides the Kraken answered. "No!" Ms. Bellcamp paled, covering her head in remorse. "Not them. Not again."

A skittering of claws came up the side of the ship, and creatures dropped onto the deck one by one.

"What are they?" Aimee yelled, kicking one in the face. It squealed and fell over the side of the boat.

Cass grabbed an oar and used it to swing at the next one coming over the side. "They're ugly."

"Finfolk!" Ms. Bellcamp shivered. "Hellbent on destruction. If we don't stop them, they will kill everything in their path."

Everly heard the conviction in her voice. "It's Crypthaven all over again." She grabbed one of the ropes and used it to swing and knock another one into the ocean. Everly landed and turned to look at her teacher.

Ms. Bellcamp's head dropped, and her lip quivered. "I'm great at summoning. Not so good at controlling."

The boat shifted again as the Kraken's tentacles wrapped

around them, looping over the top. He squeezed, and the ship began to crack under the pressure.

Ian returned with multiple harpoons. He tossed one to Hunter and Aimee, giving them numerous darts. One was even a whaling harpoon with a cable. Ian lifted the first dart and sighted in on the closest tentacle.

He aimed, pulled the trigger, and missed.

"Leave the fishing to professionals." A deep voice chuckled and pulled the harpoon out of Ian's hands.

CHAPTER 25

Roy stood on the deck, a dangerous gleam in his eyes after being reunited with his skin; there was a different aura about him, one that would gladly take on the Kraken. Behind him fighting the finfolk was his clan of selkies from the *Jolly Dodger*. They had returned and, this time, were decked out with genuine blades and swords and were gleefully fighting the finfolk creatures of the deep.

A short finfolk streaked past Everly with a spear in hand and stabbed a taller one about to take a bite of Everly's leg. Then the finfolk shifted into Cass; she wiped the blood off her face, shifted into another one, and disappeared into the battle.

"Take this, you big piece of sushi!" Roy yelled. "This is for Pike!" He pressed the trigger, and the harpoon shot straight, finding its target.

A bellow of pain followed, and the tentacle retreated, but a second one came down, knocking Roy backward into the arena pit.

It looked like they were winning for a few minutes, but

nothing could take down the Kraken. The tentacles emerged from the water and wrapped around the mast. Splintering wood filled the air as the mast cracked and fell onto the deck, bringing down the sails and lighting rigging. When it crashed into the deck, there was a spark of fire, and it caught.

Everly recognized Rob as he jumped onto one of the working trampolines and launched back into the air, slicing through a tip of the tentacle.

A second barrage of Kraken attacks came down from the air, breaking and bursting the ship apart. One went through the hull, and Everly felt the boat lurch to the side as it took on water.

Ms. Bellcamp stood at the bow and tried to control the Kraken again with her singing. Tears were in her eyes, and she stood there, challenging him. A tentacle wrapped around her waist and pulled her up into the air. It squeezed, and Everly saw Ms. Bellcamp go limp. He flung her into the ocean, and her teacher's body slowly sank into the sea.

"Ms. Bellcamp!" Everly yelled as she sank beneath the dark waves.

A terrifying roar filled the air, and then her teacher's body began to rise out of the water. Beneath her was a scaled form that lifted her to safety and deposited her on the deck of the ship.

"Lucerne—er, uh, Lennox," Everly breathed in awe at seeing the great sea dragon challenge the Kraken. He was almost as big as the Kraken, and Everly felt the ship be tossed aside as the Kraken turned on his actual victim—the great sea dragon. Eight tentacles immediately wrapped around the dragon and pulled him into the water.

Lennox growled and snapped at the Kraken but only got

a mouthful of one arm. He ripped and tore it from his body. There was a cry of pain from the Kraken, and he recoiled before wrapping even tighter around Lennox's body. He began to squeeze. Even the king of the sea dragons wasn't a match for the Kraken.

"Help him!" Everly yelled at Roy and his crew of selkies, but they were overwhelmed by the army of finfolk.

Everly tried to run, picking up another spear, and saw her crossbody bag snagged between debris and the sound equipment. Everly grabbed the bag and found Kat, just coming to, tucked into the sound booth by Ms. Bellcamp.

"Kat!" Everly patted her cheeks to wake her up. "Kat, can you play this?" Everly held up the mini record, surprised that it was still intact.

Kat's heterochromia eyes tried to focus on what Everly held in front of her. Then she looked at the equipment. Her gaze followed the cords to see that there were still speakers that were attached to the dock and the warehouse. "I think those speakers may still work, but it's whether they have..." She began to open up cupboards and found a record player. "Holy grimm, they do."

It only took a few moments before Kat got the record spinning and looked around for a cordless mic. She shoved it at the speaker, and everyone winced as Ms. Bellcamp's old solo record, titled "Tantric Echoes," echoed across the bay.

The Kraken froze, stopped fighting the sea dragon, and released him, one tentacle at a time. But Lennox had lost the fight, and he slipped into the sea.

Everly held her breath as the record worked. This wasn't a command but a song. She watched as even the finfolk lost their desire to fight and jumped into the ocean, disappearing into the dark water.

Ms. Bellcamp made her way to the sound booth, her face bruised and bleeding. "Where did you get that?" she asked in awe. "I haven't sung like that in years."

"My aunt has a peculiar taste in music."

"Well, bless her heart, she may have saved the day. The Kraken is retreating." Ms. Bellcamp wiped at her eyes. "It's not his fault that he is cursed to kill because of me. I just wanted the sea dragon Lucerne to love me. That's all I wanted to do, but the Kraken answered my call and instead tried to kill what Lucerne loved."

Then the record hit a deep scratch, and the needle went off track with a loud screech. The Kraken stopped retreating.

"Put it back on!" Ms. Bellcamp yelled frantically, reaching for the needle and fighting Kat, who was also trying to take control of the sound. They fought over the mic; it flew from Kat's hand and landed on the ground. The bottom of the mic broke, and the battery fell down a hole to the next floor below.

"Smooth move, Ex-Lax!" Kat yelled.

"I don't even know what that means!" Ms. Bellcamp cried out.

"It means what you did was a sh—"

Hunter reached for Everly. "Do you still have the treasure you took from Howler's Cove? I have a plan," he rushed out, ignoring the fighting between the others.

"How did you know I took the necklace and ruby?"

He gave her a wry smile. "I knew." He held out his hand, and she put the two pieces next to the bracelet he had taken from her at the hospital. He closed his fist around the treasure. "I'm sorry," he whispered, leaning over and kissing her. "It's not a very good plan." Then he darted out of the sound booth and jumped over the side onto what was left of the dock. He ran up the street and along the shoreline.

"Hey!" Hunter yelled, waving his hands. He was racing along the shoreline, causing a commotion. In his hands, he held all the cursed treasure.

"Hunter, don't do it!" Everly yelled as she realized what he was attempting to do. He was trying to lead the Kraken away from them. He was sacrificing himself for his team. For everyone. "No!"

Aimee was climbing a rope ladder to one of the still intact sails, a finfolk with a spear on her heels. When she saw Hunter leading the Kraken away, she grabbed one of the ropes, swung out to the dock, picked up one of the finfolk's rusty spears, and chased Hunter.

With a specific target in mind, the Kraken pulled a portion of his body out of the water, crawled over a yacht, sank it, and knocked a tugboat out of his way. It was destroying everything in his attempt to get to Hunter. As the Kraken drug himself across the shallows, he left deep welts in the sand where his smaller arms snaked along the ground.

Everly stared at them and the familiar pattern they made. It was the same as the one when they were saved and appeared on the beach. *Did that mean the monster saved me? But why?* When she had a piece of the cursed treasure on her. It meant that it should, by all standards, have killed her.

What was the reason that the monster saved her?

"You commanded him to." A voice spoke into her mind.

"I did not," Everly replied, looking up at the dark skyline and searching for Corvis.

He was flying above, watching them all, circling.

"You did. You commanded him to save you."

"But how?"

"Because your gift lies in your power over omens. Remember the choosing ceremony? You claimed me without one."

"The Kraken is an omen? I can't control *that* thing," Everly said, feeling doubt fill her.

The Kraken pulled the rest of his giant body out of the water, revealing his head for the first time. It was a cone shape with giant black beady eyes and a beak that opened and closed, able to snap a body in two.

He let out a howl and pulled himself further on land. His tree-like arms slammed in front of Hunter, blocking his route. Hunter turned, and a second one blocked his escape.

Aimee had almost caught up to the Kraken and threw the spear, aiming for his eye, but a tentacle knocked it away.

"You can," Corvis argued. "I couldn't have done what I did in the ceremony without you. It was your strength I used, not my own."

Everly knew she would lose two people she cared about if she didn't do something fast.

She focused her attention on the Kraken. "Stop!" Everly commanded, and nothing happened.

Hunter swung a sword, and it only scratched the surface of the Kraken's skin. Aimee rolled under the arm and stood back-to-back with Hunter, protecting him.

"It's not working!" Everly cried out, worrying about why Hunter wasn't running away.

"Try again!"

She did, focusing all her attention on the creature. "Stop!"

He shivered like a dog shaking off water but kept going forward.

Then, Everly saw Ms. Bellcamp appear next to Hunter and Aimee. Standing in front of the monster, she held her hand out as she faced off against the beast.

She opened her mouth, and it echoed as if she were using a megaphone, half screeching like a hawk, half song—similar to the record. "Stand down! You will not harm the children!"

The Kraken paused at the sight of her.

"This isn't what I want. I never wished for the destruction of innocents."

The Kraken seemed to be having a fit, writhing in agony, but she again repeated the commands. "No more. I was wrong. I didn't mean to cause so much harm."

The Kraken's arm grabbed a boat and used it like a club. A shadow appeared over Ms. Bellcamp, and then she disappeared among the rubble of the crushed boat.

"Ms. Bellcamp!" Hunter screamed and ran to help her, but the Kraken wrapped a tentacle around his feet and hoisted him into the air.

Aimee jumped up, digging her sai into the Kraken's skin, riding the arm, refusing to let Hunter go alone. Everly stared in terror as the Kraken brought them closer to his mouth.

Aimee cried out as she pulled a second blade from her hip sheath and stabbed over and over into the arm holding Hunter.

"No, Aimee! Let go! Or it will get us both," Hunter

yelled as he tried to push against the arm to release him. Then he pushed at Aimee, who was crying.

Aimee looked up at Hunter and turned to see the Kraken's face looming toward them, the beak opening as it brought them closer. Aimee pulled her sai, shifted her weight, and let go.

The world stopped as she fell and landed on the Kraken's head; she ran up the head and, with a mighty swing, stabbed it in the eye. Blood spurted out, and it recoiled, tossing Hunter through the air, and he hit the side of a flipped boat. Everly saw his body go limp as he slid into the ocean, disappearing into the foam.

Aimee still clung onto the sai and was about to let go when the Kraken's arm found her, the one who caused him pain. He ripped her from his eye and dragged her under the ocean waves. She didn't come up.

"NO!" Everly screamed and tried to rush forward.

Strong hands gripped her around the waist, and Ian pulled her back. "No! You can't help them now. They're gone."

"No, let me go." She collapsed to her knees. Her heart was in her throat. *Not Hunter and Aimee.*

Then, a figure burst out of the ocean. Hunter! He swam against the water, racing for the spot where Aimee disappeared. He dove under the water.

"Hunter!" Everly clawed her way to her feet and was going to run after him, but Ian pushed her down.

"Stay! I'll go!" His blue eyes met hers. "Please, just this once, listen to me. I'll bring him back for you. I promise."

In a blink, Ian was gone. She noticed that the finfolk had stopped their attack, and soon she was surrounded by selkies.

Marnie, Roy, Cleo, Rob, Kat, and Cass stood by her and watched as Ian raced toward certain death.

He wouldn't reach Hunter in time.

As Hunter came up for air, the tentacle moved, the water rushing up on either side of him. He stopped and saw his death coming. He turned and searched the ship until he saw Everly on the bow. Their eyes met as if it was the last thing he wanted to remember.

"Keep swimming!" she begged but knew it was useless as the arm rose out of the water, completely hiding him from view.

"No!"

Lennox reappeared from the ocean's depths with a mighty roar, bloody and covered in open wounds. He launched a final attack, clamping his great jaws onto the Kraken's head. In a death grip, he held, and the Kraken cried out and tried to swing his body to release the great dragon when they dove back under the water.

After the creatures disappeared, Everly saw Hunter was gone.

She screamed. Her whole body went weak, and she fell to her knees. Her mouth opened, and a silent wail fell forth, her hands clawing and grasping at anything as she tried to process what just happened mentally.

"Stop!" Her mind sought the Kraken, and she ripped his consciousness away. She saw the shattered, broken bits of his mind destroyed by the siren song. Just like the Kraken squeezed his victims, Everly took hold of his mind and squeezed. She was forcing him to obey her.

"Leave! Go back to the depths and never return to the surface again!"

She felt him surrender even as he fought against the sea dragon. He wanted to escape, and in a final effort, he squeezed out of the dragon's grip, shooting like an arrow out of a crossbow back into the deep. Although he tried to get rid of her, she didn't lose him. Just like Corvis could always tell where she was, Everly grasped the Kraken's consciousness and followed him as he dove deep underwater.

She could feel the cold surrounding her as all the light disappeared. It was hard to breathe as she felt the Kraken search the deep for a crack deep in a cavern to crawl inside of so he could hide and recover.

She tore at her shirt, unable to breathe beneath the great weight of the deep. She was feeling everything he felt. The confusion. The command. It felt like she was suffocating under the immense pressure. He wailed from the pain. So Everly held on even further, delving into his mind.

"Your duty is done. You are free. No longer will you hunt the treasure."

There was a rebuttal as he tried to fight her. "NO!" Everly doubled down. Her hands were splayed out on the deck, and she could feel spots dancing across her eyelids and sweat beading across her forehead. "Obey!"

Then, he let out a sigh.

"Sleep!" she commanded and felt the omen comply. It relaxed and closed his eyes as Everly felt herself do the same, and she collapsed onto the deck.

CHAPTER 26

ONCE AGAIN, WHEN THE MORNING CAME, DEATH HAD touched the town of Echo Bay. But instead, it went under the guise of a tsunami. The townspeople who heard the storm remembered the sound of a train and a great wave that hit their shore in the middle of the night.

Those who dared to come outside to investigate only saw the waves knocking the ships around like they were toy blocks. Cars along the roads were washed blocks away, and some of the houses were flooded, but the worst damage came to the *Jolly Dodger* ship and warehouse, which was destroyed and sunk into the bay.

"Why is she still asleep?" Kat muttered.

Everly's eyes fluttered open to see that she lay in the master bedroom of their house. Sitting closest to her, Hunter had his head buried in his hands. Ian stood by the door, hesitant to enter the room. On her right, Aimee was sitting quietly, fiddling with a plastic wrapper in her hands, while Kat sat beside her, looking protective. Seeing her loved ones around her bed brought comfort to Everly's heart.

There was a quiet tension in the room.

"Hey, she's awake!" Kat leaned forward.

Hunter's head snapped up, and he reached out to grab Everly's hand. It was warm and reassuring, and his fingers slid between hers like they belonged there. He gave her hand a loving squeeze, and Everly's heart melted.

"You're alive?" Everly was surprised, and she looked toward Ian.

"Hey, I told you I would return him to you." Ian gave her a sad smile. "I kept my promise."

Everly's lips trembled, and she looked at Hunter. "Are you okay?"

"That's what I'm supposed to be asking you." Hunter leaned forward and brushed a strand of blonde hair from her face.

"You were the one being stupid." Everly sat up, and her head complained, sending a zillion fiery flashing lights behind her eyes. "Oh." She laid back down. "I think I need to not move. What happened?" Everly asked. "Did we win?"

Ian answered without looking at her. "When Ms. Bellcamp died, the finfolk disbanded."

"So I didn't imagine that." Everly felt her eyes start to burn. "And the Kraken?" she asked, unsure if she just dreamed of his retreat.

"It's over." Dr. Peter stepped inside the room. His right arm was in a sling, and there were a few bandages and stitches on his cheek. "I followed him to his lair and sealed him within his home. I will make sure that my brethren take turns guarding him. He's sleeping for now."

"We will see in seven years if he returns," Ian said bitterly.

"No, it won't," Dr. Peter said. His blue eyes met every single one of them in promise. "I have learned from my past and buried my treasure where no one will ever discover it again."

"That's what you did last time, and others have paid the price," Ian argued.

Dr. Peter pulled off his glasses, held them with his injured arm, and polished them with his one good arm. "Oh, I think it will be very safe; no one will dare attempt to steal what is mine ever again." He put his glasses back on, and there was a glint in his eye, or maybe it was a reflection, making that one comment seem so much more sinister. "I think it will be quite safe."

Kat's eyes narrowed suspiciously. "Where."

"With the Kraken, of course." Dr. Peter smiled crookedly.

"So does that mean it's over?" Kat asked. "No more grimm tide. And to think it was all because of Ms. Bellcamp."

Dr. Peter's head dropped. "Sirens are wholeheartedly selfish, even more so than dragons. It was her desire to control me that led to this whole grimm tide mess."

"You're wrong." Ian's voice was low. "She did care for us... me. She protected me from my werewolf curse. She taught us and died protecting us."

"Yes, maybe nurture over nature won out this time, but in the end, she did something I never suspected her to do. She died protecting others, and that is not in the siren nature."

"Not in a dragon's nature, nor pirate's either," Everly

corrected, her eyebrow rising to point out that he also risked his life to protect their teacher.

He coughed and shifted his shoulders. "Well, we did love each other once, long ago. She wrapped me around her finger, and I almost crashed my ship numerous times because her song was impossible to resist, but then she realized I wasn't the weak human she thought me to be. I resisted, but she persisted. It became a game between us. I would roam the seas, pillaging, plundering, devouring to my heart's content, but then I would return every seven years to the shore, where I would meet up with her, and we would—" He coughed.

"Wait!" Kat cupped her hands over Aimee's ears to shield her.

Dr. Peter laughed. "Make beautiful music. I loved her but loved the sea more. She tried to come with me, but I refused. The longer I was gone, the more bitter she became. Then, I became injured in a battle with another dragon over my gold and had to sleep for a century. When I returned with my hoard, the world had changed; she had changed. Her jealousy changed her song. She tried to control me with her siren song, and it back-fired. It didn't harm me but affected my treasure. Then that beast came and attacked my ship. Killed half my selkie crew."

"Selkies?" Kat leaned forward. "So they were part of your crew."

"Selkies, oh, they are strong, of the sea, and when they mutiny, they taste delicious."

Kat made a face. "You're lying?"

"Maybe." He grinned. "Maybe not. But how do you think they ended up with my ship?"

"The *Jolly Dodger?*"

"It was left in the care of my first mate, and it was passed down from father to son for years. When I finally returned to Echo Bay, everything had changed. The curse had not lifted. That stupid beast was still hunting down my treasure. I no longer felt safe in the sea. So I changed my appearance and took on another job but stayed close to my treasure and watched my former crew mock my life with song and dance. Their dishonor weakened me."

"No," Everly corrected. "It's because you've lived as a human for nearly a century. You're forgetting your dragon self. I learned from another dragon that the longer you live as a human, the more human you become."

"Hm, I wonder... Yes, that would explain why I was so out of shape. I probably could have taken the Kraken if I had been up to my usual strength."

Everly pinched her lips together to hide her smile, but then she looked at her clasped hands, and worry filled her heart. "But what about Dylan?"

"He's been released. I spoke to Detective Howard and explained that he couldn't have possibly killed those teens since another victim appeared with the same markings while he was locked up."

The room fell quiet as Dr. Peter spoke of her greatest fear. "Another victim? Who?" Everly's mouth lost all moisture, and she struggled to form the question. Her eyes met Hunter's, and she saw the redness, the swelling. The way Ian couldn't look at her, and she knew. Her eyes scanned the room. Cass wasn't there.

Before she could ask, Hunter spoke. "Aimee," he choked

out, his eyes flickering to the brunette sitting beside her and immediately away—the sight too painful to bear.

Everly sucked in her breath, and her head swung to Aimee sitting next to Kat. She saw the mints in her hand and realized it wasn't Aimee but Cass in her form. Now, she understood the silent tension.

The guilt Hunter was feeling. The guilt they were all feeling.

Aimee died saving Hunter's life.

Hunter pulled away, his hands sliding from hers. "I can't be here." He flashed an uncomfortable look at Cass wearing Aimee's form and left the room.

"Hunter." Everly tried to pull the blanket back and go after him.

"Don't," Ian warned. "He needs to mourn. He lost a teammate and will blame himself for her death. Seeing you will only make him feel more guilty."

"Why?"

"Because he couldn't love her the way she loved him. The way she deserved to be loved. She gave her life for him; that is a debt that he can never repay." Ian's words filled Everly with dread as she realized that her love would never be able to compare to Aimee's sacrifice.

CHAPTER 27

THE GRAVEMARK CHURCHYARD WAS SHROUDED IN A thick blanket of fog that dreary morning, making it difficult to see the rows of headstones. The mourners arrived dressed in somber black, their faces hidden behind umbrellas as they paid their final respects to Aimee Stilwell. Aimee's parents, accomplished surgeons, stood tall and composed as they said their goodbyes. Amid the crowd stood a figure in a long tan jacket—none other than Gerald Petrovich. Despite the solemn occasion, he stood out with his tan coat and overly observant eyes.

Everyone was in attendance. Even her grandma Birdie and all the omens. Everyone... except Holland Abernathy.

The public would only know that Aimee drowned in a wakeboarding accident, according to Dr. Peter, who would take care of all the paperwork. Only the grievers and staff of Gravemark would know that she had drowned in a battle with the Kraken.

Ms. Bellcamp's body was never recovered, and Ms. March said that's because when sirens die, they become seafoam. So they held a private memorial for her at the ocean side.

But this funeral felt different from her father's. It was another griever funeral, a reminder that it could have been any of them. Their time was short, and Everly desperately needed to patch things up with Holland.

> Holland. Why are you ignoring my texts?

> Don't be mad. I can explain.

> Please don't make me choose.

As Everly sent off the last text, she felt Hunter slide his hand into hers. She couldn't help but glance up in surprise at that exact moment to see Lacie Duvall lean over and whisper, pointing to her and Hunter holding hands. Her expression was one of disgust.

Everly's stomach began to roll with uneasiness. She did not like being the center of attention. Few knew that Aimee and Hunter had broken up before they went on a reaping assignment to Echo Bay. Everyone knew of Aimee's sacrifice for Hunter and began to romanticize it, turning Everly into the evil villain who stole the prince's heart.

She pulled her hand out of his awkwardly. She glanced up to see his reaction, but he didn't even seem to notice. His eyes were focused on the ground. When they got back inside the school, he seemed lost. Unsure where to go.

Her stomach dropped even further when she heard another mean whisper come her way.

"How could she do that to her? Aimee's barely in the ground."

A painful stab hit Everly in the chest.

"Hunter, we need to talk." Everly pulled him into an alcove of the foyer and away from prying eyes.

"What's wrong?" Hunter whispered.

"Us," Everly cut out quickly. Too quickly.

The corner of his mouth twitched downward. "What's wrong with us?"

"You're my best friend's *brother*."

Hunter turned, putting his hand on the wall behind her. She felt trapped, his long, athletic body filling the small space. She could smell his aftershave, and she took a deep breath. He leaned closer to her, his eyes meeting hers, and her heart fluttered. His voice dropped to a whisper. "'Best friend's brother.' That's not what I would call me. Not after..." His eyes flicked to the mourners still coming in, and he understood. "You're drawing a line between us. Why?" He sounded hurt.

Her heart was racing, and she wanted to deny it but couldn't. "Because I don't want to hurt Holland. We need boundaries, a line we can't cross."

"What if I want to cross that line?" He tried to smile, but it didn't come fully. She could tell he was surprised by her sudden announcement, but was that also a hint of relief there?

"You can't until Holland fully accepts us, and you can forgive yourself." Everly shook her head and glanced toward the mourners. Hunter tensed when he caught others looking at them. "It's too soon, especially because of what Aimee did for you," Everly admitted. "You know it, and I know it. You're just pretending right now, but I know your heart and head disagree because you feel guilty about Aimee."

"Everly, please don't do this," he begged.

"I have to. It would help if you understood how you felt about Aimee. You dated for a long time; you can't tell me you don't have feelings for her right now. Feelings that are plagued by guilt when you look at me."

His head dropped. "I thought I was hiding it better."

"You tried your best."

"Why do you have to be so good at reading people?" He sniffed.

"It's a blessing and a curse."

He shuddered and lifted his head. Seeing fresh tears stain his cheeks, she knew she had made the right decision.

"Okay, so you're just my sister's best friend." Hunter removed his arm and stepped back, retreating behind the friendship line Everly drew. Hunter was so good at reading her facial cues and worry. He knew how to calm her and put her at ease. He knew her better than she knew herself, which only made her heart swell with emotion and heartbreak. "For now," he added. The corner of his mouth lifted in an attempt at a smile, but he couldn't hold it. It wavered and broke.

Hunter was giving her space, and suddenly, she wanted to cry because it was exactly what she wanted and not at the same time.

"Th-thank you," she whispered, her voice trembling.

How could life be so unfair?

Everly felt her emotions crumble, so she sucked it in, leaning against the window to stare at the rain. Hunter turned toward her, draped his arm over her shoulder, and hugged her.

"Hunter, I—" Everly started, but he silenced her.

"I'm just *comforting* my sister's best friend. Besides, you said I give good hugs. And Holland would kill me if she found out I made you cry."

Everly nodded and turned her face into his suit jacket to hide her tears and emotions. She swore she felt the barest nuzzle against her head.

She pulled back. "You do give good hugs," Everly said, wiping at her eyes with the back of her hand.

"I'm sorry," Hunter said softly. His hand reached for hers, but then he pulled away as soon as they touched. "I'm sorry I made you cry."

She shook her head. "No, it's just sometimes... I didn't know getting your wish could hurt so badly," she said, secretly referring to when she made a birthday wish over the surprise chicken and hot sauce pizza Hunter had gotten her. Why did wishes backfire?

Hunter leaned back and wiped at the stray tear in her eye. "It hurts because you care so much, and I get it. I'm hurting and confused—and I'm unintentionally hurting you."

Everly gazed up into his green eyes and saw his sorrow; then his jaw clenched. "I promise I'll do a better job at protecting your heart." He let his thumb brush ever so softly across her lips. "And mine," he breathed out.

Exiting the alcove, he walked past Kat, who seemed utterly immersed in a game on her phone. She had her headphones on, and Hunter had tried to prevent her from noticing the intense conversation that had just transpired.

Everly felt her chest tighten, and she wanted to grab Hunter's hand and pull him back to her. How could she want something and yet not want it at the same time? And how could he understand her so well?

There was movement in the darkness, and she knew she wasn't alone. There was another that was hurting as well.

"It's okay, boy." Everly kneeled, and Shadow, Ms. Bell-camp's omen, came and nuzzled her.

"It hurts," Shadow said, and Everly knew he meant the bond. Since it was broken, he was destined to go mad.

"It will. I know."

"Go now?" he asked, looking to the woods.

"Yes, go." She opened the door and stepped out into the rain. "You can go now."

Shadow took off and ran through the rain and into the woods. She hoped he would find freedom, hoped he wouldn't go mad. Everly dusted off her knees and let the rain mix with her tears.

EPILOGUE

"Holland? We need to talk. You can't keep avoiding me forever!" Everly pounded on her dorm room door. Silence came from the other side, which could be Holland performing one of her silent treatments. "You can't hide from me. I will find you!" Everly pulled out her phone and dialed Holland's number but heard nothing.

"Oh, come on, I know you're in there." Everly tried the door handle, but it was locked. Feeling a bit perturbed at how her friend was not even letting her explain her side was just silly. Just yesterday, Everly and Hunter called it off after the funeral. It was painful, but that should count for something.

Everly wasn't going to let her get away with it anymore. No more excuses. Everly pulled out her lockpick kit and in record time was in what looked like a disaster movie.

Granted, without Holland's housekeepers to clean up after her, her room was really pretty messy, but this felt different. This felt tossed.

"What happened?" Everly found Holland's laptop. The screen was cracked, and she put it back on the bed. Her hand hit the trackpad, and green lines of text flew across the black screen, directed to Everly.

HELLO, EVERLY!
HOLLAND FELL DOWN MY RABBIT HOLE.
TO SAVE HER, YOU MUST PLAY MY GAME.
DO YOU WANT TO SAVE YOUR FRIEND?
<YES> or <NO>

Everly stared at the screen. Surely, this must be a joke by Holland? She was trying to get her to follow a scavenger hunt type of game to make her find her so they could make up. She had done things like this before for her birthday. This had to be a new game, but Everly was tired of playing to Holland's commands and every whim.

She almost hit the No button.

But at the last second, she hovered over the Yes.

As soon as she clicked the button, a video of Holland in a dark room with no windows appeared. A light flickered on, and Holland covered her hand over her eyes. "Hello?" Holland's voice was weak with disuse. "Is someone there?"

The camera flickered off.

Everly's phone buzzed.

THAT'S ALL FOR NOW. TO FIND HER,
YOU MUST PLAY MY GAME.

ARE YOU READY?

Everly's heart dropped into her stomach.

OH, AND ONE MORE THING.

YOU CAN'T TELL ANYONE.

I'M WATCHING YOU

READ WHAT HAPPENS NEXT IN
THE GRIMM HACKER
COMING 2024

ABOUT THE AUTHOR

Chanda Hahn is a NYT & USA Today Bestselling author of The Unfortunate Fairy Tale series. She uses her experience as a children's pastor, children's librarian and bookseller to write compelling and popular fiction for teens. She was born in Seattle, WA, grew up in Nebraska, and currently resides in Waukesha, WI, with her husband and their twin children; Aiden and Ashley.

Visit Chanda Hahn's website to learn more about her other forthcoming books.
www.chandahahn.com